"Dee Henderson had me shiver[...] closer to his victim. The message that we have nothing to fear as long as God is in control was skillfully handled, but I got scared anyway! I highly recommend this book to anyone who likes suspense."

TERRI BLACKSTOCK, BEST-SELLING AUTHOR OF *TRIAL BY FIRE*

"Dee Henderson is quickly rising to the top of Christian suspense! Ms. Henderson's sparkling characters and superb plotting in *Danger in the Shadows* sweeps the reader along to a breathless conclusion. You'll want to keep the light on for this one!"

LORI COPELAND, AUTHOR OF *THE ISLAND OF HEAVENLY DAZE*

"Dee Henderson's romantic suspense is a satisfying read. She's tweaked the story line just enough to keep the tension taut and the romance springy."

ROMANTIC TIMES MAGAZINE

"A Masterstroke! Dee Henderson gives the reader not one but two irresistible heroes; a rare occurrence that should not be missed by serious romance readers."

COMPUSERVE REVIEWS

"Romantic suspense fans, if you also crave an emotionally-charged, inspirational read, *Danger in the Shadows* is the perfect blend. This book goes on my keeper shelf—it's a winner!"

BOOKBUG ON THE WEB

"An excellent read for those looking for a nail-biting read with lots of heart."

ALL ABOUT ROMANCE

"Dee Henderson has meticulously woven an intriguing tale of faith, love, and suspense."

WRITERS CLUB ROMANCE GROUP ON AOL

"I read *Danger in the Shadows* last night and it was great. I picked it up in the evening and didn't go to bed until 2:30 when I finished it. The story had twists you couldn't see coming and a touch of real romance with a spiritual base. The surprise ending had me holding my breath." —A. B.

"I absolutely LOVED *Danger in the Shadows*—now I am hooked. Count me a new Dee Henderson fan." —P. G.

"I loved it! I could hardly put the book down and can't wait for more." —E. L.

"Thanks for the great read. I love being able to read romance and suspense and learn more about God at the same time." —T. P.

"I really enjoyed the book!!! The plot, the characters, the suspense, and the romance were wonderful. I'm already anticipating the O'Malley family series. You keep writing and I'll keep reading." —V. C.

"It grabbed my attention at the very beginning. I love that in a book. This was the first of your books I have read but it will not be the last."

"I just completed reading *Danger in the Shadows*. It was so goooooooood! —M. M.

RITA Award Winner—*the highest national award given for excellence in romantic fiction*
National Reader's Choice Award Winner
Bookseller's Best Award Winner

DANGER
IN THE
SHADOWS

PREQUEL TO THE O'MALLEY SERIES

DEE HENDERSON

TYNDALE HOUSE PUBLISHERS, INC.
CAROL STREAM, ILLINOIS

Visit Tyndale's exciting Web site at www.tyndale.com

TYNDALE is a registered trademark of Tyndale House Publishers, Inc.

Tyndale's quill logo is a trademark of Tyndale House Publishers, Inc.

Danger in the Shadows

Published in 2002 by Multnomah Publishers, Inc. under ISBN 1-57673-927-9.

Cover design by Chris Gilbert/UDG DesignWorks

Cover image by Getty Images

Background cover image by Photodisc

Scripture quotations are from: *Revised Standard Version Bible* (RSV) © 1946, 1952 by the
Division of Christian Education of the National Council of the Churches of Christ in the
United States of America

ISBN-10: 1-4143-1055-2
ISBN-13: 978-1-4143-1055-8

Printed in the United States of America

11 10 09 08 07 06 05

21 20 19 18 17

Titles by Dee Henderson

THE O'MALLEY SERIES

Danger in the Shadows (prequel)
The Negotiator
The Guardian
The Truth Seeker
The Protector
The Healer
The Rescuer

UNCOMMON HEROES SERIES

True Devotion
True Valor
True Honor
True Courage

COMING FEBRUARY 2006

The Witness

Fear not, for I am with you,
be not dismayed, for I am your God;
I will strengthen you, I will help you,
I will uphold you with my victorious right hand.

ISAIAH 41:10

CHAPTER | 1

The summer storm lit up the night sky in a jagged display of energy, lightning streaking and fragmenting between towering thunderheads. Sara Walsh ignored the storm as best she could, determined not to let it interrupt her train of thought. The desk lamp as well as the overhead light were on in her office as she tried to prevent any shadows from forming. What she was writing was disturbing enough.

The six-year-old boy had been found…. Dead.

Writing longhand on a yellow legal pad of paper, she shaped the twenty-ninth chapter of her mystery novel. Despite the dark specificity of the scene, the flow of words never faltered.

The child had died within hours of his abduction. His family, the Oklahoma law enforcement community, even his kidnapper, did not realize it. Sara didn't pull back from writing the scene even though she knew it would leave a bitter taste of defeat in the mind of the reader. The impact was necessary for the rest of the book.

She crossed out the last sentence, added a new detail, then went on with her description of the farmer who had found the boy.

Thunder cracked directly overhead. Sara flinched. Her office suite on the thirty-fourth floor put her close enough to the storm she could hear the air sizzle in the split second before the boom. She would like to be in the basement parking garage right now instead of her office.

A glance at the clock on her desk showed it was almost eight in the evening. The push to finish a story always took over as she reached the final chapters. This tenth book was no exception.

This was the most difficult chapter in the book to write. It was better to get it done in one long sustained effort. Death always squeezed her heart.

Had her brother been in town, he would have insisted she wrap it up and come home. Her life was restricted enough as it was. He refused to let her spend all her time at the office. He would lean against the doorjamb of her office and give her that *look* along with his predictable lecture telling her all she should be doing: puttering around the house, cooking, messing with the roses, doing something other than sitting behind that desk.

She did so enjoy taking advantage of Dave's occasional absences.

His flight back to Chicago from the FBI academy at Quantico had been delayed due to the storm front. When he called her from the airport out East, he cautioned her he might not be home until eleven.

It wasn't a problem, she assured him, everything was fine. Code words. Spoken every day. So much a part of their language now that she spoke them instinctively. "Everything is fine"—all clear; "I'm fine"—I've got company; "I'm doing fine"—I'm in danger. She had lived the dance a long time. The tight security around her life was necessary. It was overpowering, obnoxious, annoying…and comforting.

Sara turned in the black leather chair to watch the display of lightning. The skyline of downtown Chicago glimmered back at her through the rain.

With every book, another fact, another detail, another intense emotion, broke through from her own past. She could literally feel the dry dirt under her hand, feel the oppressive darkness. Reliving what had happened to her twenty-five years ago was terrifying. Necessary, but terrifying.

She sat lost in thought for several minutes, idly walking her pen through her fingers. Her adversary was out there somewhere, still alive, still hunting her. Had he made the association to Chicago yet? After all these years, she was still constantly moving, still working to stay one step ahead of the threat. Her family knew only too well his threat was real.

The man would kill her. Had long ago killed her sister. The threat didn't get more basic than that. She had to trust others and ultimately God for her security. There were days her faith wavered under the intense weight of simply enduring that stress. She was learning by necessity how to roll with events, to trust God's ultimate sovereignty.

The notepad beside her was filled with doodled sketches of faces. One of these days her mind was finally going to stop blocking the one image she longed to sketch. She knew she had seen the man. Whatever the consequences of trying to remember, whatever the cost, it was worth paying in order to try to bring justice for her and her sister.

She couldn't force the image to appear no matter how much she longed to do so. She was the only one who still believed it was possible for her to remember it. The police, the FBI, the doctors had given up hope years ago.

She fingered a worn photo of her sister Kim that sat by a white rose on her desk. She didn't care what the others thought. Until the killer was caught, Sara would never give up hope.

God was just. She held on to that knowledge and the hope that the day of justice would eventually arrive. Until it did, she carried guilt inside that remained wrapped around her heart. In losing her twin, she had literally lost part of herself.

Turning her attention back to her desk, she debated for a moment whether or not she wanted to do any more work tonight. She didn't.

She slipped the pad of paper with her draft of the book chapter into the folder beside her computer keyboard. When it had begun to rain, she turned off her computer, not willing to risk possible damage from a building electrical surge should lightning hit a transformer or even the building itself.

As she put the folder away, the framed picture on the corner of her desk caught her attention. Her best friend was getting married. Sara envied her. She could feel the sense of rebellion rising again. The need to break free of the security blanket around her rose and fell with time. Ellen had freedom and a life. She was getting married to a wonderful man. Sara longed to one day have that same choice. Without freedom, it wasn't possible, and that hurt. Her dream was being sacrificed with every passing day.

She opened her desk drawer, retrieved her purse, then picked up her briefcase.

Her office had plush forest green carpet and ivory walls. The furniture, European; the bookcases, mahogany. This was the office where H. Q. Victor, the internationally known British author, worked.

She lifted her raincoat from the stand by the door. With the London Fog coat, she even looked British.

As she stepped into the outer office, the room lights automatically turned on. They illuminated a massive receptionist area where the walls displayed children's books—thirty-five of them—by Sara J. Walsh. Sara reached back and turned off the interior office lights.

There was a second office twenty feet away, where the name Sara Walsh had been stenciled in gold on the nameplate. She wrote the children's books there, illustrated them, had fun. The office behind her had no nameplate. When she locked the suite door, an electronic beam triggered behind her, securing the office.

Her suite was in the east tower of the business complex. Rising forty-five stories, the two recently built towers added to the already impressive downtown skyline. Sara liked the modern building and the shopping available on the ground floor. She disliked the elevator ride for she didn't like closed spaces, but she considered the view worth the price.

The elevator that responded tonight came from two floors below. There were two connecting walkways between the east and west towers, one on the sixth floor and another in the lobby. She chose the sixth floor concourse tonight, walking through it to the west tower with a confident but fast pace.

She was alone in the wide corridor. Travis sometimes accompanied her, but she had waved off his company tonight and told him to go get dinner. If she needed him, she would page him.

The click of her heels echoed off the marble floor. There was parking under each tower, but if she parked under the tower where she worked, she would be forced to pull out onto a one-way street no matter which exit she took. It was a pattern someone could observe and predict. Changing her route and time of day across one of the two corridors was a better compromise. Hopefully she could see any danger coming.

Adam Black dropped the pen he held onto the white legal pad and got up to walk over to the window, watching the lightning storm flare around the building. He felt like that inside. Storming, churning.

He had lost more than his dad—he had lost his confidant, his best friend. Trying to cope with the grief by drowning himself in work was only adding to the turmoil.

The passage in Mark chapter 4 of the storm-tossed sea and Jesus asleep in the boat crossed his mind and drew a smile. What had Jesus said? "Why are you afraid? Have you still no faith?" Appropriate for tonight.

He rubbed the back of his neck. His current commercial contracts expired in three months. A feeding frenzy was forming—which ones would he be willing to renew? Which new ones would he consider? What kind of money would it cost for people to get use of his name and image?

The tentative dollar figures being passed by his brother-in-law Jordan were astronomical.

The stack of proposals had been winnowed out, but the

remaining pile still threatened to slide onto the floor.

All he needed to do was make a decision.

God, what should I do?

The decisions he made would set his schedule for the next five years of his life. If he said yes, he was by default saying no to something else. Was it that he didn't want to make a decision or that he didn't want to be tied down?

It was hard to define what he wanted to accomplish anymore. He was restless. He had been doing basically the same thing for three years: keeping his image in the public eye and building his business. It had become routine. He hated routine.

His dad would have laughed and told him that when the work stopped being fun, it was time to find a new line of work.

They'd had eight days together between the first heart attack and his death. Eight good days despite the pain— Adam sitting at his dad's hospital bedside and talking about everything under the sun. They had both known that time was short.

"I'll be walking in glory soon, son," his dad would quip as they ended each evening, never knowing if it would be their last visit. And Adam would squeeze his hand and reply, "When you get there, you can just save me a seat."

"I'll save two," his dad would reply with a twinkle in his eye that would make Adam laugh.

Adam glanced at the red folder he had placed between the picture of his father and the glass-encased football on the credenza. No, he wasn't reading the list in the folder again tonight. He already knew it by heart.

It was time to go home. Time to feed his dog, if not himself.

Sara decided to take the elevator down to the west tower parking garage rather than walk the six flights. She could grit her teeth for a few flights to save time. She pushed the button to go down and watched the four elevators to see which would respond first. The one to her left, coming down from the tenth floor.

When it stopped she reached inside and pushed the garage-floor parking button but didn't step inside. Tonight she would take the second elevator.

It came down from the twenty-fifth floor.

Sara shifted her raincoat over her arm and moved her briefcase to her other hand. The elevator stopped and the doors slid open.

A man was in the elevator.

She froze.

He was leaning against the back of the elevator, looking as if he had put in a long day at work, a briefcase in one hand and a sports magazine in the other, his blue eyes gazing back at her. She saw a brief look of admiration in his eyes.

Get in and take a risk; step back and take a risk.

She knew him. His face was as familiar as any sports figure in the country, even if he'd been out of the game of football for three years. His commercial endorsements and charity work had continued without pause.

Adam Black worked in this building? This was a nightmare come true. The last thing she needed was to be near someone who attracted media attention.

She hesitated, then stepped in, her hand tightening on the briefcase handle. A glance at the board of lights showed he had already selected the parking garage.

"Working late tonight?" His voice was low, a trace of a northeastern accent still present, his smile a pleasant one.

Her answer was a noncommittal nod.

The elevator began to silently descend.

She had spent too much time in European finishing schools to slouch. Her posture was straight, her spine relaxed, even if she was nervous. She hated elevators. She should have taken the stairs.

"Quite a storm out there tonight."

The heels of her patent leather shoes sank into the jade carpet as she shifted her weight from one foot to the other. "Yes."

Three more floors to go.

There was a slight flicker to the lights, and then the elevator jolted to a halt.

"What?" Sara felt adrenaline flicker in her system like the lights.

He pushed away from the back wall. "A lightning hit must have blown a circuit."

The next second, the elevator went black.

Ten seconds clicked by. Twenty. Sara's adrenaline sent her heart rate soaring. Pitch black. Closed space.

Lord, no. It's dark. Get me out of this box!

"How long before they fix it?" She tried to keep her words level and steady. She had spent years learning the control, but this was beyond something she could control.

"It may take a few minutes, but they will find the circuit breaker and the elevator will be moving again."

Sounds amplified in the closed space as he moved. He set down his briefcase? She couldn't remember if there was a phone in the elevator panel or not. How could she have ridden in these elevators for three months and not looked for something so simple?

"No phone, and what I think is the emergency pull button seems to have no effect."

Sara took deep breaths, trying to slow down her heart rate. Neither her cellular phone nor her signaling beeper would work inside this elevator.

"You're very quiet," he said eventually.

"I want out of here," she replied slowly to hide the fact her teeth were trying to chatter.

"There's nothing to be afraid of."

She wanted to reply, "You've never been locked in a pitch-black root cellar and left to die before," but the memories and the panic were already overwhelming her. Her coping skills were failing when she needed them most. Her hand clenched in the darkness, nails digging into her palm. She could do this. She had no choice. It was only darkness.

"Consider it from my viewpoint. I'm stuck in the dark with a beautiful woman. There could be worse fates."

She barely heard him. *Lord, why tonight? Please, not this.* The darkness was so bad she could feel the nausea building.

"Sorry, I didn't mean any offense with that remark."

She couldn't have answered if she wanted to. One thought held her focus fast—surviving. The moment she needed clarity, her mind was determined to retreat into the past instead. A cold sweat froze her hands. Not here. Not with someone else present. To suffer through a flashback when her brother Dave was around was difficult enough. To do it with a stranger would be horrible.

Adam didn't understand the silence. The lady had apparently frozen in one position. "Maybe it would help if we introduced ourselves. I'm Adam Black. And you are…?"

Silence. Then a quiet, "Sara."

"Hi, Sara." He reached out a hand wondering why she was so tense. No nervous laughter, no chatter, just frozen stiffness. "Listen, since it looks like this might actually take some time, why don't we try sitting down." His hand touched hers.

She jerked back and he flinched. Her hand was like ice. This lady was not tense, she was terrified.

He instantly reviewed what he had with him. Nothing of much use. His sports coat was in his car, his team jacket still upstairs in his office. What had she been wearing when she stepped into the elevator? An elegant blue-and-white dress that had caught his attention immediately, but there had been more…a raincoat over her arm.

First get her warm, then get her calm.

"Sara, it will be okay. Sit down; let's get you warm." He touched her hand again, grasping it in his so he could turn her toward him. Cold. Stiff.

"I'm…afraid of the dark."

No kidding.

He had to peel her fingers away from her briefcase handle. "You're safe, Sara. The elevator is not going to fall or anything like that. The lights will come back on soon."

"I know."

He could feel her fighting hysteria. The tremors coming through her hands were growing stronger. He didn't have to be able to see her to know she was heading for deep shock. "You're safe. I'm not going anywhere. And I'm no threat to you," he added, wondering what would make a grown woman petrified of the dark. The possibilities that came to mind all made him feel sick.

"I know that too."

He carefully guided her down to sit with her back leaning against the elevator wall. He spread her coat out over her and was thankful when she took over and did most of it herself, tucking it around her shoulders, burying her hands into the soft warmth of the fabric.

"Better?"

"Much."

He couldn't prevent a smile. "Don't have much practice lying, do you?"

"It sounds better than admitting I'm about to throw up across your shoes." There was almost the sound of an answering smile in her reply.

He sat down carefully, close enough so he could reach her if necessary but far enough away so she hopefully wouldn't feel any more cornered than she already did.

"Try leaning your head back and taking a few deep breaths."

"How long has it been?" she asked a few moments later.

"Maybe four, five minutes."

"That's all?"

Adam desperately wished for matches, a lighter, anything to break this blackness for her. "We'll pass the time talking about something, and the time will go by in an instant. You'll see. What would you like to talk about first; do you have a preference?"

Silence.

"Sara. Come on, work with me here."

He was reaching out to shake her shoulder when she suddenly said through teeth that were obviously chattering, "Sports. Why did you retire?"

Adam didn't talk about the details of that decision with many people, but under the present circumstances, she could have asked him practically anything and he wouldn't have minded.

"Did you see the Super Bowl we won?"

"Of course. Half this town hated you for months afterward."

He didn't have to wonder if that was a smile.

"I liked the feeling of winning. But I was tired. Too tired to do it again. It wasn't just the physical exhaustion of those last games, but the emotional drain of carrying the expectations of so many people. So I decided it was time to let the next guy in line have a chance."

"You got tired."

"I got tired."

"I bet you were tired the season before when you lost the Super Bowl to the Vikings."

He chuckled. "I was."

"Your retirement had nothing to do with being tired." She sounded quite certain about it. Her voice was also growing steadier. "You won that Super Bowl ring to prove you were capable of winning it; then you retired because the challenge was gone. You didn't play another season because you would have been bored, not tired."

"You sound quite certain about that theory."

"Maybe because I know I'm right. You're like your father.

'Do It Once—Right—Then Move On.' Wasn't that the motto he lived his life by?"

Adam's shoulder muscles tensed. "Where did you hear that?"

"You had it inscribed on his tombstone," was the gentle reply. "Sorry, I didn't mean to touch a nerve."

Adam didn't answer. When and why had this lady been to the cemetery where his father was buried? It was outside the city quite a distance, and it was an old cemetery where most plots had been bought ahead for several generations. That inscription had not been added until almost a month after the burial.

She was a reporter. The realization settled like a rock in his gut. She had executed this meeting perfectly. Setting up this "chance" encounter, paying off a building maintenance worker to throw a switch for her, giving him every reason to believe he was going to be playing the hero by keeping her calm while the lights were out. He had been buying the entire scenario, hook, line, and sinker.

"I like the quote and the philosophy of life it contains."

"Sara, could we cut the facade? What do you want? You're a writer, aren't you?"

Silence met his anger.

"What kind of writer would you like me to admit to being?" The ice in her voice was unmistakable.

"Just signal for this elevator to start moving again, and I'll consider not throttling you."

"You think I caused this?"

"Not going to try denying you're a writer?"

"I don't have much practice lying," she replied tersely, echoing his earlier words.

"Great. Then I would say we are at an impasse, wouldn't you?" He waited for a response but didn't get one. "When you get tired of sitting in the dark, just signal your cohorts that we are done talking, and we'll go our separate ways. Until then, I have nothing else to say to you."

"That's fine with me."

And with that, there was nothing between them but a long, cold silence.

CHAPTER | 2

S ara hated feeling afraid. And she was afraid. Every
memory in her past was coming alive. Trust that God
was still there, in control, had withered under the
pressing weight of the darkness. Trust and faith were easy
words until the pressure came; living them was hard. She was
going to shatter like crystal. Terror was in control. She
couldn't stop the panic. She was looking into ink-black noth-
ingness and she couldn't handle the closed place.

*Lord, turn the lights back on. Please. I can't relive those days
again, not here, not in this small place.*

Think about something else.

She had been doing that while Adam talked and it
helped. But now he was silent, angry, and that emotion resonated with fears so deeply buried that Sara could not put
words to their source. She scrambled to think of something
safe.

The children's book due to her publisher next month.
Beautiful drawings. A baby sea horse exploring its world. The

story focused on the basics of how to make friends. The idea had just been there as she sat doodling on her art pad one Saturday morning—the first four sketches and the entire story line had come in twenty minutes. She already loved the book. It would inspire thousands of children to learn about the sea.

Nausea suddenly overwhelmed her. She hunched forward, curling in on herself, stifling any sound. She would never finish the book. The truth hit her like a brick. It had been a story she had told to her sister Kim.

The flashbacks were beginning, and there was nothing she could do to stop them.

The cellar had a dirt floor. It made Sara shiver because she knew there were spiders here.

"Sara, I'm c-cold," Kim said.

Sara tried but she couldn't reach her sister. The ropes kept them apart by only eight inches, but it might as well have been a mile. "I know, Kimmy. We just have to pretend it's warm; that helps a lot. They will bring us blankets when they bring the peanut butter sandwiches tonight."

Sara wasn't courageous, wasn't brave…but in the last twenty-four hours she had slipped into that role. She was the oldest, if only by a matter of minutes, and Dave would expect her to look after their sister. She wished her brother were here, wished she could be afraid and let him be the brave one, but she didn't know what had happened to him. He had been shoved away from them as they were yanked into the van.

"Why hasn't Dad come yet?"

Because he doesn't love us. "He's coming, Kimmy."

"But why did those men grab us? I don't understand. I want out of here. It's dark and I'm cold."

"Be brave, Kimmy. Dad will come get us. You'll see."

Sitting stuck between floors in a pitch-black elevator was not Adam's idea of a fun way to spend an evening.

He was tired. Hungry. Annoyed. He could use two aspirins and a long ride on his motorcycle to let the wind shake the cobwebs from his mind.

Until five minutes ago, Sara was exactly the kind of lady he would have enjoyed getting to know. But trustworthy and honest were nonnegotiables on his list.

Why did fame have to come at such a high price? It came with so many positives but also many negatives. Tonight was just another reminder of why he couldn't take someone at face value.

He let the hurt linger because it was late and he was in a bad mood. He was getting tired of women with agendas coming through his life. It was like walking through a minefield.

For years it hadn't been such a big deal. He'd had his career and that had been his sole focus. The situation was different now.

His dad had been right. More than anything else, it was time for a wife and family. He had spent his football career traveling practically every weekend, living like a nomad. He had more of a routine established when he stayed at a hotel than he did in his own home. It was time to settle down for good, sink some roots.

The idea of getting married was an attractive one. Being

asked to share the newspaper over breakfast, having someone meet him at the door when he got home and say, "Hi, Adam, welcome home." He wanted that person in his life.

He had paid a steep price to make a future marriage important in his life. It had been a wonderful yet incredibly lonely twelve years playing professional football because his guard had to be up all the time. The ribbing from his teammates had been intense.

But now that he was retired, the situation was different. He wasn't traveling constantly. He had the luxury of being able to settle down.

The red folder and its list of qualifications for the ideal wife had been a way to keep his father amused and focused on something other than the pain while he lay there in the hospital bed. But there was also a great deal of truth to that list of fifteen items the two of them had put together.

There was no woman in his current circle of friends who qualified. The best candidates didn't think they had a chance, so they didn't come forward. He would find her. He just had to start seriously looking.

Adam smiled. His interfering sister would love to see that list.

"Kimmy, are you awake?" Sara rubbed her tears on the torn sleeve of her dress.

There was movement in the darkness across the small room. "I'm awake." The voice was tired and scared and hoarse from crying.

"I want you to have my blue hair ribbons." Sara could feel the drooping satin brushing her cheek.

"But those are your favorites."

"I know. That's why I want you to have them."

There was silence between the twins. It was a significant gift. The ribbons had come from Dave.

"Thanks. I'll treasure them. Is there any more water left? I'm so thirsty."

The men had left one plastic water bottle between the girls, and if they were careful, they could roll it to each other. Sara had not drunk any even though she said she had. She knew what Kimmy didn't. The two men were not coming back.

Kimmy had to be okay when their dad found them.

The silence was chilling. It was a disquieting sensation that made Adam nervous.

"Sara."

She didn't answer him.

He focused his attention on what he could hear from her side of the elevator. He realized what had been steady breathing twenty minutes ago had turned ragged.

"Sara, are you okay?"

She still didn't answer him.

He reached over. His hand touched her shoulder and strands of her hair. She jerked away so violently, he heard her head pop against the elevator wall.

He grasped her face with both hands. Her forehead was soaked with sweat.

Lord, what happened? What have I caused?

He pushed aside the coat.

Her hands were clenched in tight fists.

"Sara," he snapped at her, with the same volume and

force he used on the playing field to call a play. She came out of the stupor.

"Turn on the lights. Please." It was a whispered, broken plea—and in a voice such as he had never heard before. Woman. Child. Pleading. Resigned.

It broke his heart.

"I can't, Sara." He wished he could.

He felt the fear engulf her again, felt her sliding back into that place she had been hiding and was helpless to prevent it. *God, give me some ideas here. What do I do?*

"Talk to me, Sara. What can I do to help?"

No answer. He tucked the coat back around her, keeping her hands in his. The muscles in her clenched hands were beginning to spasm in cramps. He gently worked them straight, rubbing warmth back into them.

He sat as close as he could, wrapping his arm around her. Apologies for what he had accused her of would come later when they were out of this crisis. Right now, he was seriously afraid she was going to pass out. The remorse cut deep. If he hadn't made such an angry accusation, hadn't stopped their conversation, all of this might have been avoided. *God, calm her down. I'm not equipped to deal with this.*

"Did you grow up in Chicago, Sara?"

He shook her to get an answer.

"No."

He could barely hear her.

"I bet it was London, then, given your accent," he teased, in any mood but one to tease.

"Lots of places. Texas mostly," she whispered.

Tremors began shaking her frame. Nothing he tried could subdue them.

"Was Texas a nice time in your life?"

"Yes."

"Then shut your eyes and forget this place and think about Texas. What was nice about it?"

She subtly relaxed. "Frank taught me to draw."

"Are you any good?"

"Yes."

"Did you learn to ride?"

"I rode all over the ranch on Golden Glory. Frank gave her to me on my eighth birthday."

"Sounds like a wonderful gift."

"It was. But it wasn't the gift I wanted."

"What did you want?"

He thought for the longest time she wasn't going to answer. "My brother back."

Don't touch it. The warning came—intense, forceful, urgent—and Adam stopped his next question before it was asked. He shifted the coat around her.

"What did you do last weekend for the Fourth of July?"

"Worked."

"On what?"

She gave a slight shrug.

"Just worked."

Okay, that topic was out of bounds. He racked his brain for easier questions to keep her talking. "Do you live in the city or are you a suburban commuter?"

"Commuter."

"Lived there long? Married? Have kids?"

"Yes, no, and no." Her hands crept up to her face. "How much longer, Adam? I can't stand this."

His arm around her tightened.

"It has to be soon. The guards check every floor and every elevator on their rounds, including the parking garages. They are going to restore the power, Sara."

He tried to keep her talking, but she kept drifting away from him, back into the panic-filled void that seemed to paralyze her.

Adam did what he could, rubbing some warmth into her arms and frozen hands.

"Kimmy, are you still there? Why don't you answer me?"

Adam heard the whispered desperate words, and the voice sent a chill up his spine. This wasn't someone just dealing with a stormy night and a dark elevator. Wherever her mind was, it was now scaring both of them. *Lord, please, get us out of here.*

Moments later, the elevator began to move down at its normal speed, the lights still off with the exception of floor lights now clicking over the doorway. The elevator stopped at the letter *G* and the doors slid open. Adam reached up and pulled the emergency stop button.

The parking garage was fully lit, lights on every post and concrete column driving the shadows away. Only a few cars remained in the massive structure.

Adam watched Sara blink against the light coming through the doorway. It was like watching a newborn kitten finally learn how to focus. He could see her processing the nightmare that had just happened, working through it as the light took away the terror. She unfolded her stiff body with care but did not move entirely away from him.

"Thank you."

Adam gently brushed her hair back as she looked toward the light. Her hair was wet around the fringes. "You're welcome." He wanted to know who Kimmy was, why Sara was so afraid of the dark, and what had happened to her in the past. It was not the time to ask.

God, thanks for intervening.

He suspected Sara wasn't going to be able to stand, at least not in the high heels she wore, until the shock had faded some more. He blocked her path temporarily as he moved their briefcases aside and got up himself.

"How long were we stuck?"

A calm, polite question. No explanation for what had happened. No relieved chatter now that they were safe. Adam could see the poise returning that had marked her stance before she stepped onto the elevator. She was doing her best to elegantly cover and dismiss what had happened. He glanced at his watch. "Thirty-eight minutes."

She tucked her feet beneath herself, preparing to rise. Adam stepped to her side, getting a firm hold on her forearms to help her.

She gasped in pain. "My legs are asleep."

"I thought they might be by now. Stand easy and let me take your weight. The blood will start to circulate again."

He could tell by the way her breathing changed that she didn't like the proximity to him. She was nervous in his hold and doing her best to cover that fact. What had happened to make her terrified of the dark? "I'm sorry I assumed you arranged for the elevator to shut down."

She looked up. "Thank you. I didn't do it."

"But you don't deny being a writer."

"No, I don't. I gather you've had some problems with them?"

"I've had problems with the more unscrupulous members of the press for years."

"Well, I can promise you, I'm not doing a story on you of any kind." She eased back a step, and Adam found he missed her weight resting against his hands.

"Whom do you work for?"

"Myself."

"Freelancer?"

"You could say that."

Her words were obviously selected with care. Adam hesitated and chose not to pursue it. "Why don't you have a cup of coffee with me at the hotel across the street before you try to drive home? Give yourself a few more minutes before you face the traffic and the bad weather."

"Adam, I'm fine."

Lord, I could use some help here. She's ready to leave and that's the last thing I want to happen.

Thunder rumbled outside.

"Twenty minutes. It will give the storm time to pass." He lived only eight blocks away; the rain was not an issue for him.

He could see her hesitate. "Please."

Sara needed poise now, to act as a shield between her and the questions while she tried to pull her tattered nerves together. She wanted to get out of here. But her vanity didn't want his last impression to be of a woman who fell apart in the dark. It shouldn't matter so much, but it did.

Coping meant she dealt with it and kept moving. It was the number one rule she had to live by. To stop would let this experience paralyze her. She needed time to calm down. Time to sort through flashbacks still vivid in her memory.

Space to push back that sense of being smothered in the darkness. But before all those things, she had to prove to herself that she was still able to keep moving.

She glanced at her watch. There was nothing special about it except for an unusually wide band. The doctors had never been able to totally remove the scars. It was nine-fifteen. She could have that cup of coffee and still be home before Dave.

The idea of something hot to help settle the chills was a welcome idea. But to do it in Adam's company…there would be questions. Questions she had to avoid.

It was worth the price.

"Okay, Adam." She retrieved the cellular phone she always carried from her purse. Dave's private number was speed dial number one. His voice mail picked up on the first ring. "Dave, it's nine-fifteen. I'm stopping for coffee at the Marque Hotel until the storm passes. I'm fine. Expect me around ten-thirty."

Dave now knew she was with someone. She'd ensure someone on staff at the hotel knew she was with Adam Black. It was simple security.

Had Adam not been at her side, she would have said who she was with and where they had met, but he was there holding both of their briefcases in one of his hands.

He was frowning.

Okay, so now he thought she was living with someone. Well, he could stuff his opinion of her morals. She hadn't been judging him or his lifestyle. He had played professional football for twelve years for goodness' sake. If she could withhold an opinion until she had the facts, then so could he.

She could call Travis and ask him for an escort. That

would really give Adam something to wonder about.

She didn't act on the idea. She did not need those questions.

"If you'll point out your car, I'll drop off your briefcase." Adam's voice was that of a courteous stranger. If Sara didn't want that cup of coffee so desperately, she would reverse her answer to his invitation.

"Put them both in your trunk for now, and I'll get mine when we come back from the hotel."

Adam nodded and stopped at a blue sedan. The briefcases went into the trunk and he took out an umbrella. Sara slipped her coat on properly.

The rain pounded down. Few pedestrians braved the weather. Cars passing by flung water onto the sidewalks.

The hotel was directly across the street. Sara didn't mind walking near Adam as they shared the umbrella. Any personal interest had disappeared into the polite actions of a gentleman.

Sara knew the hotel well. She knew the manager by name, the security chief and the entire security staff, the doorman, and most of the restaurant staff. Dave wanted her to have a safe public place for the occasional business lunch and dinner she needed to have—this was a compromise. She knew the hotel well enough to know when something or someone was out of place, and she knew the escape routes if she felt there was something wrong.

As they reached the restaurant, it was evident that Adam was well known here too.

"We're here just for coffee, Charles," Adam told the maître d' helping Sara slip off her coat.

"Of course." The man looked with interest between them. "Your usual table, Sara?"

"Please."

She followed him through the elegant restaurant to a back table that gave a view of the room and took the seat by the wall. "Is Gail working tonight?"

"She is. Desserts tonight."

"Add a piece of apple pie to go along with my espresso?"

The maître d' smiled. "Done. Mr. Black?"

Adam had to pull his attention back to the man beside him. "Just black coffee, Charles."

Sara had caught him off guard. She sat across from him, one hand resting lightly on the crystal water glass, the other resting in her lap, calmly surveying the room and the other guests. He would not have expected this to be her normal table. Someone who was on a first-name basis with the maître d' and the pastry chef could pick anywhere in the restaurant, yet she chose essentially to hide in a corner.

She was calm. And it wasn't a false calm. In less than fifteen minutes she had gone from a woman who was struggling to keep her sanity to someone who was poised and self-assured. That suggested she had lived through enough episodes like the one he had seen tonight to learn how to deal with them quickly and move on.

And being seen with someone who was, to a certain degree, famous did not fluster her. He knew his name had been whispered behind them as they crossed the restaurant. She didn't seem to care. She was certainly not in awe.

Her dress and understated jewelry were elegant on her, higher quality than what most women might be able to afford, but not extravagant. Her shoulder-length chestnut hair was styled to outline and highlight her oval face.

Everything about her said she was older than she appeared. He had started the evening guessing at a college degree and about five years' work experience. Now...he had no idea. It also wasn't a polite question to ask a lady.

"Adam?"

Her voice stopped his reflections.

"If you hadn't been in that elevator with me, I would have gone crazy."

"Sara..."

"It's the truth. I just wanted to know if I could say thanks in a tangible way."

Adam had rarely felt so uncomfortable in his life. He could understand her desire to say thank-you with more than just words, but it wasn't necessary. Yet to say so could hurt her feelings. He tried to come up with a suggestion that felt appropriate but couldn't think of a single thing. "Your thank-you is quite sufficient, Sara. Seriously."

"Come on, isn't there one thing in life you don't have that you would like?"

You.

Adam blinked. Where had that thought come from?

"What kind of music do you like?"

"Country. Contemporary gospel. Some blues," he replied, grateful for the easy question.

"What are your favorite hobbies?"

Her smile tugged the answer from him. "I go to a lot of sports games. Football, obviously. Baseball. Basketball. I like to get out and run just for the pleasure of it."

Their coffee arrived along with a generous piece of the apple pie. Sara let out a grateful sigh as she took her first careful sip from her china cup. "You have no idea how much I needed this."

"I think I can guess." Adam was pleased by the simple pleasure he saw on her face. It had been a grueling day and the coffee was very good.

"What's your favorite way to relax?"

Adam had hoped the interruption had thrown her off the subject. "Sara, this isn't necessary."

"Of course it is. Come on, give. What are your favorite ways to relax?" Her eyes were laughing at him as she leaned forward against the table, holding her cup of coffee.

Adam thought carefully about how much he wanted to tell her. She was a self-admitted writer whom he had known less than three hours. "I take my dog down to the beach and find some secluded place where I can sit and watch the clouds drift by. It doesn't matter what time of day it is, although late at night with a full moon is probably my favorite. I like to stretch out on my couch and read a good book cover to cover. I like to spend time with my family." *In the past, I used to go hang out with my dad.*

"Do you have a big family?"

"A younger sister who has three kids. You?"

"An older brother."

"Does he live close by?"

She didn't reply. Was family not a comfortable subject? He was surprised at that, and after a glance at her tense face, he let the silence linger. It could often do what a question could not.

What was she supposed to say? Admit she lived with her brother? It was a topic she didn't want to touch. "He lives nearby," she finally answered and left it at that.

She wished her life were different. She was so tired of the dance, of not being real, of hiding who she really was. She hadn't even been able to correct his impression that she was a reporter, to tell him she primarily wrote children's books. Would there ever be a time when she could simply tell the truth without the need for constantly policing her words? Could she even handle it if that day arrived?

She suddenly felt exhausted. It was beginning to feel as if she had been hit with a bulldozer tonight.

She pushed back her plate, unable to eat any more of the pie. "I think it's time I went home." She met his gaze and was glad she had not let the topic of conversation shift toward what had happened during those thirty-eight minutes in the elevator. His eyes showed too much interest. Give him a little and he would work to figure out the rest, making all the wrong assumptions along the way.

"Of course."

He held her coat for her, then paid the bill.

"Charles, please tell Gail the pie was delicious," Sara said as they passed the maître d' on the way out.

"I'll be glad to, Sara. Thank you both for stopping by."

The rain had stopped while they drank their coffee. A chilly wind met them as they stepped outside. Adam kept his hand on Sara's forearm as they walked, not knowing if she needed the assistance, not willing to risk letting her stumble.

At the parking garage, he opened his trunk and retrieved her briefcase. It was odd that there were no initials on it given the hand-tooled scrolling on the leather case. He handed it to her. "Thanks for joining me for coffee."

"I needed it and you knew it. I still owe you a thank-you," she replied as he watched her intently.

Adam stilled. She had the most beautiful eyes. Indigo blue. Sparkling, alive.

When Sara rested her hand on his arm and reached up, Adam instinctively bent down.

She softly kissed his cheek, her breath lightly touching his skin. "I'll be seeing you." With that, she turned away and walked across the expanse of the underground garage, walking confidently and not looking back.

He heard the electronic alarm on a gray sedan disengage as she walked toward it. Her only hesitation was a brief one when she neared the car, and he thought for a moment she might turn but she didn't. She opened the driver's door and tossed the briefcase inside, removed her coat, and slid behind the wheel.

She raised a hand as her car pulled out of the south exit. Adam noted the license plate since the car was such a common make and model: BI 691.

He leaned against the side of his own car and thought about that kiss. It had been as gentle as a dove's feather and she hadn't teased him. With that dress and that smile, she could have pushed the attraction but she didn't. *What do You think, God? And who's this Dave who is expecting her home at ten-thirty?*

Adam was not going to jump to conclusions. She didn't wear a wedding ring. Something in her past had made her terrified of the dark. There could be simple explanations. He was going to hope for the best and find out some answers.

He only had one major problem.

He didn't know her last name.

Sara struggled to remember how to make tea. Dave had pre-programmed the coffeemaker to turn on early in the morning, and she just wanted it to turn on now and give her hot water. Giving up, she filled her mug from the tap and placed it in the microwave. Her eyes shifted to the window over the sink and the darkness outside. It didn't matter that security was solid here at the house; she was on the first floor and she wanted to be somewhere harder to reach. The timer sounded and she retrieved her mug, dropped in the tea bag, and let it steep enough to make the water turn a cloudy brown. She added more sugar than normal, spilled some, and swiped the counter with a paper towel.

Kissing Adam had been a mistake.

Sara laughed at herself. Riding the elevator had been a mistake. She wouldn't be forgetting tonight for a very long time.

The kiss had been an impulse. She surprised him but she surprised herself even more. Adam's arm under her hand had been firm muscles. She was thirty-one, and she had a crush on a guy she had just met. It was embarrassing to find herself acting like someone who was sixteen.

She didn't date. Her circumstances, who she was…it all made a normal relationship nearly impossible. When security required her to disappear, the friendships could not continue. Contacts had to be broken.

She would be glad when she was able to forget tonight. She turned off lights in the kitchen. At the security pad, she activated zones for the ground floor and headed upstairs. Dave would be home soon. She kept reminding herself of that as she grasped the handrail and climbed the stairs. This house was big without him present—way too big.

Dave tightened his seat belt as the plane finally came out of the holding pattern and began its descent into O'Hare Airport. It had been a long flight, most of it spent waiting on the ground out East for the weather to finally clear. The plane settled out of its descent and touched down, the tires whining under the speed on the wet runway. Dave grimaced. The pilot had set down a little too fast. Dave preferred to be at the controls when he flew.

He looked out over the runway sweeping by and could see across the tarmac to the buildings that housed the private jets. He should have taken the private jet; he would've made better time.

No. As much as he would have enjoyed making the flight, he didn't like to take the plane and leave Sara without a means of fast exit. When they had to yank her from a location, the ability to be in the air within twenty minutes made all the difference in the world.

When the plane eventually came to a stop, Dave stood along with the other passengers in first class. He retrieved his briefcase from the overhead compartment. Sara was probably waiting up to hear about his trip. It was going to be at least another hour before he was home.

He had news to tell her. He still wasn't sure how he wanted to broach the subject. The FBI lab had generated a lead on the last package.

The packages were a nasty reminder from the kidnapper stalking Sara. He liked to taunt, send mementos, reminding everyone he was still free. This time he may have made a mistake. Dave sincerely hoped so. He had spent a lifetime working to keep Sara safe while also trying to break the case.

The man they were looking for had broken pattern and used a different kind of tape. The guess was a pretty simple one. He had run out of the previous roll. Still, the type of weave and number of threads in the packing tape were distinct. Dave already had agents doing the footwork with possible manufacturers.

The odds of it shipping to only one locale were slim. But this was a game played on slim odds. With time, one of those slim leads would be gold. How did he break the news to Sara without getting her hopes raised too much?

She'd buried her disappointment when leads went cold, but every time he'd raised her hopes and then they didn't pan out, it hurt him as much as it did her.

As Dave walked down the long terminal concourse to the baggage claim, he placed a call on his cellular phone to check messages. He would have been paged had anything urgent come up.

His jaw tightened as he listened to Sara's message. She had gone to have coffee with someone but left no name. Red flags went up. She wasn't with someone they knew. He had to tamp down his aggravation as he placed the next call. Even with Travis along for security, she should have avoided the public place.

His gut clenched when Travis reported she had waved him off tonight. It was fear now, not just anger. What was his sister doing? She knew better than this.

Dave disconnected and placed the next call, his pace picking up. "Ben, is she home?"

"Yes. Half an hour ago."

Dave let himself exhale. "Everything quiet?"

"Just fine, boss. The security grid hasn't even picked up that stray cat tonight."

Dave took the stairs rather than the escalator down to the baggage claim level, hurrying around other passengers. "I'll be there in an hour."

"I'll be expecting you," Ben replied.

Dave understood why Sara was fighting the security restrictions, but he couldn't accept it. Procedures and planning kept her alive. The burden he carried was heavy enough without her adding this kind of foolish risk to the equation.

He couldn't accept someone he loved putting herself in danger. That was the bottom line. She just had to do it on a day he was out of town. They would be having words tonight. He didn't understand why she would do something so foolish as to wave off Travis. She might chafe under the burden of the security but she didn't disregard it, not with her history.

Dave picked up the case that had come through special baggage handling. Firearms on an airline got their own baggage compartment and security procedures.

This situation felt wrong. It was out of character for his sister. It was definitely out of character given the package that had been recently sent. He went back to his voice mail and replayed the message.

He could hear the thunder in the background of her message. She hadn't used the one word change that would alert him to the fact she felt threatened. So who was she with? And why hadn't she called Travis?

He wanted to see her face when she answered him. His

sister was too good at masking things for him to believe everything she told him over the phone.

Dave pushed the speed limit on the tollway home, willing to risk having to explain the situation to a fellow cop.

Fifty minutes later, he pulled up to the security gate and Ben stepped out to meet him. The stray cat had come across the drive, but otherwise the security grid was clear.

The grounds were enclosed in a stone fence, but the real security was in the beams that invisibly crossed the lawns. Security cameras also covered the entire grounds.

"Anything in particular I should know about, boss?"

"Just my normal unease after being away for a few days," Dave replied. "What's the code word for tonight?"

"Angels."

"I see her theme is still holding."

"I'm expecting Gabriel sometime soon."

"Thanks, Ben. I'll see you for coffee in the morning."

Dave drove up to the house and pulled around the circle drive so the car was positioned by the front door. He set down his bags inside the entryway, glancing at the alarm panel. The downstairs zones were active. "Sara."

"Upstairs."

He set the security codes for the night and went up to find her.

She was in her sitting room, curled up on the love seat, reading a book. She was dressed in black sweats, her hair pulled back by a white bow—not her normal work attire. "I was beginning to think you got lost," she teased, then his expression obviously registered. "What's wrong?"

"I was just going to ask you that." He leaned against the doorjamb and waited.

She set the book on the table to keep her place. "I had an interesting night."

"Elaborate." The terse word was about the best he could do. They didn't get mad at each other very often. But when they did, the fights tended to be explosive. He felt like exploding at the moment. He wanted some answers.

"You might want to take a seat."

One eyebrow rose. *That interesting?* He set down his briefcase and took a seat in the chair across from her.

"Lightning blew a circuit and stopped the elevator. I was stuck in the dark for thirty-eight minutes."

Sara had the ability to separate emotions from facts. She only did it when the event was traumatic. There was no emotion in her voice at all tonight.

His anger evaporated. Next time, he was staying in town. He ran through the situation and understood all too well what must have happened. "Who was with you?"

"Adam Black."

His eyes widened.

"Yes, that Adam Black. Apparently he works in the building."

"Oh, this is just great." They would be finding her new offices tomorrow. New offices, new security routes, a change in routing for her mail.

She grimaced. "I agree. It wasn't a pleasant situation."

"Does he know?" It was a quiet way to ask the tougher question.

"I froze up on him, but no. He just thinks I'm a little afraid of the dark."

Her attempt to inject a little humor into her voice didn't work. Sara was more than afraid of the dark. To put it mildly, she was terrified.

"How are you doing?"

She held up her teacup. "Fourth cup. Tonight, I almost wish I drank. Adam talked me into a cup of coffee because it was obvious I was a ball of nerves. I switched to tea when I got home."

"Sara, you should have called Travis as soon as the elevator reached the garage."

"It would have raised more questions in Adam's mind. There were enough as it was. It was late. The storm was bad. The hotel restaurant only had six other patrons. The security risk was minimal."

"I'm glad Adam was kind enough to make sure you could drive home safely. It doesn't change the fact you went into a public place with a well-known public figure without anyone covering you. You were too close to the trauma to make the right security call, which is why you should've called Travis. He could have at least alerted hotel security."

"I did what I thought best."

It wasn't worth pushing tonight, not while she was this shaky. He would bring it back up tomorrow. "Tell me what you talked about. How you left things when you parted."

Sara looked down at her teacup. She told Dave all of it except for the kiss, not just because he had asked but because he needed to know. She told him about the story she had remembered telling Kim. She told him about her conversation with Adam during the half hour and then later over coffee.

It felt good to have someone to talk to.

She could see Dave was bothered by what she'd told him.

The entire situation had him on edge. "I'm sorry I didn't call Travis."

Her brother attempted to smile. "As long as you agree to call him next time."

"Next time I get stuck in an elevator, I'll call him." Sara laughed at his determined expression. "No, don't even tell me what you are going to do to those elevators tomorrow. I don't want to know. I can already see it in your face."

She got to her feet and crossed over to his side. She grasped his hand. "Dave, I'm fine."

"Think you'll sleep? I'll be glad to stay up and talk for a while if you'd like."

She looked at him with a knowing smile. "Since your body is still on East Coast time, I know it feels like 2 A.M. to you. Other than a little too much caffeine, I'm fine. We've been through events like this before. I am coping with this one remarkably well. Go to bed. If I can't sleep, I'll just read for a while longer."

Dave brushed her hair back from her face. "I'll pray you have peaceful dreams."

"Thank you," she whispered.

She was amused and somewhat relieved when Dave did a security sweep of her bedroom, just to reassure himself he said. When he left the room, he left the bedside lamp on, the door open, and the hall light on. They were never shut off when she was on the second floor of the house.

Sara woke up screaming at five in the morning. Dave was there immediately, halfway expecting it. Her nightmares always returned after packages were delivered. He came through the bedroom door crouched low. The last time the screams had come, there had been a .45 in her hand, cocked, safety off, pointed at whoever came through the doorway.

It was a two-edged sword—she needed the gun because the stalker had once gotten into her home past their security, but when the terror hit, she wasn't always rational in the first few waking moments.

"Easy, kid, easy."

He held her still, his arms wrapped around her from behind, grasping the back of her wrists to still her hands. Her breathing slowly eased from terrified…to afraid…to aware.

The shudders started.

Dave dropped his head down against her hair. Tears burned his eyes. "It's okay, Sara. It's okay." If only the kidnappers hadn't been able to shove him away from his sisters…

"Kim…"

"I know. I know." Dave gently drew her tighter against him. "You don't have to blame yourself. It wasn't your fault."

"I rolled the water jug…. I rolled the water jug, and it rolled out of her reach."

Dave felt the tears begin to flow from her, and he turned her to his chest.

It did no good to remind Sara that if she had drunk any of the water during her turns, there would have been nothing left to try to give Kim.

It did no good to remind Sara that Kim would have died in another few hours even if she had been able to drink the three tablespoons of water left in the bottle. All Sara could remember was that her twin sister had died inches away from her because she had rolled the water jug just beyond Kim's reach.

Dave wrapped her in her robe, gently slipped her from the bed, and carried her into the bathroom. He turned on the shower as hot as he thought she could handle.

"Thanks, Dave."

Her smile was shaky but her eyes were clearing.

"Sure, Sara." He hated feeling this helpless. There was so little he could do.

He found her jeans, a sweatshirt, tennis shoes, and a jacket. There was only one place where his sister found any peace, and it was several miles away.

Sara eventually joined him. She didn't ask where they were going. He deactivated and reactivated security zones in the house as they made their way to the garage. He pulled the keys to his motorcycle from his pocket.

She slipped onto the bike behind him, her arms hugging him. He put on his helmet. He would have insisted she wear one as well, but she had her head buried between his shoulder blades, and he was not going to let an accident happen this morning. Not this morning.

He took them north, knowing they would eventually turn west toward the cemetery. As he rode, he felt tears soak the back of his shirt.

Life without parole was a hollow sentence for the one kidnapper they had caught. Sara lived the same sentence.

CHAPTER | 3

"Her car is here." Adam gestured to the gray sedan with the familiar license plate as he walked with his brother-in-law toward the elevator.

Jordan turned to inspect the car Adam had indicated. "I can't believe you managed to spend two hours with the lady and not get her last name."

"Believe me, no one regrets that fact more than I do. I can't find her." Adam's frustration was acute. He was hoping his brother-in-law, who also happened to be his lawyer, would have a few good suggestions.

"She doesn't work normal office hours. Sometimes the car is here at 7 A.M., and other times it doesn't appear until noon. She's normally gone by five, but occasionally it's as late as ten. I don't know where she works. She doesn't go to any of the first-floor restaurants for lunch."

"What about the maître d' at the hotel restaurant? He would surely know her last name."

"Too embarrassing." He seriously wanted to see Sara

again, but the only sure way to get her last name he rejected because he would feel foolish—it said something not too pleasant about his ego.

"Why not just wait down here for her to show up?"

"I tried that. On one of those days her car was here late, I waited until past midnight. She never showed."

"You said she got on the elevator on the sixth floor. It would make sense that she worked on that floor."

"There's an architect firm, a dentist office, two private law offices, and a publishing distributor."

"Perfect fit—a publishing distributor. She's a writer."

"The receptionist claims no one named Sara works there. I even sent a large bouquet of flowers, and the deliveryman got the same answer. No Sara. I did the same with the other businesses. Same answer."

The elevator took them up to the twenty-fifth floor.

"Okay, then you've got two choices: wait on luck to bump into her again or start doing a systematic search to find her."

"I want to know where she works and I want her last name. I'm ready to try just about anything to accomplish that."

He hadn't told Jordan everything.

Since that night, Sara had been on his mind constantly.

At first, he had thought it would be a simple thing to find her. They worked in the same building, parked in the same garage, likely ate lunch in the same lobby restaurants. He had hoped she would want to see him again too. Crossing paths should have been simple to arrange.

But after three weeks, Adam knew the opposite.

She didn't want to see him again.

Three days after the incident, he had left a note under the windshield wiper of her car, asking her to call him. He worked on edge the entire next day waiting for her to call.

She hadn't called.

That night, however, there was a small brown paper bag set on the hood of his car with a note inside.

"One tangible thanks. That big husky of yours will love it. Sara." It came from a specialty dog shop in Lake Forest, and as he hefted the rubber ball he had to smile. It even smelled like the inside of an old shoe. How she found out he owned a Siberian husky was not something he wanted to ponder too long.

The next week he left another note and his business card, asking her to stop by. He would like to take her out to lunch at her convenience.

The note, but not the business card, was tucked under his windshield wiper that same night with a simple no written beneath the invitation.

The next day his secretary asked him point-blank what had put him in such a foul mood.

He thought his third invitation, left with a single white-red rose, was accepted until he walked into the coffee shop on the first-floor lobby where he was to meet Sara and found the waitress wearing the rose pinned to her uniform. She told him his coffee was already paid for, but Sara was unable to stay. The message had been a polite way of saying, "I'm not coming." There was a note on his car that night saying, "Please, no more invitations."

It was driving Adam crazy.

He had never pursued when someone told him to back off. And she couldn't have been more clear in her request, but his heart refused to leave the problem alone. It wasn't right. He wanted to meet her, at least once, under normal circumstances. If she told him to his face to get lost, then he'd do it. His gut told him her denials were coming from sheer embarrassment over how they had met, and that they had little if anything to do with him.

He wanted her found.

"What would you do, Jordan?"

"Follow her to see where she works. She parks under this tower, so that cuts the search area in half. It wouldn't be that hard, just time consuming. Have someone in the garage wait for her car to arrive, then have him follow her."

"What's Thomas doing? Can you spare him for a few days?"

"The kid will love it. He's been buried in law books for the past four weeks."

The park was deserted at two in the afternoon. Sara was grateful. The solitude allowed her to drop her guard a bit. She would never be totally comfortable in a park again—she and Kim had been playing on a set of swings when a van swerved toward them and men grabbed them.

Security was with her now. Ben was jogging along the track that circled the park. He liked to work out. She was always in his sight, and he could inspect the woods that encircled the park without drawing attention. Dave was somewhere around too, though Sara doubted she would spot him.

She owed Adam an apology. That bit with the rose and the coffee had not been handled tactfully at all. It had been downright insulting, now that she thought about it.

He didn't mean anything threatening by his actions. But after so many years of trying to stay out of someone's sights, to suddenly have someone focused on her was not only wonderful, it was also terrifying.

Dave didn't know about the requests. She had managed to talk him out of changing her office location, but just barely. If he had even the *suspicion* that Adam was trying to get in touch with her, her office would be relocated. She did not want to move. It had taken a lot of time to put together her studio. The regional FBI office was in the same building; a fact that made life easier on her entire security team. She didn't want them having to live with all the hassles that came with working at two locations. She had worked at the office complex for three months without meeting Adam. There was no reason to believe she couldn't continue to slip past him.

And if she did see him again, what then? It bothered her that she couldn't envision what she would say. All these invitations were making her freeze.

Adam's first note had been a surprise. His handwriting was strong, sharp, clear, except for his signature, which showed the result of having signed autographs for twelve years. Sara had looked repeatedly at that note during the following two days, tempted to call and yet always pulling back when it came time to dial the number.

The invitation to lunch had come next. The fact he was so interested in seeing her again made her hesitate even more.

She had spent a long time sitting in the rose garden behind her home that night, looking at the stars, talking to God, trying to figure out what she should do.

She wasn't a coward. If she were, years before she would have retreated back into her shell and pulled back entirely from life. She was a fighter. Life knocked her down, and she coped by getting up and moving on. But right now she was on ice so thin she had no idea how to step without crashing through. Guys didn't exactly appear in her world. There were safety concerns. Background checks. Precautions to keep her out of the public eye.

She didn't have the option of accepting. Her position put her in the situation where nothing in her schedule happened spontaneously. To accept would open doors she simply did not want to open with Adam. She would have to trust him with an awful lot of information in order to let him into her life. She winced just imagining that initial conversation. Sometimes playing it safe was the smart and only thing she could do.

She didn't trust Adam's reaction—that was the bottom line.

At times she had to struggle to trust God, and He was perfect in all His actions. Even events like getting stuck in the elevator figured somewhere in His sovereign plan. With a few days to shake off the aftereffects of that evening, she was willing to trust that there was some good purpose behind the event.

It was interesting, reading her own faith journey as captured in her journal. Fear was a nasty problem to overcome. She thought she had made progress, then got hit with another challenge. And she found she wasn't on quite as solid ground as she'd thought. It wasn't a battle she could win once and get past. She longed for the day when she could face a crisis without the panic winning.

She had to live with life as it was. Security. A very real

threat sat waiting in the shadows. Her faith sometimes met the challenge and sometimes did not.

Her decision for today wasn't that difficult. Adam might want to have lunch. There was no likely reason he would want to see her again after that. Taking so many risks for a single meal was a bad idea. The best strategy was to simply keep the door firmly closed.

There had been a brief glimmer of hope in the last week. News of the packing tape discovery had come at a vulnerable time. After all these years, she was careful to take news for what it was, not to go beyond the actual information.

This time, the hope had been in full bloom before she could stop it. Dave had burst that bubble last night. The tape had been a general lot number shipped to twenty-two states. She had wanted the freedom to answer one of Adam's requests without having the baggage of her past hanging over her head. It wasn't to be.

She needed to apologize to Adam for that rose. Avoid him, but apologize.

"No gray sedan license BI 691. She didn't come to work today," Thomas reported at 3 P.M.

Adam tried not to let his disappointment show. The way his luck was going, Sara was a writer who frequently got sent out of town on assignments.

Lord, should I just drop this? Everything is conspiring to keep me from meeting her again.

He didn't feel a hard-and-fast conviction one way or the other. He just knew he wanted to see her. He wasn't ready to give up trying.

"Take the rest of the day off and try again on Monday, Thomas," Adam said quietly.

All I want to do is talk with her. Is that too much to ask?

He tried to push aside the disappointment and stay focused on work. It had been a full day of meetings and more still to come, but at least the next one was with former team-mates over at the sports club. It wasn't easy. His thoughts kept drifting to the plans he had. Lunch with Sara had become a mission, and not one that was easily set aside.

Four-fifteen finally came. Adam gathered up his notes and slid them into his briefcase, glad the meeting gave him an excuse to get out of the office.

The message was waiting for him at his car.

The note was on white linen paper, slipped into a matching envelope with a deep blue border around it. The windshield wiper left a slight smear across his name.

"My mother never approved of rudeness. Forgive me for giving away the rose? Keeping it would have generated questions I could not afford to have asked. Sara."

There were two tickets to the sold-out Friday night charity basketball game along with the note. Good seats too. It was quite an apology.

He scanned the garage and felt a deep sense of relief when he saw her car. She was somewhere in the building.

Acute frustration warred with responsibility. Canceling his meeting wasn't an option. Some of his friends had flown in to attend. He had already told Thomas to go home, and Jordan was out of the office. There were no good options.

He finally did the only thing he could. Scanning her note, he wrote one in reply. She had cracked her solid wall of saying no. If he could keep her talking…

"Sara, apology accepted. But freelance writers don't have several thousand dollars at their disposal, and those tickets are going at twenty-five hundred dollars apiece on the street. Take them back, please."

He put the note on her car windshield and hoped he would be back in time to see her retrieve it.

No such luck. When he got back from his meeting, her car was gone.

When Monday evening came, there was another note waiting for him. He had been somewhat prepared for it. He knew she had been at work today. Thomas had lost her this morning in the lobby shops. He opened it slowly, hoping for the biggest wish of all—a phone number.

"Adam. Enjoy the game."

Her car was already gone. If he hadn't been saving her notes like a kid in high school, he would have crumpled the elegant card in frustration.

He drove home, wondering how his timing always managed to be off just enough that he kept missing her. He had hoped to at least get a chance to ask her to go to the game with him, but that apparently wasn't going to happen.

He let the valet park his car.

He still lived in a condominium, even though since his retirement he'd promised himself a house with several bedrooms, a large yard, and a view of something other than the city skyline. His condo wasn't a small place. There were advantages to living so close to work; he often walked to the office.

His dog met him, padding in from the living room. Adam greeted the animal with an affectionate welcome.

His sister Mary Beth had helped decorate this place. She

managed to turn it into a comfortable home. He liked it well enough, but there were days he wished there was someone else who lived here as well, who would occasionally mess up the place. When he returned in the evening, it was always as he had left it in the morning. It got boring.

Adam dropped his briefcase by the couch and walked to the kitchen to retrieve a cold drink. He was tired. Tired inside where his hopes and dreams lived.

He sank down onto the leather recliner that faced the entertainment center but didn't bother to turn on the stereo. Instead he sat in silence while he drank the cold soda.

Sara, why do you have to be so stubbornly hard to find? A nice dinner and you would probably stop haunting my dreams. At the moment you are playing havoc with my life.

Sara looked down at her glass, biting her lip, then raised her head. "Ellen, are you sure about this? Being a politician's wife?" They were having dinner at her best friend's home, going over the wedding reception plans. Sara had been trying hard not to ask the question all evening. It was unfair, for Ellen was deeply in love with Richard—his occupation shouldn't matter. But Sara had to ask. Had to raise the warning one last time.

Her friend leaned forward and set her own glass on the table. "Yes."

Ellen looked back at her with sympathy in her eyes; it had never been pity, or they never would have become friends. They had met in Switzerland as teenagers, both there on vacation. Sara had hung on to that friendship, one of the few she was able to keep despite the frequent relocations.

"Your father was, *is,* an ambassador, Sara. That's an entirely different game than being a state official. Richard would be comfortable being a mayor someday, or maybe a state senator. But he honestly has no desire to go into national politics. I won't let my children be put into that public spotlight."

"Hold him to that, Ellen. Don't put your children at risk."

"What's going on? This is a lot more than your persistent fear of a child you know getting snatched. You want to tell me what has been going on since that experience in the elevator? You were looking over your shoulder when we were shopping today."

"I'm jumping at shadows. I thought someone was following me yesterday."

"What? Where?"

"I was on my way upstairs to work, and I suddenly felt like I was inside a fishbowl, like someone was watching me intently. It scared me badly enough I used one of Dave's cutout routes to get to my office."

"What did Dave have to say?"

"I didn't tell him. By the time I reached my office and realized there was no one following me, I felt like a fool."

"You should have told him immediately."

"I feel like a fool just telling you. It was nothing but my nerves. Ever since that elevator ride, I've been jumping at my own shadow. What are we ordering in for dinner?"

"Chinese. Quit changing the subject. Your instincts are good, Sara. You have to tell Dave when he gets home tonight."

"He got called to San Jose for a consult on a case. He'll be back in a couple of days."

"Call one of the others on the team."

"When there is even the slightest evidence to support the feeling—a face I see in different places, someone following me—believe me, I'll hit the panic button. Until then, it's nothing but my nerves getting frayed. I'm always like this at the end of a book."

"You've finished it?"

"Two more days. Like to read it?"

"Absolutely. It's going to be your next international best-seller."

"It's the best book I've written to date," Sara replied, knowing it was true, knowing it would likely bring record sales. The money made very little difference in her life now. The story represented more memories put to rest. It had accomplished that—it was enough.

Again she considered telling Ellen about Adam. Ellen was her best friend, and yet Sara had mentioned nothing about the notes or the rose. She was hiding the truth because she was afraid to hear Ellen's response.

Ellen would tell her to accept, to open the door. She didn't understand the emotional pain that came with always having to say good-bye. Sara had learned to protect her heart from that constant bruising.

No, it wasn't something she wanted to discuss with Ellen. Whatever possibilities there had been were over. Even Adam was unlikely to persist much longer.

"Has Richard hinted at what kind of honeymoon arrangements he's making?"

"His only instructions have been to pack for ten days. I can't get a clue from him as to our final destination."

Sara wished the envy would fade. Her journey with Adam was over. Her final destination had been a dead end.

"Mr. Black, I think I know why it's been so hard to find her. She doesn't work in this tower," Thomas said, his face flushed with excitement.

"I was on my way back from delivering those papers to the Pratt and Getty law firm in the next tower when I saw her step out of the elevator carrying her briefcase. She crossed the concourse to this tower. I followed her down to the garage and watched her leave."

Adam leaned back in his desk chair. "You're kidding."

"No, sir. I can't explain why she's been taking this tower elevator to different floors in the morning, but I'm convinced that if I wait on the sixth floor concourse, I'll pick her up on her way to work."

"Good work, Thomas. Great work, in fact. Try it again tomorrow."

"Yes, sir."

Adam got up and moved to the office window to look down at the street.

Sara, you and I are going to be saying hello tomorrow. I hope you're ready for it, because after the past weeks of trying to find you, I certainly am.

CHAPTER | 4

Someone was following her.

Sara's heart rate jumped. Her steps accelerated. It was just a glimpse. Just a glimpse of a color. A man's suit jacket. A man's face. But every sense in her body suddenly focused.

She had seen him before.

Several times.

Like last week in the garage.

Two days before in the other tower elevator.

Yesterday.

Yesterday he had followed her down to the parking garage.

Her hand was already pushing the panic pager in her jacket pocket. She was on the concourse standing in front of the elevators. She had three prearranged routes to choose from. She chose the second, slipping into the ladies' rest room with an abrupt move.

She had never thought any one of these contingencies

would ever be used. Her pulse pounded in her ears as she rushed to the other rest room entrance. *Lord, it's been three years since he's gotten this close. Why now?*

The elevator across the corridor was just opening.

Go, or not? What should she do?

He knew she was in this room. She raced for the open elevator.

He'd seen her.

"Thirty-four, I'm late," she gasped out to the other occupant of the elevator—needing the doors to close—desperate to have the doors close.

At the last minute, she knew she had made a fatal mistake. The elevator doors were not going to close in time.

God is my refuge in times of trouble. The words first memorized in her childhood flooded her mind as someone bumped into the man she feared.

The elevator doors closed.

She was safe. For the moment. The lady with her in the elevator gave her a curious look but Sara ignored it. The cut outs and the safety routes, changing floors and using the stairs, would only delay her from getting where she was to where she needed to be. As soon as she pushed that panic page, her entire life had changed.

Her sole objective now was to reach the thirty-fourth floor. They were already responding. They knew which elevator she was in, knew she was moving up. They would be coming to meet her.

She was beginning to shake, but now it was with anger. For three years she had been safe, and now he was on her heels again. She deserved to be angry.

Come on, follow me, she prayed as she rocked on her

heels, watching the floor numbers tick by. If they could catch him, her nightmare would be over.

The elevator doors opened on the thirty-fourth floor. Sara stepped out. A glance up showed one other elevator moving up, now passing the thirtieth floor.

Let it be him. Please, let it be the guy following me. The last thing I want is a drawn-out search to find the man I saw.

She walked at her normal pace down the hall to her office suite, adrenaline pounding high, passing a man waiting to get on the third elevator. A lady was arranging a large bouquet of flowers in the hall display. The agents had been fast. They had made better time than in any of their frequent drills.

She heard the elevator door open behind her just as the security lock on her own office door clicked open and she stepped inside.

A voice behind her called her name. She ignored it.

A hand on her left shoulder moved her silently to the side and another body moved in front of her.

"How many?"

"One," she whispered back. The hand on her shoulder gave a gentle squeeze.

"FBI! Freeze!"

"Down on your knees!"

It was over.

A panic page from the daughter of a U.S. ambassador, with a known stalker still active against her, could and would bring down the wrath of more than a few agents. Sara had left a very scared young man who could not be more than twenty-three sitting cuffed on the couch in the reception area of her office suite, answering questions coming at him from five very protective agents. She escaped downstairs to the FBI offices on the eighteenth floor. She paced the private office of the FBI regional director.

"Would you care to explain how you can now recall four encounters with this man who followed you, yet you mentioned none of them to your brother?" He leaned back against his desk. He wasn't mad; he was furious.

"My ultimate safety rests solely with me, Mr. Marshall. I made the call when I felt there was a reasonable threat. Until that point, neither you nor my brother needed to know." She spoke as the ambassador's daughter she was and did not bother to hide the British accent nor the formality of her next order. "I would like to know who he is and why he was following me. I would also like to speak with the agents who responded so promptly, if you would not mind. They did an excellent job."

"Agent Richman!"

The door opened and her brother Dave came in. He had been one of the three agents waiting inside her office when she had stepped inside, his body the one that had moved between her and the threat.

"Escort her upstairs."

"Yes, sir."

Dave draped his arm around her shoulders as they left the office together. "I love it when you get British, squirt."

"Stuff it, Dave," she replied affectionately, leaning against him.

He squeezed her shoulder. "Making it okay?"

She was a trembling mess. But it was over. Patching over

the shakes was becoming all too common for her. "I could use some tea."

"That I can probably arrange." He gestured to another agent in the open bullpen of desks.

They went up to the thirty-fourth floor together. The suspect had just been taken downstairs.

"What have you found out, Dave?"

Her brother gestured toward the office where she created her children's books, and they stepped inside. He shut the door behind them. "His name is Thomas Berman, and he was following you because he was instructed to do so. Apparently Adam wants to know your last name and where you work." Dave said the last with something of a smile.

Sara sat down abruptly at her drawing table. "All of this—" she looked around, then shook her head, not sure whether to laugh or cry—"All of this was because of Adam Black?"

"Mr. Black."

Adam looked up with a start. It was flat unheard of for his secretary to interrupt while he was on the phone.

Until now. "You are *never* going to believe this. Thomas Berman has just gotten himself arrested by the FBI!"

"Lance, I'll call you back."

Adam dropped the phone and ran both hands through his hair. This couldn't be happening. All he wanted was a date.

A short time later, he was sitting with Jordan in the FBI office of agent David Richman, being questioned by an agent who had identified herself as Susan Vernon.

Adam was not used to getting stonewalled. "I would like to see my employee."

"Of course, Mr. Black. You'll be able to in due time. We are still trying to sort out exactly what happened."

"What did happen, if you don't mind my asking?"

"Let's just say that little red light above your head went red at 8:17 A.M., and life got a little interesting around here for a while."

"What did Thomas do, interrupt a vice presidential speech?"

"Adam." It was a quiet warning from Jordan.

"He followed and posed a threat to a lady we protect with a great deal of diligence," replied a voice from the doorway. "Enough of a threat that she tripped a panic code. She hasn't felt the need to do that in over three years."

Adam swung around in the chair. "Sara?"

"Sara," replied the man.

Adam wanted to swear but instead tightened his hands and deliberately relaxed them. "Is she okay?"

The man in the doorway relaxed his weight against the door frame, the shoulder holster he wore visible under his jacket. "I left her sketching dragons and fireflies," he replied. "Susan, I'll take back my office. Thanks for the assist."

She smiled as she handed him the paperwork she had begun. "Anytime."

Adam watched Agent Richman move around the desk and take a seat.

The man looked back at him, studying him. "So, you want to know her last name and where she works. Why?"

"Does it matter?"

"Adam." It was another soft warning from Jordan.

The FBI agent waved away the warning. "Don't worry about it. Let's see...there was an incident in an elevator that went dark and stopped, followed by coffee at the Marque Hotel, an invitation to phone, a ball for your dog, an invitation to lunch, an invitation to coffee accompanied by a rose, an apology accompanied by two basketball game tickets—tickets which I would very much like to know how she obtained—and finally, a decision by you to try to tail her from her car to the place she worked in order to learn the information you sought. Would that be a fair summary of events?"

Since the man had given the list from memory and certainly not from any paperwork, Adam raised an eyebrow. "May I presume you are the Dave she speed dialed to tell she would be home at ten-thirty?" Adam ignored the fact Jordan had turned and looked ready to throttle him. Most of what the agent had just said, Jordan was hearing for the first time.

"Let's just say Sara and I don't have too many secrets." The agent tapped his pen against the pad of paper on his desk. "However, your employee Thomas appears to have been one of them. She hadn't mentioned to any of us the impression she was being followed. She hit a panic code this morning, and Sara hasn't done that in the last three years."

"Who is she?"

"No one you would know, I assure you. She writes children's books for five-year-olds. And where said five-year-olds are concerned, she is quite famous."

"But that's not why she has you and all of this." Adam gestured about him.

"No."

"What is Thomas Berman being charged with?" Jordan asked.

"In light of the...unusual nature of what occurred, we'll discuss it. In all likelihood, no formal charges will be made."

Adam felt relieved at that news.

He leaned forward in his chair and considered the man across from him. Dave. His competition? His adversary? Or his potential ally? Dave clearly knew what had happened to Sara in the past, and Adam knew with absolute conviction that he wanted—no needed—to know every detail of that information. "May I see Sara?"

Dave considered for a moment and then nodded. He picked up his phone. "Sara, I have some guests who would like to see you. May we come up?"

He made a face even as he smiled, turning slightly in his chair. "You are driving a hard bargain, lady. Are you sure?"

"Okay, okay. Anything in particular sound good?"

"Done. We'll be up in a few minutes."

He hung up the phone. "Let's go meet Sara."

Dave led the way. "Susan, would you call Dirk and ask him to cater us lunch here and in Sara's suite? She's making me buy again, for everybody, so make sure he knows he's catering for about thirty people."

Susan laughed. "Glad to."

"You know she's doing this deliberately just so I'll go broke one day."

"With your private expense account? That'll be the day," Susan replied. "Tell her thanks from all of us."

Thomas had been right. Sara did work in the east tower. They took the elevator to the thirty-fourth floor.

They had to pass two FBI agents to enter Sara's office suite. The gold stenciling on the plaque outside simply said: SW, Ltd.

Sara's secretary met them with a smile and a Texas accent as she asked if they would like something to drink. Adam declined. Jordan, with an answering smile, asked for a soft drink.

"Have a seat, gentlemen." Dave motioned and moved to a closed door where he tapped softly.

Adam was impressed with Sara's suite. The reception area was a profusion of flowers and fauna, the couch, chairs, and tables placed together for a visitor's comfort.

It was a beautiful, comfortable, relaxing room.

The wall displayed children's books, the covers enticing one to linger and browse. Several of the covers carried the gold medallion of a major award. Interesting. It wasn't what Adam would have placed as her profession, yet it fit. Her work was exceptional.

Her secretary brought Jordan his drink. A phone rang and she retreated to an open office off the reception area to answer it.

"Adam, you really should play it cool when you see Sara. Apologize profusely. These guys are close to having legal rights to charge you with harassment."

"They won't."

"Probably not, but they could make your life miserable. As your lawyer, as well as your brother-in-law, I strongly suggest you promise to keep your distance and never seek her out again."

"She's not going to take it that way."

"Oh, really? You said she was really terrified by that experience in the elevator. How do you think she felt this morning at the moment she hit that panic code? Fine? You managed to scare the daylights out of her. Don't expect a nice reception here."

Adam already knew that. He had known it the moment the agent had said Sara had sent a panic code. He had seen her cope with the incident in the elevator and pull herself together so quickly it made his head spin. He only hoped she had coped in the same way with this morning's incident.

Adam would never knowingly have caused her trauma…but the hard truth was that he had. It was inexcusable. He owed her more than just an apology, but he didn't want his actions to cause her yet more grief.

"Come on in, gentlemen." Dave gestured from the now open doorway.

It was obviously Sara's domain. There were sketches and storyboards all around, large work surfaces laying out books in progress. It was a place that any child would have found enthralling. The pictures and sketches conveyed the talent of a world-class artist. The room was vibrant in colors and the flowers were profuse.

She was sketching, a colored pencil in one hand, a cup of tea in the other.

Dave walked over and set his hand on her shoulder. He looked at the sketch. "This one is pretty neat."

She smiled, still looking at the sketch, then she glanced up at them and lowered her gaze back to the sketch.

Adam did not like the tense look in her face that had yet to fade.

She set down the cup of tea, pulled the sketch from the pad, and handed it to Dave. "Add it to your collection."

"You're going to make me rich with all these free drawings."

Sara squeezed the hand on her shoulder. "Right. You're already rich."

Adam saw her take a deep breath and reach for her cup of tea before she looked over at him.

"Please, gentlemen, have a seat." Her tone of voice was formal. There were several stools around the room, as well as conventional chairs. She smiled at Jordan when introduced.

Dave remained standing, leaning against the drafting table by her side.

"Dave, has Mr. Berman been released yet?"

"Soon."

"Adam, please apologize to your employee for me. I'm afraid he got more than he bargained for when he tried to approach me. These gentlemen stop you forcefully and ask questions later."

"I will, Sara. You have my word."

"I feel bad for him. He was clearly just the messenger."

"Are you okay?"

Adam was surprised to find she looked up at Dave before she answered. "Fine."

She wasn't. He wondered what was going on in her mind. He wished they were alone, not being watched by his brother-in-law and her protective FBI agent. He wished she were relaxed, not so tense her fingers were white as they held the cup of tea. "I am so sorry, Sara. I would never have knowingly frightened you."

"Tomorrow it will be forgotten."

He doubted that.

She smiled, seeming to collect herself. "Since you went to such extreme lengths to learn where I worked, would you be interested in seeing the place?"

Her invitation clearly took her some courage to offer. There had been more than a little damage done to this lady this morning. His error. His responsibility.

"Yes, I would," he replied, knowing he was starting at ground zero with her again.

Dave took the teacup from her as she got to her feet. "I'll get you some more tea."

"Thanks, Dave."

"Jordan, why don't you and I talk about Mr. Berman for a moment," Dave requested.

Sara led Adam to the far wall and the story line sketched there. "This is my next book."

God, what do I say that will help her? You are the only one who really knows where she's at inside. What does she need to hear?

Adam looked at the charcoal sketches and the few she had done in color and could see a playfulness to her work that made him smile. "It's good, Sara."

"I think so."

She showed him several of the stories she was working on, and he asked some questions, learning how a children's book was produced. He also heard her relax as she was pulled into a world that was obviously a passion in her life.

"Is there any way I can apologize?" he asked quietly when her words tapered off.

He had been watching her hands. They were clenched together or pushed into the pockets of her jacket when they were not gesturing as she described something. She was trying to stop them from trembling. She was relaxing, but she had a long way to go before she was steady. He desperately wanted to make today fade from her memory.

"I'm fine, Adam. Believe me, I have been through much tougher mornings."

"But it never should have happened." Adam gently touched her hand and felt the soft tremor in it. "I didn't know. But that is hardly an excuse." From the corner of his eye he saw the FBI agent moving toward them.

Adam was glad Sara had the protection she obviously needed, but it felt quite stifling to know his every move anywhere near her was being closely watched and reacted to.

His own life in the spotlight had felt nothing like this. There had been a lot of team security and at times a lot of personal security around him. But this was different. This was protective coverage, not general security.

"Dave's quite protective," he remarked, admitting the obvious with a reluctant smile as he dropped his hand.

Sara smiled. "He's also my brother."

Adam felt like she had dropped a bomb. "You're serious?"

"It makes security easier. I can trust him."

Adam felt one enormous weight lift from his shoulders. Dave was not his competition.

"When can we have dinner together?"

"Adam…"

"I'm not taking no for an answer, not after nearly getting one of my best employees arrested just to ask the question." Adam knew what he wanted to secure before he left this office. He wanted, no *needed*, time with Sara, and he would have it arranged before they parted company today. If he didn't, he knew she would have time to put obstacle after obstacle in his path.

Sara bit her bottom lip. Eating out meant security. It would never work. Adam might be able to adjust to the watching eyes, but her conversation would at best be stilted. She would never be able to be herself when men she had known for five, and some of them ten, years watched every move she made and every move around her. The men would be discreet, kind, and she knew them well enough to know there would be no unnecessary intrusions on her evening. But she would know they were there, and that would be enough to turn her into a flustered ball of nerves.

Sara made up her mind. "Come for dinner Friday night. Security is easier on my own turf."

Adam's smile told her it had been the right decision.

"I can't believe you invited him to dinner."

"Dave, why won't you let the subject drop? It's not like I'm going on a date. I just want somewhere private to explain why I'm not interested in seeing him, to ask him to back off."

Her brother checked the rearview mirror again. "Sure."

"Why do I get the impression you're not buying a word I'm saying?"

"Because I'm not."

"I might feel a certain…attraction," Sara admitted, "but he's a public figure. A *well-known* public figure with all those commercials he has made."

"Don't forget the magazines."

"Exactly my point. He was voted Most Eligible Chicago Bachelor last year for goodness' sake. There is no way we could ever have a relationship. You and I both know it. Why do you think I kept turning down his invitations? One photo, one too-inquisitive journalist who tried to go into my past, and my life, my privacy here would disappear. I like him, okay? I'll admit that. But I don't like him *that* much."

"Sara, we can't let the trail lead to you. Right now that second kidnapper doesn't have a name or a location. Sara Walsh has no connection to Sara Richman. Our mother's marriage to Peter Walsh, your adoption papers, have been so deeply buried that no one is going to make that connection without access to sealed documents. Don't do something foolish that will change that."

"Dave, I promise. On Mother's grave. I won't let there be a lapse in security. Now, is the lecture over?"

Dave reached over and squeezed her hand. "I know this is hard for you. I know that, but we are going to catch this guy one day. His last package to the embassy had the necklace you were wearing when you were snatched. All the profilers say he is becoming more and more obsessed with what happened. Every package and letter he sends gives another clue to work with. We will either catch him or convince his partner to give him up."

"After twenty-five years, do you honestly expect the kidnapper who was convicted to say a word?"

"No," Dave admitted. "It would be too easy. I think his partner got to him and convinced him to keep his mouth shut or he would wind up dead."

CHAPTER | 5

S o this is your place. I have to say, Sara, I'm impressed."
"Actually this was my grandmother's home. She left it
to Dave and me," Sara commented as she closed the
front door behind him.

The property was not large enough to be classified as an
estate, but the five acres of open land allowed the house to be
set toward the back of the property. Large flower beds land-
scaped the grounds around the house.

"Think you'll keep this one?"

She blushed as she accepted the white-red rose. "Yes, I
will. Thank you."

"You're welcome." As she looked flustered, he got practical.
"What's for dinner?"

She laughed. "Italian. But I warn you, I'm cooking so it
could be an interesting meal. Come on back to the kitchen."

He liked her dress. She liked bold colors. He had noticed
that the first evening they met, seen it in the statement she
made with her office, and now in the dress she wore tonight.

Solid blue on top, to a four-inch red sash at her waist, into a flowing skirt that flared with multiple colors. She was in high heels again—to put her closer to his height?

Adam looked around the house as he followed her, finding it an intriguing mixture of European and early American furniture—walnut and redwood dominating. The home was light and airy, the profusion of plants and flowers making the home a warm living place. The paintings on the wall were bold in color and placed to attract the maximum attention. Family pictures and snapshots were displayed on polished tables. This was the home of a family who had wealth and had had it for many generations.

It was also clear they lived here. In the den there was mail on the end table and a suit jacket tossed on the couch and a sprawling stack of magazines on the coffee table.

The kitchen was spacious and smelled of olive oil and browning garlic. The cutting board was covered with freshly diced tomatoes, peppers, and olives. She was fixing a pasta dish, and the smells were heavenly. She moved to check the tenderness of the simmering pasta.

"Help yourself to something to drink. Sodas are on the bottom shelf. That fruit juice stuff Dave likes is somewhere in back."

"What are you having?"

She reached over to stir the sauce simmering on a back burner. "Ice water." She grinned. "At least for now."

She wasn't in a hurry in her own house; her movements were fluid, graceful, and relaxed. Charming.

She didn't mind that the meal wasn't ready when he arrived. She seemed intent on having a relaxing evening with him, and Adam couldn't find the words to express his gratitude. He had been afraid the evening would be stiff and formal and touched with the unfortunate history of their first two meetings. She seemed determined not to let that happen.

He slipped off his suit jacket and draped it over one of the kitchen chairs. "Can I do the salad?"

"Sure. Oh, and find us some music—there is a radio tucked by the bread maker."

The radio was already tuned to a jazz station.

"That's Dave's preference. See if you can find some country."

Adam tuned in to a station he liked.

"Thanks."

There were breadsticks ready to go in the oven and fresh-grated Parmesan cheese for the pasta already prepared.

Adam cleared a section of countertop and took an interested look over the salad options she had set out on the counter. He liked to cook when it was going to be for more than just one. When it was just him, he didn't bother.

Sara leaned past him to retrieve some fresh oregano.

"Can I ask you a question?"

She popped an olive in her mouth. "Sure."

"Why the invitation to come here instead of somewhere public?"

"You would have seen a different me in a restaurant. As you seemed to be determined for us to spend a couple hours together, I thought it was best that you not see the wrapper but the real me."

"The security?"

"Yes. But also the fact I would be sitting there exposed. That knowledge sets me on edge. I don't have the security for the fun of it."

Adam considered what she had said. "Will you tell me

someday why you need the security?"

Sara momentarily stopped moving. "I don't know. There are only about a dozen people in the world who know all the details, another couple dozen who know bits and pieces."

"That's not many people."

"It's been going on for twenty-five years, Adam," she said simply. "Security is part of who I am and how I live. It's either private or professional security, depending on my father's job at any point in time, but it's always there. You're going to have a tough transition to learn what that means. To you, the public spotlight is your career; for me, staying out of the public spotlight is an absolute necessity for staying alive."

Adam absorbed that statement with some shock. Twenty-five years was practically her entire lifetime.

"Sara, can you get this tie straight? I swear you bought this particular one deliberately." Dave interrupted them, coming into the kitchen, dressed for a night out.

Sara smiled as she wiped her hands. "You look quite elegant in black tie."

"Stuff it, squirt, and just fix the blasted thing. Next time you send ballet tickets to my girlfriend, I'm going to throttle you myself." Dave held still as she fixed his tie. "Hello, Adam."

Adam grinned. "Hello, Dave."

Sara patted Dave's chest. "There. You're all set."

"Thank you. I think. What's the password for tonight?"

"Chili peppers."

"Got it. Security is hot in zones four, seven, and ten in the house and all the grounds. Travis is principal for the night." Dave kissed her cheek. "Be good. Don't do anything I wouldn't do."

Sara laughed and pushed him toward the doorway. "Out. Or you're going to be late picking up Linda."

He glanced at the clock and grabbed his keys. "You're right. And she absolutely hates that. Night, you two."

"Would you like to eat in here or the more formal dining room?" Sara asked as her brother left.

"The difference being?"

"The formal dining room is the white tablecloth, candlelight, china, et cetera."

Adam leaned against the kitchen counter and grinned. "And here?"

She shrugged, grinning back. "It's comfortable."

"With you, I think I prefer comfortable."

She gestured toward the cabinet to his right. "Plates are there."

The phone rang. She reached around and snagged a cordless phone from the counter. "This is Sara."

Her back stiffened and she straightened, her smile disappearing. "Hello, Father."

Adam was startled by the tone in her voice. It had turned cool and formal. Her father? It was obvious as the minutes passed that what she was listening to was not pleasant. She spoke few words, just listened. Her accent caught his attention. He had heard it before and not made the connection. The phone call ended and her jaw was tense. It was a moment before she set down the phone.

Adam hesitated before he said anything. "You're British?"

"I hold dual British-American citizenship," she replied, lost in thought.

She shook her head slightly and gestured toward the kitchen table. She put the breadsticks into the oven and set the timer. "Let's eat. The bread will be done when we're ready for the pasta."

Adam didn't push the subject.

The salad was eaten quietly.

They put the pasta together over the stove, passing plates back and forth. Adam bumped her shoulder as they moved toward the table. "Sorry."

She looked up, and the distant look in her eyes dropped away. Okay, maybe his move had not been that subtle.

"Adam, you're as bad as Dave." She slid onto her seat. "Sorry. My father raised some subjects I would have rather dealt with tomorrow."

"I'm sorry."

She smiled. "So am I. It interrupted what was becoming a nice evening."

"Sara."

She met his eyes.

Adam smiled. "Enjoy your meal. It's still going to be an enjoyable evening."

Her look was one of amusement. "Yes, I think it will be."

"The pasta's good." He was surprised to see a slight blush form as she accepted the compliment. So she didn't cook for many men besides her brother. He would be lying to say that fact didn't please him.

"Tell me how you got into writing children's books," he asked, moving the conversation to a subject he knew she was comfortable with.

Sara choked on her water.

Adam came around the table to help her as she struggled to get her breath back. "Okay?"

She nodded, tears still wet in her eyes. "Sorry."

"Sit back easy and take a few deep breaths."

She finally did so and Adam felt some of his panic fade.

"Your question surprised me. I apologize."

She hides behind formality when she gets uncomfortable. The realization made him want to smile. If they had been beyond a first date he would have reached over and stroked her chestnut hair back from her face, told her to relax. Instead, he took his seat and watched her with a slightly raised eyebrow, waiting for her to explain.

"When my parents divorced, my mother married Frank Victor, and we went to live in Texas. Frank was the one who taught me to draw." She hesitated. "I had been telling stories all my life, putting the two talents together seemed a natural fit. My first book as Sara Walsh was published when I was twenty."

"That wasn't Frank on the phone."

"No. Frank died when I was fourteen. That was my father, William Richman."

Her face showed so much tension when she thought about her father. He could never imagine feeling that way about his dad. "Was the divorce bitter?"

"On the contrary. My parents were so polite about the thing, it was barely even mentioned in the papers. One day we were in London and the next we were in Texas."

Adam tried to put together the pieces she had told him. Sara's family had been living in London when her parents divorced. She and her mother had returned to the United States. A couple whose divorce would be worth a journalist's time and a newspaper's space...

"Your father still lives in London?"

"He's still there."

Dave. That was the key. Adam remembered now. In the elevator. When Sara had whispered that what she had wanted most for her eighth birthday was not the horse Golden Glory but her brother back... "Dave didn't come back to the States with you and your mom, did he?" Adam asked quietly. "He stayed with your father."

"He stayed with my father."

The pain had to be over twenty years old, and yet it still looked so raw in her eyes.

"I made a cheesecake for dessert. Let's take it into the living room."

Adam rose politely when she did, accepting the coffee and dessert she offered him.

William Richman was Sara's father. For some reason the name was familiar, but he couldn't place it.

The living room was a beautiful room, an extension of the rest of the house in its formal yet livable decor, the white carpet contrasting with gleaming polished wood. The bookcases were filled with mysteries and suspense novels; two books with bookmarks were stacked on the end table. Sara sank down on one end of the sofa, and Adam chose a comfortable chair across from her.

Richman. Dave's last name. Her mother had then married Frank Victor. So how had Sara's last name become Walsh? Now that was an interesting puzzle. Had it ever been formally changed, or for security reasons had everything simply been changed overnight to Walsh? Adam froze.

"Sara, you've never been married have you?" He didn't know a polite way to ask the question.

He was grateful she looked puzzled and not offended. "No."

"Your last name is Walsh. I was trying to figure out how that transpired."

He was getting used to her hesitations. It was as if she were mentally censoring what she said. "After Frank died, Mom married for a third time. I was adopted by Peter Walsh when I was sixteen."

"You don't sound happy about that."

"It pleased my mother," Sara replied, leaving it at that.

His life had been one of consistency and steadiness; hers sounded like a life being shuffled from pillar to post. Different countries. Displaced siblings. Frank's death—she spoke of him with great fondness. Yet a third home before she was eighteen. He couldn't even imagine the toll that had taken on her as a child.

He gestured to the pictures above the fireplace mantel. "May I?"

"Feel free." Sara continued to sip her coffee as she sat curled up on the couch, having slipped off her shoes.

Adam got up and studied the pictures. They were informal shots, most of them pictures of her and Dave taken in the last few years. Sara was laughing at her brother in most of them. There was one of them on skis, snow flying up toward the camera as they both turned to an abrupt halt at the same instant. A second picture showed them apparently taking part in a game of touch football, for Sara had the football poised ready to throw as her brother rushed her—the picture had been taken an instant before they would have made contact. One that held his attention for some time was of a dusty, tired, sun-browned Sara wearing chaps, work gloves, boots, and riding a beautiful mare. Her brother rode a quarter horse. It didn't look like a pleasure shot; the two of them gave the impression of coming back from a hard day's work.

Adam moved on. This picture had to be Sara and her mom. "What was your mom's name?" Adam asked softly, already sensing what Sara had not told him directly, that her mother had passed away sometime in the past.

"Michelle."

"She was a beautiful woman."

"Yes. She died in a car accident."

The picture third to the right stopped him in his tracks. "Your father is the U.S. ambassador to Britain." Adam was more than stunned; he was speechless.

"Yes."

Protective security. Someone was actively threatening her.

Adam swung around and looked at Sara. She looked back at him calmly. "My life is not as neat as yours." She half smiled. "You only have half the nation that knows your face and name and thinks you are a superstar. I've got one man out there somewhere who would like nothing more than to see me dead."

"Why?"

"Sit down, Adam. You're intimidating when you pace," she said quietly. "I need your word that you will not repeat what I'm going to tell you—that includes your lawyer and your sister."

"My lawyer also happens to be my brother-in-law, but you've got my word."

"Children are targets, pawns, very effective ways to influence and pressure political figures, and I became one of those statistics when I was six. My father had just been appointed to the British post, and there were some extremely sensitive negotiations going on with China at the time. My parents' marriage didn't survive the kidnapping, and I didn't talk for two-and-a-half years after the event.

"One of the men is serving a life sentence in a federal prison, but the second man has never been apprehended. I know his face, buried somewhere in my mind, and I would put him away for life if I could remember it. He knows it. But rather than lie low, every few months he keeps taunting my father with...mementos...of the event. Worse, he's daring the FBI to catch him. The psychiatrists think he is going insane."

Adam's eyes closed. *Lord, tell me what I'm hearing didn't happen...please.* He looked over at Sara who sat there calmly, her coffee cup resting in her relaxed hands. Other than her stumble over the mention of mementos, she had told him the facts with no discernible emotion or change in her voice. Could she even really feel after all the trauma she had just described, or had her emotions been so suppressed that this was the only way she could cope—to detach and say everything is okay when it could never truly be okay inside?

"Sara."

She looked up.

Adam came over and sat beside her, noticing the slight tightening of her posture. He took the coffee cup and held her hands in his. "Is that when you got these?"

The scars on her wrists were more like tight bands of skin than ridges. He had noticed them as they fixed dinner, and they would've gone unmentioned until she chose to tell him, if not for the opening she had just given him. If she was six when the scars had occurred, it would explain the appearance of the skin now. As she had grown, the scarred skin would have been too tight to stretch naturally.

She tried to pull her hands away, but after a career where

hand control was a necessity, he could feel the nuances of her movements before she could make them, and he deliberately countered every one of them. She was very uncomfortable having him look at the scars. "I don't mind the scars, Sara. I'd just like to know how they happened."

She bit her bottom lip. "The left wrist was from the initial struggle to get free of the ropes on the first day; the right wrist…it was later."

"How long were you held?"

"Nine days."

The tremors were back in her hands now, the ones he had felt in the elevator, the ones he had felt the morning he tried to apologize in her office. "Come here." He drew her toward his chest.

Her entire body stiffened. His hand moved her head down to his shoulder; he wrapped his arms around her, then forced himself to go very still.

She couldn't break his hold. "Adam, I don't want this."

"Tough."

"Why are you doing this?"

"Because you need it." He rubbed her back.

It took almost three minutes before he felt her relax.

She had been six when all this had happened. The details of her past were not going to change in the next few days or weeks. There would be plenty of time for questions and answers. And he'd need to understand them. He instinctively knew the biggest obstacle he had was not her past, but her ability to trust him.

She trusted Dave.

She could learn to trust him.

"You are an obstinate man."

He smiled into her hair. "So my sister tells me frequently."
She tried to push away from him again, and he simply shifted his hold.

"Adam, my coffee is going to get cold."

He let her turn in his arms and retrieve her cup.

"Better?" He brushed her hair back behind her ear so he could see her face. He liked her earrings, for they sparkled with every turn of her head. He was now willing to bet the emeralds were real.

Her bent head lifted to give him a rueful smile. "Yes." Her blue eyes were clear.

She was such a beautiful lady.

"What did your father want?"

"I'm maid of honor for my best friend's wedding, and he's not pleased with the idea."

"Security?"

"He just likes to be the one in control, that's all. Her fiancé is the grandson of a former governor. There may be some press in attendance. He thinks it's a bad risk."

"What does Dave think?"

"It can be managed. There is no easy way to trace Sara Walsh to Sara Richman, and the picture will only make the local papers."

"Get me a wedding invitation."

"What?"

"I'd like to meet your best friend."

Sara grinned. "I can guarantee Ellen would like to meet you, but I hardly think a wedding invitation is necessary."

Adam gently squeezed her shoulder. "Then how about a quiet restaurant where you and I can have dinner with Ellen and her fiancé?"

He was surprised at her sudden stillness. She pulled away from him and rose to her feet, moving to the far side of the room before turning. "We won't be seeing each other after tonight. It just felt wrong not to at least explain my reasons after what happened the other morning." The formality was back in her voice. "Adam, you are a public figure. You are noticed wherever you go. I cannot afford to be around you."

He got up. "There are many quiet places away from the public where security is not a problem."

"We have no future. You have to accept that. I have no choice in this. If you continue to push it, Dave will simply take me from level two protection to level three, and not only will you never see me again, I'll be stifled to death by their presence. At level four, not even my father will know where I am. Don't make this difficult for me, Adam. Please."

Accept it? Hardly. "Do you like me?" He moved away to pick up his coffee.

"What?"

He looked over at her. "It's a simple question. Do you like me?"

"Yes."

"Then quit being so defeatist before we've even explored our options. We're going to get to know each other, Sara."

"And if I don't want to get to know you?"

He walked across the room to stand in front of her. The hand under her chin was infinitely gentle. "You do." He leaned down and kissed her, felt her tremble. "Find a movie you want to watch from your collection. I'll be back with more coffee and the required popcorn."

He let the kitchen door swing closed behind him and stopped. He tried to collect his thoughts. It was hitting him too fast to absorb, like calling a play and realizing as the ball was snapped that he was getting blitzed by four defensive linemen.

Sara. What am I going to do with you? You are the most intriguing woman I've ever met, with a history so complex it's going to take months to understand all the layers, let alone all the facts.

He would give anything at this point to be a decent psychologist rather than a former professional quarterback. There had been rules to that game; there were no rules to this one.

What had happened to her during those nine days? Did he dare ask her any questions? If he avoided the subject would she think he didn't care? If he did, would he be reopening old wounds?

"I didn't talk for two-and-a-half years." Her simple statement covered a wealth of implications. She had felt so threatened she had withdrawn inside for two-and-a-half years. He didn't know if he was ready to hear what had happened during those nine days even if she had the courage at this point to tell him.

He worked a little more on the timeline of events and hated what it told him. She had been kidnapped at age six, nine days later it had been over. Her parents divorced when she was seven, and by her eighth birthday, her mother had married Frank Victor, leaving her brother behind in London. Sara had not spoken a word from the time she was rescued until she was eight-and-a-half. She would never have been able to cry and talk and express the pain of all those losses.

Was that why she spoke with so much affection when she mentioned Frank? Had he been the one who finally gave her the courage to speak again? Was Frank the one who had finally made her feel safe? "Lord, I need wisdom. Desperately," he whispered. He rarely felt this uncertain about what he should do.

He fixed the popcorn, cheating by finding a bag he could fix in the microwave, then refilled their coffee mugs.

"So what did you choose?" he asked, rejoining her.

She had two videos in her hand. "Your options."

He tilted his head to read the titles. *Star Trek* or *M*A*S*H*.

"These are the early *M*A*S*H* episodes with Trapper John, and the *Star Trek* tape has the classics like the Tribbles episode."

"There's no contest." He met her eyes and saw the disappointment. "We're watching both tapes."

Her disappointment was replaced with a look of relief and a giggle…. A giggle.

"Do that again."

"What?"

"Giggle."

"I can't giggle on demand," she replied, her face turning red.

"It was a delightful sound. Try."

"Adam, give me my coffee and go sit down," she said, trying to hide what had become a grin.

With a sigh he did as he was told. She put in the *Star Trek* tape and brought back the remote with her.

She sat on her side of the couch, something Adam let last as long as it took for him to set down his coffee, reach over, and lift her to the middle of the couch next to him. "That's better."

She made a face at him. "Enjoy being the director for a night because we won't be seeing each other after tonight."

"Quiet, Sara. I'm watching TV."

He heard her drawn-out sigh. A few minutes later she shifted her weight and made herself comfortable against him, trapping his arm behind her back. Adam didn't mind a bit. She was light and warm and smelled of honey shampoo.

He reached back to shut off the end table light reflecting on the TV screen. She flung her hand across his chest to grasp his arm and stop him, scattering popcorn in her wake. "No, leave it on. Please."

There was panic in her voice and certainly panic in her eyes. He slowly lowered his arm. "I'm sorry. I didn't think."

She wasn't afraid of the dark—she was petrified of it. Even in her own home with the TV and the hall light on, she still panicked at the thought of the light being shut off.

She buried her head against his shirt and fought to regain control. Hating the fear he had triggered by not thinking, he tentatively soothed his hand over her shoulder.

He felt when she accepted that she was safe, and he didn't say a word as she carefully moved back and began to pick up the spilled popcorn. When she started to say something, he stopped her words with a finger to her lips. "No. No apologies. No explanations. I don't need them tonight." Her fear of the dark was something they were going to talk about in the light of a bright, sunny day, at the right time, and in the right place. This wasn't it.

She hugged him. It surprised him, and from the look on her face, astounded her.

He put the cup back in her hand. "Finish your coffee."

"So, have you two been good tonight?" A voice from the doorway made Sara lean her head back against the sofa to look behind her.

"Stuff a sock in it, Dave." She had to stifle a yawn. She had never been so comfortable in her life. Somewhere at the start of the second tape she had cradled her hands against Adam's chest and rested her head against his shoulder, turning him into a big, warm pillow. He had tugged a throw cover across her feet. There was no question she would love to enjoy more peaceful evenings like this.

She knew they couldn't continue to see each other, but that fact had only intensified her desire to ensure she enjoyed the one evening she did have with Adam all the more.

Dave laughed and walked into the room, dropping into the seat near the couch.

Sara watched Dave remove a holstered gun from his side and set it on the end table. Only one. Normally he carried a second behind his back.

"Did you and Linda have a good time?" she asked, feeling tired.

"Dinner was worth it." Dave shared an amused look with his sister.

"If you're going to date someone who loves the arts, you'll have to widen your horizons a bit."

She didn't bother to move away from Adam's side. She was too comfortable, and her brother could draw his own conclusions. She was sure she would hear his opinion later.

"All quiet tonight?" Dave asked.

"Yes."

—∞∞∞—

Adam could tell that Dave's relief at Sara's answer was genuine. It was plain the man didn't trust someone else to protect her—and he immediately understood the feeling.

"I see she's already got you watching her favorite tapes." Dave met Adam's gaze with a challenge in his eyes.

"Oh, I can't say I've minded." Adam watched Dave's eyes narrow. Good. Her brother was more than playing games about this protection business. Sara did not need someone who was more words than actions.

Sara shifted in his arms to look up at him, a puzzled look on her face. She didn't understand the byplay of two guys defining turf boundaries. That was okay; she didn't need to understand. She still thought they wouldn't be seeing each other after tonight.

There would be time to correct that impression another day.

"It's time for me to leave and time for you to go to bed properly," he told her, enjoying the way she blushed. If Dave wasn't sitting there, he bet she would've been willing to come back with a one-liner of her own and put him in his place, but for now she simply pushed herself off him, covering a yawn she couldn't prevent. "Sorry, Adam. I don't know why I'm so tired."

Dave chuckled. "I do. You were working until 4 A.M., remember?"

"Would you believe I actually forgot that book for a few hours?" She rubbed her eyes. "I don't think that has ever happened at this late stage of editing."

"When is it due to the editor?" Dave asked.

"I told Helen she would have it in her hands by Tuesday afternoon. I've already got plane tickets for Judy to hand deliver it."

"Sara, are you crazy? That's only another four days."

"I want this book finished and out of my hands. I know what I committed to."

"Do you normally hand deliver your children's books?" Adam asked.

"Sometimes." Sara and Dave exchanged a look.

Something was not being said. Adam didn't push. "Come on; walk me to the front door."

Sara escorted him to the front door and deactivated the ground's security. "I'm glad you came for dinner."

He brushed back her hair. "I enjoyed it a great deal. And if you ever change your mind, all you have to do is call. My invitation for coffee or dinner is still open."

She tentatively fingered the lapel of his jacket. "I'm sorry, Adam. It's not possible."

His fingers entwined with hers. "Someday it will be. Think about it. We can work something out." He bent and kissed her. It was something he rarely did on a first date, but the possibility of its being the last one was lingering too close in the back of his mind. "Good night."

The beach was deserted. Adam walked along the shore, deep in thought. His dog loped ahead of him, exploring.

The night was comfortable. The moon was full, casting a bright trail across the lake water. Adam typically enjoyed the view. Tonight it barely registered. He had a problem to solve.

His normal approach was not going to work in this situation. Sara wasn't going to accept an invitation for a date; she wasn't likely to be more forthcoming with details of her past.

She didn't know him well enough to trust him.

Adam picked up a shell on the beach and rubbed it with his fingers. Trust was going to be hard to earn. The complexity of Sara's past stood like an insurmountable mountain. Like the fine lines in the shell he held, her past was layered deep.

Her past had made a pearl. Rather than break her, the pressure had made something beautiful.

He sighed.

He could walk away. It was what she wanted. He certainly understood her reasoning. The complications her security needs introduced could destabilize any hope of having a relationship.

He had never been one to walk away from a challenge. He *liked* her. She had a class about her that was much more than just her appearance; it went deep into her character. He liked how she expressed herself, how she related to her brother.

There was complexity to her. He was tired of shallow people. Over the last decade he had seen all he wanted to of fame, the gloss, the surface. He didn't want that for his future.

Sara held the promise of something real. Her life forced her to live with carefully chosen priorities. She couldn't afford to live at the surface in her relationships. As he had listened to her talk about her brother and her friend Ellen, he had heard the depth she had established in those relationships. He wanted to be part of that circle. He wanted a chance to really know her.

What did he have to offer her? Others were attracted to his fame, his accomplishments. To Sara, they were real obstacles. His wealth, which might help with the security, was not a plus either. Her family came from old wealth. She didn't lack for what money could buy.

He knew she would gladly trade that wealth for what she didn't have: a relationship with her father, freedom.

Adam paused.

Besides her brother, she didn't have any close family. She didn't have freedom of movement. She didn't have the luxury of taking a dog for a walk on the beach late at night.

He had a great family. The fact he had lived in the public eye for so long had also taught him some invaluable lessons about how to ensure privacy when he needed it.

Sara didn't realize the extent to which her life would be better with him in it. So how did he convince her to take the chance?

Dave.

Adam's eyes narrowed. Yes, Dave would be the key. Nothing happened around Sara without his security coverage.

Could he turn that to his advantage?

Lord, I want to get to know her. What is the best way to approach this? I'm only going to get one chance.

Dave had finally gone upstairs to bed shortly before midnight. Sara had assured him she was going to be up in a few minutes and that she would set the security codes.

She pulled the throw cover down across her feet again and curled up on the couch, the room as dark as she could tolerate.

She wiped at tears slipping down her cheeks.

This was the third time in her life a good man had

crossed her path who could be both a good friend and possibly more. And for one reason or another, she had to stop it before the relationship could form.

Lord, why didn't You let me die in that root cellar, too, if I'm to remain a captive to that event for the rest of my life?

The grief tasted bitter.

She didn't know if she even would want a relationship with a public figure like Adam, but she would at least like to make the choice.

If it were just a risk to herself, she might consider it. But the risk to those around her? to Dave? to Adam?

She knew what the FBI experts said. The second kidnapper was obsessed with the crime, with her. If he found her, if he realized there was someone important in her life, that person would become an immediate target of his jealous insanity. To have a relationship with Adam would put a bull's-eye on his back.

She didn't try to stop the tears. There were times it was good to cry. She wished she had that stupid teddy bear Dave had given her when she was ten. It was packed in the suitcase on the plane, waiting for the next time she got yanked at a moment's notice out of life as she knew it. It would be good to have that bear to cuddle. She wiped at her tears with her sleeve.

She shouldn't be whining. It had been a great night. It was what she asked God for and He delivered it beyond her expectations. Dinner came together well. She had been nervous about that. Adam handled most of the shocks she threw at him with tact. The end of the evening, curled up beside him on the couch, was a memory she wouldn't forget.

She had a rose to press in her scrapbook.

The tears started again and she furiously rubbed them away. *Enough already.* She couldn't change what she lived with.

"The Lord is my rock and my fortress, my stronghold and my deliverer." The words from Psalm 144 resonated with a strong reassurance. She tried to get her perspective back to match God's. His was bigger than hers. There had to be a safe way through this turmoil. There was always a path when she looked hard enough.

Lord, I can cling to Your Word as I have done all my life, but must this burden be forever? Will it ever lift?

Adam was not used to hearing no. It was doubtful he would go away peacefully. Sara winced. She wanted to spend more time with him. He was going to be persistent, and she had to find the courage to do what was right. Say no. Keep saying no. The dangers were real. He was too public a figure to be near. So what did she do? Go to the ranch for a few months and work from there?

Thinking about security was part of how she had to make decisions.

She wished she understood what God had planned. It would be so nice to have a normal life instead of this peculiar one that defied description.

She wished God didn't demand so much from her.

CHAPTER | 6

"How long, Sara?"

She was unpacking the fourth box of books Dave had carried in for her, restocking the shelter's supply of books so the kids who came could take a favorite book with them when they left. Dave's question caused her to pause. "Thirty minutes? I'll read a couple stories."

He nodded. "No longer."

Sara knew Dave hated the fact she had chosen this ministry in which to work, but he understood why, so he let her come. She had spent a lifetime trying to understand why God allowed violence; here she could both offer what she had learned and learn from others who had been forced to take the same journey.

About a dozen young children were crowded around, hoping Sara would read them one of her new stories. She smiled at them and suggested they all go to the playroom.

She picked up two of the younger ones whom she had known for several months, and they giggled as she stole kisses on their cheeks. They were happy kids even though most of them were at the shelter because their homes had been torn apart by violence.

She gathered the children around her in a circle and made sure each one of them got to look at the pictures as she turned the pages of the book she had titled *God's Butterflies*. By the inflections in her voice she could make any character, any story, come alive. She had the children giggling and laughing and fully engaged with the book within minutes.

She loved to watch a child's face as he or she heard a story for the first time. It was a delight to see. She learned something new about her craft with each group of children. She learned she could write stories that were quite complex and still have the full attention of a three-year-old.

She learned that while adults would look at the artwork and see a good picture, an overall image, a child would look at the artwork and see the details first, then the full picture.

She had changed her style of artwork when she realized that. Now her drawings were quite detailed down to the legs on a butterfly, the raindrop on a leaf, the caterpillar on a stem. An adult would turn the page when the words ran out; a child would look at the picture a long time to see all those details.

Dave stood by the doorway, watching as various mothers came quietly into the room also to listen to the stories. It was a women-only shelter, and he attracted a few curious looks that he answered with a smile.

Sara saw Dave tap his watch. She nodded and took the time to pass out copies of her books so every child had one to look at.

Outside the building, hands on her lower back, Sara

stretched, looking up at the light fluffy clouds drifting by.
"Since it's such a beautiful Saturday, would you like to go
horseback riding for a couple hours?"

"If you don't mind us inviting along some company."

Sara looked over at her brother, alerted by his tone.

"Who did you have in mind?"

"Linda and Adam."

"No way, Dave. You're not setting me up on a date. I
know you and Adam have become buddies in the last couple
weeks—playing racquetball at the health club, jogging
together, doing all that macho stuff to see who is in better
shape—but no way am I letting you set me up on a date.
Besides, it's a security risk."

She'd been hurt to learn Adam had taken her at her word
and made no further attempt to contact her, which was a
contradiction in logic that made her mad at herself. It had
been hard to admit in her daily journal how off balanced the
situation made her feel. She wasn't used to dealing with a
crush, and that was exactly what she had—on a good-looking
guy that half the ladies in the country would recognize on
sight.

She was coping by burying herself in work. In the days
since she had last seen Adam, she had finished two more
children's books. Dave was in the habit now of coming to her
office suite around 7 P.M. and ordering her to put down her
colored pencils and come home.

"Sara, we're talking about a few hours horseback riding
in the middle of nowhere. Yes, it's a minimal security risk, but
you know the Graysons or their staff would never talk about
who we invite to join us."

"Then why are you suddenly willing to take the risk?"

"Because it's my job to consider what's best for you. And getting you out of that tomb of an office is more than a need right now, it's a necessity."

"I don't need you to arrange my social life."

"You canceled out on Ellen twice. So say, 'Yes, Dave, let's go riding.' I've got the car keys, so you might as well face the inevitable."

Sara knew she had to say yes. Dave deserved a day with Linda. Horseback riding with Adam…it would be embarrassing to ask him. "Do you know if he can even ride?"

"He can."

"Then you call him. And make it very clear I had no part in the invitation."

Her brother used his cellular phone and made the call. It surprised Sara that they spoke less than a minute.

"Adam said, 'Sure, why not?' I told him we would pick him up."

Linda was free as well and eager to go.

Sara moved from the front seat to the back when they picked up Linda, and her nerves began to flutter. Adam. From the address Dave had quoted, they would be picking him up in less than five minutes.

Linda, given twenty-minutes' warning, had managed to make herself into a man's delight with colored jeans, a black belt, a top that accentuated her good looks, and her hair pulled back by a gorgeous gold-and-satin clip. Having nothing against Linda personally, for she rather liked Dave's latest girlfriend, Sara nevertheless slouched in her seat for the first time in ages.

She had planned for a workday, not to see Adam. She was wearing Dave's old flannel shirt with the sleeves rolled up and faded jeans that should have been given a decent burial months ago. It was embarrassing. Anything else in her wardrobe would have been better. She didn't mind the lack of makeup, but it was a windy day and even a simple barrette would have helped things.

Adam was waiting at the steps of his condominium complex, talking to the security guard.

Sara slid farther over in the seat.

"Thanks for the invite, Dave. It's been way too long since I've had a chance to ride."

"My pleasure, Adam." Dave pulled back into traffic. "Let me introduce Linda Olsen. I'm sure I've mentioned her on more than one occasion."

"More than one. It's nice to finally meet you."

"I had no idea Dave knew you, Mr. Black."

Adam wanted to groan at the look he saw in Linda's eyes. A fan. It couldn't get worse. Not on the one day he and Dave had been trying to get arranged forever.

"Please, call me Adam. I'm surprised you aren't getting tired of bumping into all of us. Dave knows lots of sports players from the club downtown. Did he mention he was working in a batting cage with Greg Nelson yesterday?"

Linda turned to look at Dave.

Adam understood what had just happened only too well, and he felt intensely sorry for Dave. He was falling in love with Linda, while she was more than willing to move on to the more famous and wealthy at the drop of a hat. No wonder Dave had kept her away from the sports club and the restaurant there.

Sara's mouth was stiff. Adam suspected she had just come to the same conclusion he had. He had the feeling she would like nothing better than to shove Linda out of her brother's life. The protective instincts between Sara and Dave went both ways; that was good to know.

Adam touched the hand that was curled into a fist beside him. "Hello, Sara. It's good to see you again."

Her head turned and her glare toward the front seat was changed to a polite smile. "It's mutual, Adam."

Formal, so she was nervous, but it was not the cold front that he had been expecting. "How have you been the last couple weeks?"

"Good. Busy."

He knew how busy she had been. Dave was quite forthcoming about the work schedule Sara was keeping, and his words had not been kind.

"Not too busy, I hope."

Sara shrugged.

The way she answered pleased him, for it meant she wasn't willing to lie, even to herself.

"Tell me about this farm where we're going."

"The Graysons have been breeding and boarding horses for years. They bought a few horses from Frank over the years and have always been good friends of our family. They let us board a few horses with them.

"There are several trails on their property that go for miles. There's a river that cuts across one corner of their land. It has a natural dam made by beavers some years ago. After a good rain it can be a beautiful sight. Dave and I come out here when we need to get away and relax for a few hours. Even if it's raining, I like to simply mess around in the stables."

"Sounds like a nice place to spend some time."

"It is," Sara agreed.

Adam watched Sara check that the car door was locked and then turn to rest her back against it, making it easier to face him. She was beautiful to look at simply because she hadn't known she would be seeing him today. The flannel shirt made her look soft, comfortable; and the patched jeans reflected the fact she was used to working, not just being a pretty face. Her face was bare of makeup, not that it needed any. On top of it all, her poise was refusing to let her apologize for any of it. He wanted to smile but knew she would misinterpret it—certainly not take it for the compliment it was. Not everyone could look superb in what she was wearing, and she pulled it off without even trying.

"I hear you were in Georgia last week," she offered.

"For three days. A sports-apparel convention."

"Are you thinking you might add to whom you currently represent?"

"I don't have the slightest idea what I'm going to do," Adam replied. "The contracts are coming up for renewal. I'm still deciding what I want to do at this point."

"No pressing desire to see yourself center stage during a Super Bowl commercial?"

"I'll be in one of those this next year."

She looked a little nonplussed. "Oh."

Adam shifted uncomfortably. His face and name recognition was something he couldn't undo. It was one of the obstacles they eventually would have to deal with.

They reached the farm in less than an hour. It was truly set out in the middle of nowhere, with no discernable signs to direct someone coming to visit.

"I gather some of the horses stabled here are valuable?" Adam asked Sara as they left the car.

"Very. Some go as high as seven figures."

The chief stable hand was delighted to see them. The Graysons were in Connecticut for the weekend he told them. They were going to be disappointed they had missed the chance to visit.

Sara strolled toward the nearest paddock by the barn; it went on for acres. A shrill whistle brought several horses' heads up from grazing, and a few began to wander toward the white fence. She let her hands linger on their muzzles, stroking their necks.

Adam joined her at the fence, resting his forearms on the top bar.

"This is Cobalt, Ruby, First Fire," Sara strained her arms around one that was nuzzling her shoulder, "and finally this fine creature is Archer. Any particular one you would like to ride?"

"Which do you normally ride?"

"I normally take Ruby, and Dave takes First Fire. Depends on which needs the most exercise."

"How about Cobalt then, if you think Linda can handle Archer."

"She'll have no problem. He's big but gentle."

Dave came from the barn carrying the first of the tack they would need. He handed Sara a bridle, rested the other three on the fence, and dropped a loop of coiled rope over the fence post. "Want me to get them?"

"No, I'll have no problem." Sara slipped between the rails.

Adam felt his muscles bunch ready for action. She was

getting squeezed between the animals. But it was soon clear that this was something she did with ease. He remembered that photo on the mantel and wondered what had happened to Frank Victor's ranch after his death. Sara would have spent six or seven years there. She was a natural with horses; her movements were smooth and calm and not startling to any of the animals. First Fire threatened to resist the bridle. Sara stepped back and stared at him and the animal came back to her side, seeking her favor again.

Dave and Sara saddled the four horses, both of them moving with deft hands to tighten cinches and adjust stirrups.

Linda was doing her best to start a conversation, but Adam refused to get drawn in. There had been too many Lindas in his lifetime. What he would view as polite conversation, she'd take as encouragement.

"Linda." Dave had Archer saddled, and with one last glance at Adam she went to join Dave, accepting a hand to mount.

A few minutes later, they were underway.

"Okay?"

Adam turned astride Cobalt to find Sara on Ruby prancing at his side. "Fine."

"These guys have a disdain for walking, so you'll have to hold him in check for the first bit. Once we're in the open country, we'll let them canter and use up some of their energy."

Adam answered with a smile and let Cobalt prance sideways toward her. "I fully intend to enjoy every minute of it."

Sara was magnificent on a horse. Her knees gripped tightly, the reins held lightly, and her balance shifted in tune with the animal as if she were reading the horse's mind.

They opened and closed the gates behind them, riding single file out from the stable area until they reached a large meadow.

"If you were better acquainted with the mount you rode, I would challenge you to a race," Sara said.

They were already splitting into couples, still riding as a foursome, but now with almost twenty yards between them. "If I were sure I could win, I'd accept."

Sara laughed and nudged her horse into a canter.

The day could not be more perfect—the sun was shining, the temperature was comfortable, and the sky was bright blue with drifting white clouds. Adam admired the picture Sara made, storing it away in his memory, then nudged his own mount to follow suit. Sara was headed across the meadow to a line of trees.

It felt good to ride, to leave behind the pressures of work and enjoy her company.

Becoming friends with Dave had not been planned. The first invitation to a game of racquetball had been intentional. Adam wanted to know if security was being improved for Sara's movements across the concourses, but he hadn't planned on the friendship. Now it was strong enough it would probably last even without Sara being part of the equation. They were men of like spirits, driven by love for God, care for family, ambition to make their world a better place, and a mutual enjoyment of sports.

Sara was waiting for him at the line of trees, holding Ruby still as she stroked her neck. Dave and Linda were some distance behind them now, for they hadn't joined the canter.

"Would you like to go to the river, or up one of the trails

that circles around the farm for about three miles?"

"Let's go to the river. It'll give the horses a chance to drink and us a chance to sit and talk for a few minutes."

"Dave!" When Sara had his attention, she pointed south, and Dave nodded from across the meadow.

Adam followed as Sara led Ruby into the trees. The temperature dropped noticeably, as did the breeze. There was a path of sorts, narrow, grown high with grass, more a deer trail than one riders often took.

"There is a steep descent to the trail that goes to the river. Cobalt's been down it numerous times so give him his head and let him make the choices."

Adam understood when they reached the drop-off. The river had once flowed through this piece of land, then changed course, leaving the land to slowly crumble and smooth itself back out, erosion destroying the former riverbanks.

Sara went down the embankment without fear or hesitation, her arm out to provide extra balance and her weight leaning back to give Ruby a better center of gravity. Adam really wished he had decided on the three-mile trail instead. His heart was in his throat until Sara was safely to the bottom.

Without a word, he nudged Cobalt and followed her down. He could feel the horse making decisions as different muscles bunched and relaxed. Adam rubbed the horse's neck affectionately once they were down.

"So have you thought any more about my invitations?" He watched Sara as they walked their horses side by side down the former riverbed. He hoped she had reconsidered. His question startled her. That was good. Maybe she had been thinking about them.

"I can't take the chance with the possible publicity, Adam. There is no link between Sara Richman, daughter of Ambassador Richman, and Sara Walsh without someone digging into deeply classified information. But a picture could establish the link quite easily."

"I am not followed by the press."

"No. But you are an opportunity shot. If a photographer sees you with someone, the picture will get taken, and they'll think about what to do with it later."

"How about coffee in your office then? It's private. And we could do dinner at my home, if you wouldn't take the invitation the wrong way."

She stopped Ruby. Her hands clenched tight on the reins. "If we did start seeing each other, what do you think it would be like in a few weeks? You couldn't stand the closed confines I live in. At some point it's going to get to you—the no-public policy—and you'd want us to go out, and then we'd start fighting about the risks. Either I accept the risks to myself and thereby put Dave in danger just to please you, or you give up chunks of who you are and try not to turn the resentment back on me." She blinked hard and averted her face. "Please, it won't work. I would like it to, but I simply know it can't."

"You've been in this position before." Adam knew it; her pain was too focused.

Sara didn't bother to deny it. "I met him when I lived in New York. He was a literary agent, a good one, but you don't stay in that position without having to court publicity and be seen by your peers. His job was largely parties and dinners where deals could be discussed. I think we were both in love for a time until the complications hit, and he realized how impossible it would be for him to be married yet have a wife who couldn't accompany him and be an asset to his career."

"I'm sorry, Sara."

She shook her head. "Don't be. I've learned that life comes at its own terms, and it's best that you learn to go on." She nudged her horse forward.

"Then why can't we simply be friends?"

She looked over her shoulder at him. "Do you honestly think you would be willing to settle for that?"

Adam shifted his mount toward her. It didn't take much to reach across and take her hand. "I like your company. And I would no more put you at risk than Dave would. If we can't be more than friends, then at least let's be good friends. Don't give up without giving us a chance."

The sound of horses behind them interrupted the conversation.

"It looks like you two are not getting very far very fast," Dave commented.

Sara blushed as she pulled her hand free. "We were just waiting for you two."

"I could see that." Dave nudged his horse into the lead, Linda beside him.

Sara didn't say anything as they rode the rest of the way to the river, and Adam didn't try to pull her from her thoughts.

She was right. He wanted to be much more than friends.

Adam eased his horse around a fallen tree.

He could choose not to renew the commercial contracts. It wasn't the first time he had considered making that decision. But he was not naive enough to believe it would change the equation much. The last fifteen years of his public life existed. That was the bottom line, and that was the threat to Sara. It would take years for his name and face to fade from public knowledge.

The sound of the water reached them before the river became visible. Sara shifted in her seat, nudging Ruby ahead. Adam saw the change in her posture and expression, and when he rounded the bend in the trail he understood why. The sight was gorgeous. Flowers of all varieties grew naturally along the banks of the pool, and water came flowing over the top of the beaver dam back into the riverbed proper. At this time of year, the sparkling water had to be less than two feet deep.

Dave halted his horse beside Sara and leaned over to say something. She looked at him, startled, glanced at Linda, then nodded her agreement.

Adam watched Linda and Dave move downstream. "Want to cross and pick a bouquet?" Sara asked, drawing his attention back to her.

"Where are they going?"

"There are some natural caves down the river a ways that Linda asked to see."

Caves. Dark. Not her favorite subject. Adam avoided it.

They picked their way across the stream.

"I never did tell you how much I enjoyed those basket-ball game tickets."

She laughed. "Who did you take?"

"Jordan. I can't afford to have my lawyer and brother-in-law on my bad side."

Sara dismounted with a graceful move. Adam watched her look around at the flowers and choose just a few. She was selecting the colors and styles that fit both the beauty of the creation around them and her own preference for brilliant colors.

Adam slipped from his horse and moved to lean against one of the large outcrops of rocks on the riverbank.

She joined him after collecting her bouquet, and he offered a handkerchief to use as a tie around the base of the stems.

"Aren't they beautiful?"

"Very. Sara, why do flowers mean so much to you? They touch your office, your studio, your home."

"I need the reminder that God loves to make detailed and beautiful things, and that act of creation is itself a sufficient reason to make them. These flowers will live and die here, the majority of them never seen, even though a busy road is less than a mile away."

Adam gently touched her hair, stroking it behind her ear. He could add his own reason. Sara used flowers to counter the pain her world had dealt her. At times her past must feel like a prison, but a prison didn't have flowers.

He could pretend she was who he wanted her to be, or he could start learning to honestly accept who she really was. A woman who was petrified of the dark, threatened by an unfinished past, who struggled to cope with the limitations imposed upon her, who struggled to live life despite the constant fear.

"Would you like to collect a second bouquet to take to your office?" Adam asked, watching her face as she looked down and touched the bouquet in her hands.

"I don't think so."

"Sara."

She looked up at him.

"You don't have anything to worry about, you know. I like you. There is nothing about your past that will ever change that."

"There's a lot I haven't told you."

"I imagine there is." He watched her eyes go black, reflecting her distress. "It won't change anything."

"It will. It always does."

"Try me."

Suddenly there were tears in her eyes, and she turned away to reach for the bridle of her horse.

"Sara, I'm sorry."

She shrugged away his hand as she brushed away the tears. "Let's go back, Adam."

"Dave and Linda?"

"He'll know."

Adam moved back to his mount, feeling miserable for ruining what was a beautiful day.

The climb up the embankment was not nearly as difficult for the horses as coming down. Sara led the way and Adam followed her in silence.

Okay, God, I blew it royally. I'm asking for help. I don't want Sara to end the day feeling miserable. If it will help her talk about the memories, then let's talk. If she needs the opposite, help me also to understand that.

They moved up the trail back toward the meadow. Sara pulled to a stop.

"What is it?"

She slipped off her horse. "I think Ruby picked up a stone."

In the narrow trail, Adam could do little but watch as she

lifted the left foreleg of her horse and confirmed her suspicion. "Sorry, Adam. I can't dislodge it. It looks like we're walking back."

Adam slipped off Cobalt. "How serious is it?"

"Not very, but to dislodge the stone I need a couple tools I don't have." Sara patted Ruby's neck and got a nudge back from her muzzle.

Adam knew that kind of mutual affection with a horse was not born overnight. Sara obviously spent a lot of time here, in a place she felt safe, a place where she could find some freedom in a carefree ride.

She slipped the reins forward and led her horse up the trail. Adam followed. In less than two minutes they stepped from the trail into the open meadow.

Feeling a great deal of uncertainty, Adam reached over and took Sara's hand. She squeezed it. They walked in the sunshine, sharing the warmth. "Would you be willing to tell me why you fear the dark?"

She sighed. "It's the only thing that makes the past suddenly feel like the present. My mind reverts back in time. I'm suddenly six again, in a pitch-black place, and so petrified I can't breathe. Part of that terror was real; the gag really was choking me. Despite all the therapy and the counseling and, for a brief time, medication, the fear has only been managed not cured."

"Do you think it will ever be overcome?"

"No. I have a feeling I will carry it to my death. God has given me the courage to face it, but He has not taken it away. I've accepted that."

Adam thought about that answer for some time. "I'll pray for you, Sara. God may still take away the fear." He was thinking about the verse that said perfect love casts out fear but didn't want to say it, for the words would sound like a simplistic answer. He knew she was well beyond the simplistic side of who God was and what He would do. She seemed to understand his words were a genuine desire to help, for she accepted them as such with a soft thank-you.

Adam liked walking with Sara. Her hand was warm in his and she had relaxed her pace. The horses occasionally nuzzled her shoulder, and she reached back to affectionately rub a muzzle.

"What are you afraid of, Adam?"

He had to grin. "Nothing like getting a tough question in return. When I was playing professional football, it would have been an easy answer—it was the guy rushing at me ready to knock me to the ground and give me a concussion in the process. Now," he thought for a moment, "I guess I would say making a bad decision I couldn't reverse."

Sara smiled. "Tactical answer. It could apply to anything. Quit being evasive."

"Making my sister mad."

Sara laughed, so his honesty had been worth it.

Adam rubbed his thumb across the back of her hand. "Can I pry a little more?"

"As long as you accept the fact I might not answer."

Adam took a deep breath. "Why didn't you speak for so many years after the kidnapping?"

She was not going to answer. Adam released her hand and draped his arm around her shoulders, intending to offer a reassuring hold, only to find her literally shuddering. He stopped and pulled her close, pressing her head against his shoulder, holding her tight. "You don't have to answer, Sara."

She pulled away. "I was too afraid to speak. The second kidnapper threatened to kill me if I whispered even one word once I was found. I believed him."

"Was it Frank who finally helped you speak again?"

She tried to smile but it didn't reach her eyes. "Yes. He was the only one who wasn't constantly trying to coax me to speak. Except for Dave. He never pushed either; Dave just held my hand. I was seven when I first met Frank, bone skinny and spooked by people's movements. The ranch was large and he was a hardworking, hands-on, quiet man.

"For days and weeks on end, he would take me with him as he moved cattle, fixed fences, and rounded up horses. He seemed to understand that I felt safer in the wide-open spaces where you could see for miles. About eight months after we moved to the ranch, I asked if I could go out to see a newborn foal. They were the first words I had spoken since the kidnapping."

Adam didn't know what to say. "Thank you for telling me."

Sara looked away as she nodded.

They were halfway across the meadow. Adam didn't want the walk to end anytime soon. He debated whether he dared risk another question while they walked together in silence.

The sound of riders approaching had them both turning. Dave and Linda rode up to join them.

"Problems?" Dave asked, already scanning the area.

"Ruby picked up a rock I can't dislodge."

"Want to double up? We can ride back at a slow pace and lead Ruby."

"Thanks, but we don't mind the walk." Adam didn't move his arm from around Sara's shoulders. He met Dave's assessing look that moved from Sara back to him.

Dave gave his horse a gentle nudge. "Then we'll see you at the stable."

"You do realize the speculation you've just raised." Sara sounded slightly piqued.

"Of course." He had been frank with Dave the day after dinner with Sara. He went down to the FBI office and told Dave flat out that he intended to get to know Sara better. Dave listened without saying much, then finally commented, "I suggest you wait a few weeks."

Adam thought he was being warned off until he looked at Dave and saw, instead of the protection of a brother and an FBI agent, the man who knew Sara better than anyone in the world. "Two weeks," Adam had agreed.

Dave gave him a half smile. "She's going to say no."

"Not if you arrange it."

Adam looked at Sara now, trying to decide if she was offended or not.

"I will say this for you, Adam Black, you are an ambitious man."

He laughed and gently squeezed her shoulder. "Good. So allow me to be extremely ambitious with a request."

"What?"

"Come to my place for coffee and a movie after we leave here. I'll even let you pick out the video from my collection."

"I don't know…"

"Ask Dave. If he's agreeable, then come."

She thought about it. "I'll ask him."

"Thank you." If the next several hours went smoothly, he might finally have this friendship on a firmer ground. If they didn't find that stability soon, he risked losing her for good.

CHAPTER 7

S ara struggled with her wardrobe, trying to find a combination that was elegant and informal at the same time. She had enough practice that she knew how to pull it off. But not for a date. It changed the equation completely.

Dave was due back soon. He had dropped Linda off first, Sara second, then left to take Adam home and have a look at the security in his building.

I can't believe I said yes to a real date....

She finally settled on a comfortable mix of clothes—a ruby red, baby-soft sweater, jeans to keep it informal, a thin fourteen-carat gold necklace and earrings. Around one wrist, she placed her wide-band watch, around the other, a white wristband.

"Sara, are you ready to go?"

Dave was back already? Sara hurriedly sprayed some of her favorite perfume. "I'm ready."

Dave was in the dining room. "I've got new batteries for your cellular phone. How much cash are you carrying?" He tucked his second gun out of sight behind his back.

Sara replaced the batteries in her phone. She placed a call to their own home to confirm it was working, then checked her cash. "Eighty dollars."

"Put forty in your pocket, the rest in your purse."

There was a map on the table. "Here's the building where Adam lives. The security is good inside. His condo is on the third floor. There are two main elevators, a freight elevator, and stairway exits here, here, and here if you need them. If we get separated, there's a department store at the corner of Lemont and Harris where it should be easy to get lost in the crowd. The police station is here."

Sara memorized what she was seeing. "The police station phone number?" As Dave told her the numbers, Sara punched them into her phone as the ninth speed dial number. "Got it."

Dave rubbed her tense shoulders. "Relax, Sara. This is routine; you do it every time for every new place."

"I can't help feeling like I'm going to be under a microscope. Where will you be?"

"I'll make sure you are comfortable in Adam's place, then disappear. There is a central security room that monitors the lobby, the elevators, all the halls, and the fire exits. Their camera security is quite good. I'll be there for the rest of the evening. Ben has offered to be an extra presence in the building lobby."

"It has to be two people?"

"Even at home there are at least two people. Don't worry about it. It's part of the job. Besides, Ben offered to swap me the time for Thursday afternoon so he could see the White Sox game."

"Buy the tickets for him."

"I already have." Dave smiled. "I would be outside the apartment door and put Ben in the security room, but having met Adam's husky, I think you'll have pretty good security between that dog and Adam."

"What's the dog's name?"

"King Henry. Henry for short. The dog must weigh seventy pounds at least. It nearly knocked me over saying hello."

The car ride to Adam's home was made in silence.

How much did she risk telling Adam? Did she keep the evening totally casual and entirely avoid the subject of her past, or did she tell him more of it? She hadn't told him about Kim or about the H. Q. Victor books. Or about the ranch. So many untold facts were piling up.

She had been a coward not to tell him about Kim. He had to know. About how Kim died. About how the second kidnapper came back after her death. Adam had to understand her past and what that experience had done to her inside.

What if he walked away once he knew? He might. They weren't pleasant memories to deal with. They still came all too often to the surface.

What should I say?

Dave pulled up to the condominium complex, and her time to decide was over.

Adam opened the door to meet them. His husky pushed around him, eager to greet the company.

"Henry, behave yourself."

Sara laughed and took hold of the massive paws that were resting on her chest. A gentle nudge convinced the dog not to stand nose to nose with her. The husky was a beautiful animal.

Sara relished the affection as the animal leaned against her.

The condo smelled of freshly brewed coffee. On the dining room table was a cheesecake that Adam managed to have delivered from somewhere for dessert.

"Thanks for coming."

She was trying not to blush at his appraisal. "It's my pleasure."

"Please, come on in, have a seat." Adam gestured toward the living room.

It was obvious why companies kept coming back to him year after year for commercial endorsements. He had changed into jeans and a black shirt. It was hard to look away.

His condo was not what she had expected. It was spacious and well decorated. Rather than highlight his career in football, it showcased his attachment to family and friends in pictures and sketches done by very young artists.

"Can I show you around?"

Sara realized to her relief that he was nervous as well. "Please."

If the newspapers, magazines, and stacked biographies were any indication, Adam spent most of his time relaxing in his den. His packed bookshelves were impressive. She would have liked to linger.

She saw her H. Q. Victor books on the bottom shelf, easy to spot, for the hardback covers were black, each with one single word written in blood red on the spine. *Shawn. Tara. Benjamin. Scott. Jennifer.*

Sara glanced at Adam who now rested his hand at the small of her back, guiding her. Would he understand if he knew that the author who wrote such award-winning children's books and the author who wrote such international bestsellers about murdered children were one and the same? They were two different parts of who she was: one a grown-up expression of the innocence and talent of who she was before the kidnapping, the other an expression of the anger and rage of who she was after the kidnapping.

They were both her. She had learned how to let the two sides of her personality coexist, accepting each, denying neither. But could Adam? Could he understand that at thirty-one, each reflected the totality of who she really was?

It had taken two decades for God to help ease her pain and anger and grief into a safe expression. When she wrote she could step back from the tragedy that was her life. She could look at it, taste it, feel it. It was something that could be examined and analyzed. The past no longer made her bleed, even if it still bound her freedom.

The man who still stalked her would probably be surprised to learn his victim now pitied him more than hated him. God had been good to her in that respect. What hatred had festered, God had lanced early. Sara now simply longed for him to be caught, for justice to be done, for her nightmare to be over.

There would be a final H. Q. Victor book someday. Her book. Kim's book. That book would be a final sign that she was truly free.

It was too complex to even approach the topic. She said nothing as Adam directed her from the den, his hand warm on the back of her sweater.

There were three bedrooms and two baths in the condo; the master bedroom was large and spacious; the guest rooms looked as if they had not been disturbed since his housekeeper had last dusted.

Back in the kitchen, the short tour completed, Adam reached for coffee mugs he had set out. "There is cream in the refrigerator and sugar in the bowl on the counter." He poured her a cup.

"Thanks." Sara accepted the drink, glad to have something in her hands.

His refrigerator was covered with snapshots of the lake, his family, men who were obviously teammates, even baby pictures. "That's an impressive collection," she commented as she stirred a small amount of cream into her coffee.

"I keep in touch with most of the guys I ever played football with and their families. Anyone who has a kid knows to send me a picture."

The man had a sentimental streak. Not many men she had met did.

"The living room?"

"Sure."

Dave had silently slipped away, Sara realized. She was grateful for that.

Rather than sit when they entered the living room, Sara wandered around the room, looking at photos.

"That one is my dad."

Adam was beside her.

There was a wealth of sadness in his voice. Sara looked up in surprise. Adam's attention was in the past.

He shook off the memories. "He died ten months ago."

"I'm so sorry."

"So am I. He was my best friend."

She absorbed that comment, knowing how that pain must feel. She moved on down the wall of pictures, asking about them.

It was obvious his family was special to him, especially his sister's three children. He talked about what they were doing for the summer, what they each liked to do for hobbies. Sara wasn't surprised to find out he often spent Saturday afternoons playing ball with them.

When they were both on their second cup of coffee, Sara finally found a seat. She chose a comfortable chair across from the couch. Adam settled down on the couch.

"It took about an hour for me to figure out you and Dave had arranged today's riding date well in advance," Sara commented.

King Henry was at her side, his head resting on her knee, gazing up at her with adorable eyes as she stroked his head.

Adam smiled. "When you know going straight ahead means meeting a blocker, that leaves doing an end run. Dave knew you would eventually make the suggestion, although you certainly kept me waiting long enough."

"You could have told me what you had in mind."

"You would have said no."

Sara had to concede Adam was right.

"Don't start thinking about security for the next time we meet," Adam warned. "Tonight is coffee, a video, and cheesecake for dessert. Tomorrow can take care of itself."

"It's habit."

"Why don't you decide on a video while I cut the dessert? That is, if Henry will let you move an inch or two. He's in love."

"So am I," Sara replied with a laugh. She got up to review the tapes in his entertainment center.

Adam returned with two plates balanced in one hand, a refill for her coffee in the other. "So what movie have you selected for us to watch?"

She held up a videotape.

"Sara, please select something else." He set down the dessert plates.

"Nope. My choice. This is what I want to watch first." It was a tape labeled Adam's Thirty-Fifth Birthday Party. She was amused at his discomfort.

"My dad was taping the entire thing and adding commentary as he went along."

"I'm sorry. I didn't think. You don't need this kind of reminder of what you've lost."

Adam's hand covered hers. "It's okay. It will probably be good in fact. Put it in."

She bit her bottom lip.

"I'll stop it if I decide it's too much," Adam told her firmly. Sara reluctantly did as he requested.

They shared the couch.

The video had been filmed in his condo, a surprise birthday party with all his family and about thirty other guests present. The tape began with hurried calls to be quiet; the photographer caught Adam's startled expression when he opened the door.

Adam narrated parts of the video while they ate their cheesecake, introducing people to her, most of whom had familiar names.

Sara was relieved that after a few tense minutes, Adam seemed to relax and truly enjoy the video.

Adam and children? Sara felt a growing sense of dread as she realized the number of interactions the tape had captured with Adam and his extended family. From the oldest to the youngest, the children all adored him. The affection was mutual. During the tour he had given her of his home, Sara had seen some of the children's handmade birthday gifts still on display.

Adam had been holding a baby during the last clip of film, carrying the infant around as he would cradle a football, the only one at the party apparently able to stop the infant's crying.

Sara felt cold. *What have I let develop?*

"What's wrong?"

Adam's hand dug into her forearm, keeping her steady, his other hand removing her coffee mug.

"I got dizzy for a second." She forced a smile back on her face. "It's already passing."

"You're white as a ghost."

Because you would want—no need—children in your marriage. And I can't have children. Can't even consider adopting. The coffin lid on their relationship had just been nailed shut, and it made her physically sick. *Lord, I should have known. He's at that age. He's a natural family man. And I never even considered it. What have I done?*

"Let me call Dave."

"No!" She took a deep breath. "I'll be fine. Just give me a minute," she pleaded, seeking a grip on his hand to stop his movement and also to still her own tremors. She scrambled to buy herself more time. "Tell me more about your father."

She could see that Adam didn't want to change the subject, but he did so at her insistence.

"He believed there was nothing impossible if you desired it enough to work for it. He loved helping people live up to their potential. He loved the outdoors and traveled all over the world, was into ecology concerns long before it became fashionable. He loved to have fun."

Sara slowly loosened her grip on his hand. "It sounds like he was a wonderful man."

"He was."

His hand brushed back her hair. "Come on, Sara, trust me. What just happened?"

"A memory, with consequences that reach far into the future."

She needed to say, "I can't have children." She needed to end this relationship before she hurt him. She couldn't do it.

The entire subject tore at her, shredding her heart, her hope.... She rose and walked toward the windows. She rarely if ever let herself think about children...about all that had been sacrificed in her life.

She knew what it was like to grow up surrounded by security. She couldn't do that to her own children. She couldn't put them at risk either. Which left one choice: no children. She had faced that fact years before. It cut deep into who she longed to be, but she had no choice.

It was late—dusk—and the city lights dominated the skyline.

She couldn't tell him.

Adam joined her, his arm encircling her waist. She was drawn back against his strength and held.

He seemed to think her on the verge of breaking apart, for his hold was the gentlest yet firmest grip she had ever felt. His touch spoke of safety...comfort.

She struggled to wrestle back control from the memories. She couldn't tell him all of it, but she had to tell him some of it. "Adam, I was not the only one snatched. They grabbed my twin sister Kim too. She died during the kidnapping."

The past slammed into her mind...the terror as she realized Kim was no longer answering her. She had known her sister was dead, but for hours couldn't accept it. She'd screamed at God for help, even as choking tears depleted her own remaining resources.

She had said it…told him the ugly truth…and it could not be unsaid. She waited for the tightening hold, the reaction.

Nothing.

Nothing but a catch in his breathing. His arm remained firm around her waist, and the hand stroking her arm continued its gentle caress.

And all she wanted to do was close her eyes and get lost in that sensation…to forget who she was, what she'd survived, and all that could never be.

Adam was afraid to move. *Lord, keep me still. Don't let me lose it. If I react wrong here, I'm going to lose her, and this door will never open again.*

He finally took a breath. "It must feel awful to be the one who survived."

A shudder rippled down her back.

He didn't bother coaxing her to the couch, he simply led her there. He didn't try to get her to raise her face or see her expression. He knew what was there—Kim—she had lost her sister. She had lost her twin sister. Nothing prepared someone to hear that. She opened a door for him into those nine days of captivity…and he wasn't sure he wanted to step inside.

God, give us the strength to get through the next few minutes.

He held her, stroking her arm, waiting.

"We were back in the States with our mom for vacation, visiting friends," Sara finally said quietly. "We were all at the park—Dave playing catch with a friend, Kim and I on the swings, our mom sitting on a bench reading. The van...it drove right between us and Mom, and two men dashed out. They grabbed us and they threw Dave to the ground when he tried to intervene."

Adam wished she needed the tissues he had reached for, but Sara was still dry eyed despite the shudders that rippled under his hands on occasion. It scared him, her ability to detach facts from emotions, and she was doing it now.

"It was almost twenty-four hours before the chaos of being moved and taken from vehicle to vehicle was over. We were hooded, our hands bound. And then we were put into hell."

Her grip tightened around his hand so hard he winced. "I learned much later after we were found that it was a root cellar, sloped, but deep enough a man could stand, built behind a farm in the middle of nowhere. They sat us on opposite sides of the cellar, the ropes binding us so that we couldn't reach each other. It was dark. Blinding dark all of the time."

"Was there a ransom demand?"

"Not for the first four days. And then they demanded six million dollars apiece."

"Twelve million dollars?"

She twisted one of the tissues he had given her around her fingers. "Dad was only willing to pay seven." Her bewilderment was plain. "Negotiations began and then broke down and then began again." She struggled to get the next words out. "Kim died on the evening of the eighth day from fear and thirst."

Adam tightened his hold around her waist, knowing she was in trouble. He tried to get her past the painful memory.

"You were found on the ninth day?"

"Sunrise. I was lifted from the hole in time to see the most beautiful sunrise God had ever created. Brilliant orange, offsetting a turquoise blue that radiated across the full sky. Someone had noticed a pickup coming out to the deserted farmhouse. A local sheriff's deputy decided it was worth checking out. They left evidence in the house. He saw the new padlock on the root cellar. A $2.49 shiny new padlock. That was what saved my life."

"Sara." He tried to stop her story, for the shock was rippling through his own system.

Her head rested against his chest. "My dad ended up paying seven million dollars and getting one daughter back. I don't know which he hates me for the worst—being the wrong daughter to survive or losing the seven million dollars he paid out, for the money was never recovered."

Adam closed his eyes. His chin rested against her hair and his hands stroked her back. No child should have to pay the price she had been forced to pay. She had been there when her sister died.... "I should never have put you into the position where you had to tell me this."

Tears flowed from her eyes now, for he could feel them on his shirt. "Shhh." He didn't try to stop the tears as much as he did the pain.

"This is who I am. This is what I live with day after day. You can't know me and not know."

"They didn't catch the kidnappers?"

"They caught one of the two, but he was the extra hand, not the brains behind the kidnapping. He was sentenced to life in prison without parole, but he has never given anything away about his partner."

She looked up and Adam saw the pain in her eyes that went beyond anything he could comprehend.

"My father did not come back from Britain. He was informed of the kidnapping, and he spoke hourly with the FBI, but he never left his post in Britain, never returned to the States. When we were found, he came back but only to attend Kim's funeral. He came by the hospital to see me for all of ten minutes."

Adam framed her wet face with his hands. "I can't explain his actions, Sara. I doubt anyone could. He must have been in shock."

She shook her head. "He didn't think Kim and I were his children. I overheard my parents arguing during the divorce discussions."

Adam closed his eyes. Did anything in her past ever work out with justice? "I'm sorry."

"So am I. I tried so hard to please him when I was young, but nothing ever seemed to be enough. He could tolerate Kim, but I was too much of a tomboy. The ironic thing is the DNA tests they did for the blood traces proved we were his children."

Sara rubbed her red eyes, probably hating the fact she had cried. She closed her eyes as she sighed, trying to collect herself. "Kim is buried in the same cemetery as your father; that's why I knew what inscription you had added to his tombstone. Mom's family plot is there. Kim's gravestone has an angel etched on the stone and a pair of ribbons and a little teddy bear."

She was weary beyond words; Adam could see it in her posture, her cloudy eyes. The memories might be twenty-five years old, but they were still raw. "Thank you for trusting me, Sara. I know how hard it must be to talk about this."

There was more. There was a lot more. He didn't think he could handle hearing it at the moment. His own emotions were churning with rage that the man who had done this was still free.

"I think you chose the wrong time to get to know me, Adam."

"Why do you say that?"

"The memories constantly intrude."

Adam hugged her, understanding the dilemma. "Don't worry about it. I can handle bad memories." He kissed her gently on her wet cheek.

They sat together for another hour, talking quietly, silence stretching between them when needed, words said when they would help. He eased her into his arms, and she rested her head against his shoulder.

Adam intentionally slowed their conversation as Sara grew drowsy. It had been a long day for her, and she had just spent a great deal of emotional energy. He waited until she was asleep before carefully shifting his arm and reaching for the phone on the end table.

"Dave, she's spending the night. Go on home. I'll give you a call in the morning."

"Absolutely no way!"

"She told me about Kim. Go home, Dave," Adam said quietly.

Sara was peacefully asleep in the guest room. Adam carried a cold soda back with him to the den, Henry trailing behind him. Sleep for Adam was a long way away.

Okay, God. What now?

His emotions were boiling, and he wished he had a football game to play, some way to wear off this anger. He wanted to throw something, feel the energy release. They had to catch this guy. It was that simple. A future with Sara depended on it.

Living with these memories was tearing her up inside; she was never able to get closure. It was a living wound in her heart.

Murderers didn't walk free while victims lived in fear, not in Adam's view of the world, not if there was anything he could do to change it.

God, I want this guy caught. I want him to pay a price for what he did. I want justice.

No, if he were honest, what he wanted was vengeance. He wanted the man dead. And he wanted it to happen slowly, painfully…to cause the monster as much agony as he had caused Sara and her family.

Adam drew a deep, shuddering breath. *I want vengeance, Lord. I'll have to settle for justice.*

For Sara's sake, he'd let justice be enough.

CHAPTER | 8

Sara woke abruptly. Disoriented, her first instinct was to reach for the end table and the gun she kept in the drawer. There was no end table on the left side of the bed. Her adrenaline surged. She rolled in the other direction and was met by sunlight coming in a wide window with sheer drapes.

Sara blinked.

The bedroom was large, beautiful. The comforter over her was soft and peach colored. Four pillows surrounded her—big, soft, with rose-patterned pillowcases. She had instinctively created a shell for herself with them.

Where was she?

Talking with Adam was the last thing she remembered.

How in the world had Dave allowed this? Had there been words between him and Adam last night? She could imagine what that conversation must have been like.

She eased back the covers. In the wrinkled clothes of yesterday, she felt the strong need for a shower and a hairbrush.

A look at the time showed it was almost quarter after ten.

Slipping from the bed, she listened quietly to see if she could hear anything from Adam.

She yawned as she opened the bedroom door. There was a bathroom across the hall, and she found fresh towels laid out, a wrapped toothbrush, and a mix of perfumed shampoo samples.

Sara looked over the selections, grateful for Adam's consideration. She took a long shower and let the hot water free her from the remains of a restless night's sleep.

She had told him about Kim. In the light of day, she could not believe she had done that.

How was Adam handling it today? Last night he had listened, comforted her, but said very little. But now? After he had a night to think about what she had said? It was hard to know what to expect. Would he say nothing? a lot? She was afraid of the questions he would want to have answered.

She had told him about her past and about Kim, and to tell him the rest would be hard but possible. He would be able to cope with it.

She could never live with the risk that one of her own children would go through what she had endured. Her wealth was so much greater than her father's, and Adam's wealth was equal to if not beyond her own. Add the factor he was a public figure, and the risk to any child would be enormous. She would never take that risk.

Sara forced herself to step from the shower. She brushed her wet hair, her hands rough when they encountered tangles.

She knew she was on borrowed time. But she didn't want to lose the friendship.

She brushed out the wrinkles in her clothes as best she could. The jeans were fine, but the soft sweater was a little more rumpled.

There was no avoiding the inevitable. She walked down the hall, the smell of coffee drawing her toward the kitchen.

"Hello, Sara."

The voice came from behind her. She spun around on bare feet. "Adam. Hello."

He stared at her for a moment, then smiled. "Relax. It's hard to be formal in bare feet."

She hated the fact he could make her blush so easily.

"Did you sleep well?"

"Yes, thank you."

He was looking for something else in her answer, but she was not sure what it was. He didn't enlighten her.

"Would you like some breakfast? tea? coffee? I can make an omelet and there are fresh muffins."

"I am hungry," she admitted.

"Then let's eat. I waited for you."

"Where's Dave?" she asked gingerly, never having been in this position before, not sure if she should say thank-you for Adam's hospitality or be upset that he had somehow convinced her brother to leave her with him for the night.

"In the living room. He showed up around six this morning, and it was obvious he doesn't get told to go home very often."

Adam's humor caused her to relax. "Oh my, I'm sure there were words."

His mouth curved into a devastating smile. "Actually, he brought the muffins. And a change of clothes for you."

"Why didn't you send me home?"

"I liked having you here," Adam brushed his hand down her cheek, "and you desperately needed the sleep."

Sara had the awful suspicion she was being treated like a kid sister again. She had to take it from Dave; Adam was a very different matter. "Feed me, Adam. Then I'll get out of your way and go home." She started walking toward the kitchen.

"Hey, what did I say?"

"Nothing."

"She's a bear before she's had a cup of coffee." Dave told Adam, handing Sara the coffee he had just poured.

"Start telling stories, Dave, and you'll be fixing your own dinners for weeks." Sara stirred her coffee with a cinnamon stick. "Did you make this?" she asked her brother, suspicious of how strong it looked.

Dave smiled. "Yes. Live with it."

She grimaced and found the cream. She selected one of the blueberry muffins and her hand covered a yawn. She never felt awake until midafternoon.

She ate, watching Adam fix himself an omelet. She was glad she had passed on his fixing her one. Everything was going into that omelet, including what looked to be very hot red peppers.

Adam looked good first thing in the morning. He was dressed casually in jeans and a soft chocolate sports shirt. His dark wavy hair ended just above the collar.

Dave was watching her. Sara shifted away from the counter.

She refilled her coffee mug and carried it into the living room, settling into a comfortable chair.

King Henry came to join her, the dog choosing to sit by her feet. Sara idly rubbed his coat with a bare foot. The dog flopped down on the floor and rolled over. Sara laughed and rubbed his belly.

She felt a lingering headache from last night. Her sleep had been peaceful, but the memories were still near the surface. Thank goodness the memories had not invaded her dreams last night.

To kill time and to keep from thinking about Adam, Sara picked up the book on the end table. She rarely read science fiction, but she opened the novel to the marked page and glanced at the text. There was a major interplanetary war going on. Having felt like she had lived through a few of them herself, Sara settled back to enjoy the story. It was interesting reading.

She heard her brother return to the living room, and a few minutes later Adam came to lounge against the doorpost.

"You need to eat more than a muffin, Sara. What else appeals? Fruit? A bagel?"

"I'm fine."

She knew he was coming across the room without having to lift her eyes from the book. Two hands settled on the arms of the chair. She glanced up with a smile into eyes that were inches from hers. Today his eyes looked like those of a wolf, a silver wolf who had his prey caught. The idea had Sara fighting a desire to laugh.

This man she knew, and she was not above flirting with him, even if her brother was present. Times with Adam were going to be few and far between. She planned to store as many memories of their time together as she could.

One of her hands moved to press against the center of his chest; her fingers curled. "I like being a skinny rabbit. It keeps me fast on my feet."

Adam's eyes lit with laughter, and his gaze moved down to look her over. "You're a pretty thin rabbit. Would you like apples or oranges?"

"You don't give up, do you?"

"Not when it's for your own good. I'm an athlete; I know nutrition."

She wanted to laugh at his expression because he was flirting back with her, but she knew her limits. "May I have a glass of orange juice then?"

"You may." His right hand lifted to the side of her face and fingered the drying curls. "You look quite beautiful this morning, in case I haven't mentioned that fact already."

Sara felt her face grow warm. "Thank you."

"Now don't go all formal on me; I think the curls are delightful."

Her hand still rested against his chest; she gave him a slight push back. "My orange juice, Adam."

She thought for an instant he was going to kiss her, but he hesitated and backed off. Sara sent a glare to her brother who looked back innocently from across the room.

"So what would you like to do today, now that you've managed to sleep through church?"

"You do realize you've managed to cost me my attendance sticker for this month."

"Blame Dave. I wasn't the only one who let you sleep in. So what *do* you want to do today?"

Sara had no idea how she was supposed to answer that. She looked back at him, raising one eyebrow.

"My nephew has a Little League game at three o'clock. Want to come and have hot dogs and peanuts and meet my sister?" Adam offered. "It will be fun."

Going to a Little League game fit what she already knew about him. She would dearly love to meet his sister. "Dave?"

"As long as we're not tailed to the park and there's not a journalist covering the game, security won't be a major problem."

"I would love to go," Sara decided, and the agenda was set for the day.

"Here, you'll need this." Sara accepted one of the lawn chairs Adam handed her from the trunk of his car. He carried two more and a cooler of sodas.

Sara had dressed for the ball game, choosing her casual attire with care: white shorts and an emerald top, her hair pulled back away from her face in a gold clip. She was meeting Adam's family after all.

"There's Mary Beth."

Sara saw a mom and two girls unpacking a sack of food on a picnic table. "How many from your family are coming?"

"Hard to tell. We've got three cousins, and a couple of them sometimes come around to see Peter's games. There's Peter out in left field practicing. The girls are Rachel and Bethany."

Sara felt the flutters begin inside. What if Mary Beth didn't like her?

Dave was walking two yards to the east of her. Behind his dark sunglasses she knew he was scanning the crowds. Dave didn't like her to be in public places. She understood it and could certainly empathize. The scar from the bullet he had taken in New York was always a reminder when he dressed each morning of the dangers that followed her. The FBI agent

Dave had recruited for the day was already mingling with the growing crowd.

Mary Beth looked up as they approached. "Adam, I was wondering if you were going to make it. When you missed church this morning, I wasn't sure what to think."

Adam set down the items he carried.

"Hi, Mary Beth." Adam gave her a hug that lifted her off her feet. "I got held up this morning," he replied. "How are my two favorite girls?" He swung up Rachel and Bethany, getting giggles from them.

Sara saw Mary Beth's eyes shift and take in her closeness to Adam, taking in with some alarm the presence of Dave. It was too warm a day for a jacket. Dave had chosen to make his presence as security known up front. He was an intimidating figure in the dark glasses, stiff posture, and visible weapon.

Adam reached over and caught Sara's hand. "Mary Beth, this is Sara. I believe Jordan has mentioned her on occasion."

Sara wasn't prepared for the sudden smile.

"He has told me only enough to ensure I just had to meet her. Sara, this is a pleasure."

Sara found herself in a hug that surprised her and startled Dave.

"Umm…what exactly has Jordan told you?"

Mary Beth smiled warmly. "That you told my brother no repeatedly when he originally asked you out. I can't tell you how wonderful it is to find out Adam has finally met his match."

Sara found herself pulled toward the table and kids and away from Adam. She sent a helpless look back at him and he just grinned.

"She's harmless, Sara; I promise."

Mary Beth laughed. "I've also been waiting to put you to work, Adam. Chet needs an assistant coach for the game. Lisa went into labor this morning, so you're up next as his replacement."

Adam hesitated a moment beside Sara, gently squeezing her shoulders. "You'll be okay here? I could ask a favor and have Frank take my place."

"I'll be fine. I'll enjoy watching you be a coach." Sara leaned her head back against his shoulder.

Adam kissed her. It was a quick kiss, one Sara didn't expect; then he was gone. She blinked her eyes, then realized if she wasn't careful she would be looking right into the sun.

He had kissed her.

She wished she were anywhere but here. Mary Beth had seen it. Her kids had seen it. Sara had to pretend it was nothing, when it was exactly the opposite. Big time. Adam had known exactly what he was doing staking that claim in front of his family, his friends. He was issuing her a challenge.

Sara wanted to accept. She would give her fortune, her name, her heart to accept, to kiss him back and match him in a dance toward making this friendship become a relationship.

But she couldn't do it. Just watching Adam as the boys gathered around him told her how much children meant to him. To deny him part of who he was would be to leave a lasting wound in his heart. She was too close to falling in love, and love required what was best for the other person.

Mary Beth kept her girls busy laying out a picnic lunch and introduced Sara to several families who came by to say hello. It was obvious the Little League games were family events. Rachel and Bethany were soon off playing with friends their own ages.

Sara took a long drink from the cold soda she held. She and Mary Beth had settled into lawn chairs to watch the game begin. Dave was standing nearby, resting his weight against the bulk of a massive oak tree, taking advantage of the shade and the view of the entire area. Sara was beginning to relax. Mary Beth had the ability to put someone at ease, and she was going out of her way to do that with her.

"Peter plays left field because he can't catch very well. He's been working so hard at it too, both with Jordan and with Adam."

"Where is your husband, if you don't mind my asking?"

Mary Beth looked around, then pointed him out. "Looks like he's going to be the home plate umpire this game. Normally he's the official scorekeeper."

"Were you as active in sports when you were in school as Adam was?"

Mary Beth smiled. "Lettered in track and basketball."

Sara shaded her eyes and wished she had brought her sunglasses. "Adam doesn't seem to attract undue attention here."

"He doesn't. He's a known quantity. Besides, he's autographed just about everything any of these kids own, from their shoes to their hats."

Sara looked around at the families watching their children as the first team came up to bat.

"If you don't mind my asking, why exactly did Adam miss church this morning?"

Sara winced. "He had a houseguest who overslept." She expected to see some censure in Mary Beth's eyes, but her look was too complex for that.

"Are you okay?"

Sara wasn't sure how to answer.

Mary Beth nodded to her left. "I know you travel with security. I also know Adam made rather a mess of it when he tried to see you. Did something happen yesterday?"

In that instant Sara understood. Adam didn't have ladies overnight at his place, and if asked, would more than likely admit that he never had before. Mary Beth knew that, so for Sara to have spent the night at Adam's condo meant some reason other than the obvious one. "We were talking quite late and I fell asleep."

"He's a good man to talk to. He isn't quick to offer a solution until he's heard the full story."

"I noticed that," Sara agreed.

"Please, tell me you passed on his offer of an omelet this morning. He likes to add a few green chilis to his."

"They were red this morning. My brother brought over muffins from the local bakery."

"Your brother?"

Sara nodded back toward Dave, surprised Mary Beth didn't know.

"Oh. I had no idea your brother was part of your security detail."

"He's been with the FBI for a long time now. I have to admit I'm grateful. On the occasions a silent alarm trips and I get hurtled to the floor, it's not quite so bad when it's your brother doing the tackling."

"Does he like working for the FBI?"

"Let's just say they like the fact he works for them." Her brother had received so many offers both from other agencies and individuals that his personnel jacket was flagged red during every review. He was one of the best, and it was a well-known fact among his peers. Dave stayed only as long as he remained head of her security detail, as long as she was in danger.

Sara wished she could release Dave from the burden he carried, the awful feeling that it had been his fault he had been unable to stop the men. As it was, they had shoved him away so forcefully he had broken his wrist in the fall.

"All right, Peter! That's the way to hit the ball!" Mary Beth's son had just knocked a single down toward third base. Given the throwing and catching skills the boys were still learning to develop, Peter made it to first base safely.

Sara grinned as she realized Adam was also on his feet, calling encouragement from the dugout. Peter was leaning over listening to the first-base coach, his face showing his thrill at having gotten on base.

It was a lively and enjoyable game. As kids struck out, they were consoled by teammates; as good hits were made, everyone called their congratulations. She added her voice, longing for someday to be at a game where it was her own son or daughter on the field.

Sara loved watching Adam. He was in the middle of things, often handing out gloves and bats, adjusting caps, earnestly listening.

Mary Beth's girls came to join Sara, shy but wanting to get her attention. She shifted her attention to them, hoping to form a friendship. They were beautiful girls, one six, the other nine. Sara made up stories for the dolls they had brought.

When the game was over and Peter's team had won by managing to hold on to a one-run lead, Adam came over to where the women sat, carrying an equipment bag. He stopped behind Sara as she sat at the picnic table sharing a sandwich with his sister.

He rested one hand on the table beside her. "How are you doing?"

He was grinning and could tell she wanted to grin back, but she kept looking around, too conscious of the eyes watching them. "I liked the game."

"That's good. It's a requirement of my dates that they like sports."

"It's a requirement of mine that they not embarrass me."

"That would clearly not be to my benefit." He slid his hands across her shoulders, gently ruffling the back of her hair. Sara had managed to do it again, look casually elegant. With her chestnut hair and deep blue eyes, emerald was a perfect color for her. She looked vibrantly alive.

Adam had watched her today as she sat talking with Mary Beth. If the laughter was any indication, they were forming a friendship. He was glad. He needed Sara to fit in with his family. He didn't let himself question why it was so important to him this early in their relationship. It mattered.

Sara eased her head back against his arms to look up at him. "Adam?"

He smiled down at her, wondering if he could steal another kiss. "Hmm?"

"I hear there is a tradition of taking the team out for ice cream after the game."

"There is."

"I want a double-decker chocolate-and-pecan crunch on a waffle cone."

"That's pretty pricey for just a date."

The palm of her hand flattened against his sweaty shirt. Adam grinned. "Do I get a taste of the waffle cone?"

"When I'm done with it," Sara replied, leaving him to infer what she was offering.

Adam's smile widened and he grasped her hand. "Come on, Sara, we have fifteen boys to collect."

The ice cream shop was two blocks away, across from the local high school. Since it was tradition that the team went there after a game, it was a fairly easy task to make sure everyone was accounted for.

Jordan and Mary Beth joined them with the girls. Peter was up ahead with his teammates.

Adam settled his group of five boys at one of the outdoor tables. He came back carrying ice cream for Sara, Dave, and himself.

Sara looked surprised at his personal choice. "Just vanilla?"

"The bottom is butter rum." He laughed at her grimace.

It was a warm day and the ice cream grew increasingly hard to eat as it melted inside the waffle cone.

Adam was laughing as he watched her finish her cone.

Her hands sticky, Sara couldn't push her hair back as it fluttered in the breeze. Adam brushed it back for her and handed her several napkins.

"Messy choice."

She wrinkled her nose at him as she wiped her hands.

The kids were focused on their own ice cream cones so

he leaned over to whisper, "Do I get that kiss now?"

Sara thought about it, then put her hand on his arm. He lowered his head to meet hers.

"Butter rum doesn't taste too bad."

For those murmured words, he kissed her again.

It wasn't a flash, it was the click of a shutter. A split second later Dave hit Sara with a shoulder in her side that sent her careening to the left.

The photographer was a high school girl, ten feet away, the camera still raised in her hands, looking stunned at the response.

"Dave, easy. She sometimes covers local events for the high school newspaper. That's all," Adam said forcefully, stepping in front of Dave, facing him. Dave clearly wanted that film.

"Cool down. I've signed several pictures for her photo album over the years. Don't blow one more snapshot for her album out of proportion. Let it go. Okay? Let it go."

"Sara?"

She nodded her head slightly, indicating her vote.

"Adam, we leave now, nothing said. Who can watch the boys for you?" Dave asked tersely.

Frank was nearby; Adam gestured him over. Very few people had actually seen what had transpired, for that Adam was grateful.

They walked back to the park, Dave a few paces ahead.

Adam reached over to take Sara's hand. He could feel her tension but didn't understand it. The picture would make a scrapbook and maybe a summer school paper. That was all. Yet Sara and Dave were leaps ahead of him imagining the worst. Adam didn't understand why and he desperately needed to.

When they reached his building, good-byes with Sara were stilted at best. Adam wanted to reassure her everything would be fine, but the look in her eyes as she turned toward him told him it wasn't.

"Adam, call me tomorrow," she requested softly.

When Adam called her the next evening, Sara was working, sketching in an artist's notepad. She tucked the receiver against her shoulder. "Hello, Adam."

"How are you doing tonight?"

"I've been better." She propped her knee up so she could steady the notepad. She had not gone into work today. Her fear of that photograph was stronger than Dave's. It was a current picture, and if Dave had happened to be in the photograph as well as Adam, it was a piece of evidence she dreaded. Had the girl learned her full name?

Sara didn't regret the decision not to take the film. It had been the appropriate one. The girl wouldn't have understood. And she could have made an issue of it that would have attracted more attention than the photograph risk was worth. What she did regret was that she agreed to be in a public setting where such a picture could be taken.

It was a waiting game to learn if any damage had been done. Sara could only hope for the best. In the meantime, she was doing the one proactive thing she could—push her memory to release the man's image.

"How are you doing, Adam?"

"I can understand why a picture is such a risk, but I've got a long way to go before I understand a situation the same way you and Dave do. Just how serious a threat is what happened?"

Sara spun her pencil in her hand. They didn't know if their adversary was willing to work with others. So far, they had no evidence he was using private detectives to aid in his search. His pattern was one of arrogance. He wanted, needed, to be the one in control. That pattern was clear from his original negotiations to his frequent packages still taunting them to find him. They were relying on that fact now to limit his ability to scan for such a small school newspaper.

"It's very slim. But the rationale is simple: Deny him any information and he can't locate me. The last time security broke down, I was living in New York under a different name. We eventually traced the source of his discovery of my location to a news clip at a bookstore, where I happened to be one of the Christmas shoppers passing by in the background. Dave got shot in that eventual encounter. We have to worry about the small things. Patterns of movements. Any contact with people we think he can tie to me. Pictures, obviously."

Sara flipped to a clean sheet of paper and began another sketch. "I've had a peaceful life here in Chicago because he hasn't been able to trace me."

"Then we should have retrieved the film."

"Not necessarily. To do so risked making a bigger news story. Dave and I are used to being extra paranoid, okay? In a week, the risk will be past. He's not a man to use others to help him. If he were, the situation would be different."

"I'm sorry I caused this."

"I made the decision to go to the game, Adam, not you. Dave and I are both intimately aware of the risks involved in any public appearance." The conversation was awkward and Sara hated that. "I really enjoyed getting the chance to meet your sister."

"Mary Beth echoed that."

Sara was grateful the tension in his voice had eased. They spoke for another twenty minutes. When Sara finally set down the phone, her frustration spilled over in the way she shoved aside the pillows. What did she say? What *could* she say? *Adam, I'm petrified?*

That's what she was. Petrified. And as she curled into a ball, hugging her knees close to her chest, she wondered if she would ever be anything else.

CHAPTER | 9

Days passed, then a week, two weeks. Sara went back to work, determined by the end of the month to finish the children's book she was creating. She spoke with Adam frequently by phone but refused his invitations out. One scare was enough.

She had to commend him for his persistence. He called every night. It was embarrassing how much she looked forward to those phone calls. They didn't talk about anything profound.

Books. Adam was an avid reader. The twelve years of constant travel and living in hotel rooms had resulted in a lifestyle where reading a new book was part of his normal evening. He preferred techno thrillers and suspense novels. Since he didn't know she wrote as H. Q. Victor, and Sara had no intention of telling him due to the security policy she had with her brother, she had to be careful in how she voiced her opinions of books they had both read. She liked to take stories apart and see how they worked. Adam was good at finding new, talented authors.

Sports. Sara was becoming very conversant about football and baseball news. She never liked to be ignorant in any subject she deemed important—even her children's books were carefully researched—so she had been doing her sports homework, much to Dave's amusement as she pestered him with questions while they ate dinner. She had to be prepared for the phone call with Adam later that evening.

They rarely talked about work during those calls. Long hours at the office appeared to be the norm for them both. They avoided bringing it into their time off.

Sara shuffled colored pencils in her hand. She was at the drawing table in her office, working on the final colors for a sketch. It was almost complete.

She couldn't find her lilac soft-lead pencil. She sorted through the ones that had accumulated on her desk. She was going to have to take a day off to clean this office and put everything back in place. The supplies wandered with her over time until she got to the point where she couldn't find anything.

She finally found the pencil she sought.

Sara picked up her teacup. Empty. Again. She set down the cup, annoyed.

She looked up when she heard a familiar four-tap knock on the door. Dave came in and Sara was startled to see Adam behind him.

"What are you two doing here?"

"We brought lunch," Adam replied, as if that explained everything.

Dave looked over the drawing. "Nice dolphin."

"Where do you want it?" Adam asked.

Sara gestured to the open work space by the window. "There, I guess." Adam looked great. She followed his movements with artist's eyes and longed to sketch a portrait.

Several times in the past two weeks, Adam had tried to convince her to come to his office and join him for lunch. She always refused the invitations for security reasons. For the same reason, she turned down his suggestion that he come over here. She didn't want them seen together, not in the building where they both worked. Obviously Dave had decided to override her decision. Sara couldn't say she minded. She had missed Adam.

Dave settled onto the stool beside her. "I'm releasing you back to level two security. So what do you want to do for a night out?"

Adam answered for her. "Go to a movie with me." He handed over a hot egg roll.

Sara accepted the food but protested the decision. "I already told you no."

"That was yesterday. You haven't said no today."

She had to finish a bite before she could reply. She had skipped breakfast and it was past two o'clock. "No. I don't want to go to a movie."

"Sara, *I* want to go to a movie," Dave inserted. "I would rather not leave you at the house with a security detail. So say yes to the man and let me set it up."

The laughter in Dave's voice was just below the surface. Sara looked from her brother to Adam back to Dave again and knew what it felt like to be pressured. They were the two guys in her life. It didn't give her much maneuvering room. "Give me one good reason why I should say yes."

"I'll give you two," Adam replied easily. "Steven Spielberg

and homemade pizza. My dad's recipe," he added for good measure. "Just tell me what you like on it."

Sara was going to lose this debate. There were some things she just knew. She gave in gracefully. "Italian sausage and black olives."

"Good. Now that that's settled, which do you want for lunch? Sweet-and-sour chicken or Hunan beef?"

Sara turned on her stool. "How about some of both?"

"Good choice." Adam handed her a plate.

"Thanks." She ate lunch, enjoying every minute of the break. "So what were you two doing when you had this brilliant brainstorm?"

"Playing basketball. I won." Dave grinned.

"You only won because I let you," Adam qualified. "I felt sorry for him, Sara. I had taken the last six games."

"We'll settle this on the court tomorrow and see who's right."

Sara grinned at them sparring back and forth. She had really missed this. Only guys related this way. "Can I come and watch?"

"No!" It came from both of them at the same time.

Sara's grin widened. It was so obvious. They were each protecting the other, like good friends did. Guys' egos were so fragile.

She turned her attention to a more pressing problem. "Do I have to dress up for this date?"

Going out to a movie was actually one of the safer public outings for Dave to arrange. She would slip in the back row of the theater just before the movie began, then leave by a side exit when the movie was over.

They met at the service entrance behind a local theater at quarter to seven. Adam waited at the doorway with a jacket slung over his arm. Sara had spent the rest of the afternoon anticipating the chance to spend the evening with him. Now that she was out in public, some of that anticipation was being washed away by fear.

She frowned. She was determined to enjoy tonight. She was safe. God hadn't changed. Hadn't she read in Psalm 3 just that morning that the Lord was a shield about her? The only reason fear was finding a toehold now was because she was letting it in. She pushed aside the emotion.

She had Dave hovering. What more could she ask for? She waited for him to signal it was all clear before she moved from the car.

She had dressed in jeans and a powder blue college sweatshirt for the evening, comfort taking precedence over style. It was a security decision. The clothes made it easy to blend into the background should there be trouble.

She relaxed as Adam caught her hand in his.

"Hi, beautiful. You timed it perfectly."

They moved down the janitor corridor between the theaters—Dave in front, Ben behind them.

"What snacks would you like?" Dave asked.

"Nachos, popcorn, and a couple big drinks."

Sara knew that when they slipped into the back row, there would be familiar faces on the end seats on both sides, blocking the row from other moviegoers.

It must be a good movie. Dave had gotten several volunteers for the evening. Sara slipped past Susan into the darkened back row and could see the theater was already more than half filled.

There were times when being accompanied by security had its benefits. The fact that Dave paid for the movie tickets and the refreshments were two of them.

Sara chose seats partway down the aisle where she and Adam would have some relative privacy. They had too much food between them to do much beyond a soft laugh as they got themselves arranged. Sara took the nachos and Adam took the popcorn. The drinks easily fit in cup holders in the seats in front of them.

Adam chuckled at her as she ate her first nacho, carefully balancing one of the jalapeño peppers in the center of it before eating it.

"You do realize that is going to make kissing you rather a challenge."

Sara held one similarly constructed up to him and nudged his arm. "Not if you try one yourself." Her challenge dancing in her eyes.

He deliberately ate the nacho.

Sara had to stifle her giggle at the tight way he suddenly tried to breathe. "Sorry. I didn't realize you had that low a tolerance for pain."

He set down his drink. "I don't. But I think you can have the nachos tonight. However, I do want my reward." He leaned over and kissed her.

"We're here to watch a movie, remember?"

Adam settled the box of popcorn against one knee and draped his other arm around her shoulders. "I would say that was one objective of the night out."

Sara slouched down in her seat, getting comfortable. "If you start getting too fresh, please remember Dave is still my older brother."

"He also thinks it's been too long since you've been on a date."

Sara straightened up in her seat. "He said what?"

Adam nudged her back down to the slouched position. "Hey, don't get offended. He meant it as a compliment."

"Sure he did."

The theater lights dimmed and the previews began. Sara rested her head against Adam's shoulder and watched the movie.

This could get addictive.

The popcorn was shared.

Sara realized partway through the movie that Adam was leaving her the buttered spots. She looked away from the screen to glance up at him and got a smile in return.

She could understand why she had a crush on him, but why in the world was he attracted to her? She had yet to come up with an answer that made sense. But if buttered popcorn didn't prove it, there wasn't much that would. Adam was sweet on her.

She was going to have to call Ellen. Her friend would freak—Adam Black!—but it would be great.

Sara smiled to herself and ate more of the buttered popcorn.

She refused to think about all the problems involved with their having a relationship. She was not going to let anything spoil tonight.

The movie was a good one to see on the big screen. Sara enjoyed every minute of it. She was reluctant to move when the movie was over. It meant sitting up for one thing, and she didn't think her back would straighten. Adam laughed and massaged out the kinks for her.

"Glad you came?"

"Yes."

They were escorted back through the same safe passage to the rear of the building.

Ben and Susan followed them in a second car until they reached Adam's condominium complex. Dave waved his thanks as he dismissed them for the night.

King Henry met them at the door. Sara laughed at his antics as Adam tried to get him to step back and let them inside.

"Is he always this hyper?" Dave asked, scanning the rooms in view.

"He wants to go run on the beach." Adam looked over at Dave, concern wrinkling his brow.

"Stay put." Dave disappeared into the dark rooms.

Sara understood even if Adam didn't. She hated to say the words that would change the tone of the evening. "The teen photographer knew who you were. If that picture became a problem, it would be your home and your office that would be the starting points for trouble."

Adam's face tensed. His grasp on the dog's collar tightened so the animal would stay with him.

Dave came back into the room after a few minutes, turning on lights. "It's clear."

"Stay for dinner, Dave," Adam requested quietly.

"I think that might be best."

Sara sighed. It was best. But it was awful too.

Dave moved into the living room to call down to the security office.

Sara had a hard time shaking off the feeling of disquiet. Her monster had been gone for a brief time; to have it reemerge, even in a false alarm, rattled her. The verse from this morning no longer pulled her back to a sense of security. The shield around her felt like it had a puncture wound. She hated the change. Was her faith so shallow it still rocked even under the false alarms? What was going to happen the next time when the threat was real? If she couldn't ground herself and trust in God, what was she planning to hold on to? Everything else could be shaken.

She leaned against the kitchen counter next to Adam, her mood subdued, as he went about the practicalities of fixing dinner. He diced onions while the smell of browning sausage filled the air. She couldn't change the reality she lived in, but it sure had ruined a nice evening.

Adam studied Sara's pensive face for a moment, considering what he could do. "Interested in making the pizza dough?"

She pushed up her sleeves. "Sure. Just tell me how."

Adam was relieved to see the distant look leave her eyes.

He couldn't afford to show her or Dave just how disturbed he was by what had just happened. They had considered the danger, determined it was safe, and were taking precautions. They lived their entire lives like this. He had just felt the threat for the first time. It had touched his home. It had been abstract until tonight.

He worried about Sara. One day the threat would be real. He didn't know how he would cope when that day came. How did he convince her to let him help keep her safe? There had to be something he could do.

For tonight, his role was to help her still have a semblance of a normal life. He turned his attention to making pizza dough.

"The key is to keep the ceramic mixing bowl warm as you work. Fill the sink with about four inches of hot water, then set the bowl down in the water."

Sara arranged it as he described.

"We'll make two large pizzas, so you'll need about a cup and a half of warm but not hot water."

Sara measured the water, added a package of yeast, and reached for a wooden spoon. "Okay, what next?"

"Add a good dash of olive oil, a couple tablespoons of sugar, oregano, and a little garlic."

Sara smiled. "Typical family recipe—an art, not a science."

He grinned back. "Of course." She rummaged through his cabinets to find everything on his list.

Adam found the black olives she had asked for on her pizza.

"Add flour until you can handle the dough without it sticking to your fingers, and you're done."

Adam watched her finish the dough as he greased the pizza pans. "Not bad."

"Thanks."

"You've done this before."

"Homemade bread. This is similar."

Adam dusted his hands with flour. He spread out the dough on the two pans with a deft hand.

Sara pinched part of the shredded mozzarella cheese from the bowl as he tilted the pans to spread the pizza sauce evenly.

"You're cheating."

"That's half the fun," she replied, grinning.

He handed her one of the pans. "Top this one while I do the other one."

Two pizzas were soon baking in the oven. They companionably cleaned up the kitchen.

When they returned to the living room, Sara started browsing Adam's library. She was already beginning to think about what would make a good birthday gift for him. She knew the date from the videotape they had watched. A book was an obvious choice. She could get one autographed for him if she knew who his favorite authors were. She idly listened to Adam and Dave's conversation about baseball as she ran her finger along the titles.

She was glad they had become such good friends. Dave needed the personal time. He might date, take evenings off, but he never really had a life of his own. Since determining that he was going to be part of her security, his life had been forced to bear the same weight as hers.

So much of Dave's life had been put on hold because of her. She hated that fact. When she was forced to move, he moved too. She knew he wanted to settle down, have a family and kids one day. When she raised her concerns about how many years were passing for him, he dismissed them with a shrug. God had a plan. He would have his family someday, after Sara was safe.

It would be easier if he said it because he didn't want to add another burden to the ones she already carried. He said it because he meant it. Dave worried, but it was not about God taking care of him.

His faith was stronger than hers. It was depressing at times.

Sara realized she had stopped at the section of commentaries Adam had on his shelf. She smiled as she fingered the book on James. Faith without works was dead. Dave was like that. His faith was in his actions. He liked to quote from James 2:18: "I by my works will show you my faith." He expected God to protect him, so he didn't hesitate to go into harm's way when he had to.

He not only had to be concerned with her safety, but with the safety of his entire team. He didn't hesitate to take the actions he felt necessary.

The oven timer went off.

Sara helped set the table.

The pizza was delicious. Sara went through three pieces before stopping to enjoy the conversation.

It was going on ten o'clock. The three of them settled in the living room with sodas to watch the evening news. Sara relaxed beside Adam, content to drink her soda and pet King Henry. She needed to think seriously about getting herself a dog. The husky was a guy-sized dog. Big. Solid. Imposing. At the moment, about to fall asleep with his head on her knee.

"He loves the ball you got him."

Sara smiled. "I thought he might." She turned to watch the sports segment on the news.

Adam had hoped to ask her to come down to the beach with him, to enjoy an evening walking the dog. He knew better now. He had to rethink when and where he could see her without compromising her safety.

They needed time to talk. He didn't want to broach the tough subjects over the phone. He needed to talk to her about how she coped with this situation, what he could do to help.

She lived under a constant threat. He more than knew it now, he also felt it. There had to be something he could do to help her. He hadn't found this lady only to lose her.

She was beautiful. Every time he saw her, that impression just grew stronger. What she wore. How she carried herself. Tonight was no exception. He liked the way the powder blue of her sweatshirt matched up with the indigo blue of her eyes.

He truly enjoyed the time he spent with her. Their long conversations on the phone were the highlights of his evenings. She had a sense of humor that delighted him. He wanted to spend more evenings with her.

"Would you like to go out to dinner next week?" He brushed his fingers lightly over a few strands of chestnut hair that had escaped from her white silk bow.

She turned to look at him. "Where did you have in mind?"

"Somewhere with a private dining room. The Hamilton Hotel, maybe."

She tipped her head slightly toward him as she considered his question. "I would like that, Adam."

"We'll let Dave set something up."

"I'm beginning to feel like your social secretary, Sara," Dave remarked, half asleep in his chair.

She grinned. "You always have been."

"Thank goodness you haven't had much of a social life lately."

Adam chuckled at Sara's expression. "Take him home, Sara. We'll kick him out on the next date."

She leaned over and gently kissed him. "Good idea. Thanks for the movie and the pizza."

"You're welcome."

Adam walked down with them and stayed beside Sara in the lobby as Dave brought the car to the door. It was a beautiful night. Adam tucked Sara in the car. "Get a good night's sleep. I'll talk to you tomorrow."

She smiled as she squeezed his hand. "I'll look forward to it."

Adam watched the car pull away. Tomorrow wasn't going to come soon enough.

Sara rested her head against the headrest as Dave drove them home. She watched the moonlight filter through the drifting clouds. It had been an enjoyable evening.

"I think Adam likes you more than a little."

Sara turned her head and smiled. "I'm beginning to think so too."

"Any idea what you intend to do?"

It was the biggest question on her mind these days. "Not really. I keep pushing off making a decision for another day."

"Maybe that's best. Take it a day at a time. He's a good man, Sara."

She studied her brother's face. "You really think I could have a future with him?"

"I think anything is possible. We will find the guy who's after you and end this problem once and for all."

Sara turned up the cuffs of her sweatshirt, frowning slightly. "You were worried tonight."

"I would feel better if Adam had security with him."

"Have you broached the topic with him?" It was inevitable for anyone who entered her world.

"Not yet. But I need to soon if you're going to continue seeing him."

Dave passed Travis at the security gate to their home. The clock on the dashboard showed it was shortly after midnight.

CHAPTER | 10

The house was quiet. Security lights were on in the hall. Dave deactivated the zones that covered the stairs and the bedrooms. "Need anything downstairs?"

"No. I'm ready to turn in."

Dave nodded and set the security for the night.

Sara walked upstairs with him, thinking about bed and at least ten hours of sleep. She didn't intend to go into the office until noon the next day. Covering a yawn, she stepped into her bedroom, reaching for the light switch.

She froze.

"Dave!"

It was instinctive panic. She felt it close against her chest.

Her eyes darted around the dark room, looking for what was wrong. There wasn't anything out of place. She was alone in the room.

Her throat tightened. She wanted to turn and flee but couldn't move.

"Sara?" Dave had one hand on her shoulder, his body moving in front of hers.

"Something is w-wrong. I d-don't know w-what, though."
She was shaking so badly she couldn't get the words out.

Dave reached past her and pushed the silent alarm, then
flipped on the bedroom lights.

He tucked her into the corner of the room with his arm.
"Stay there."

She nodded and wrapped her arms around her waist,
trying to stop the shaking.

It didn't take him long to search the room, check the
closet, under the bed, the window. His gun out, he moved
back into the hall.

Travis had arrived. Sara heard her brother give the quiet
order to sweep the ground floor.

She stood where Dave needed her to remain, determined
not to hinder what he had to do. The chill wasn't fading.

What was it about the room that alarmed her?

The apricot dress she had worn to work still lay across
the quilt rack, waiting to be hung back up in the closet. The
shoes she had discarded lay on their side by the closet. Her
bed still had that annoying crease in the wedding quilt she
had tried without success to straighten when she made the
bed that morning. The family pictures on the dresser had a
faint outline of dust at their base; they had not been moved.
The perfume bottle she had used during her rush to change
still stood in front of the dresser mirror, waiting to be
returned to the spin rack.

Everything was so normal! So why was she shivering like
a fall leaf after the first hard frost?

There was nothing here that didn't belong. Nothing
missing that she could see.

Dave was gone only a short time, but it felt like forever.

"The house appears clear. There's no evidence security was broken."

The words were not meant to reassure. Dave's tone of voice told her he was more worried than before.

"Any idea what it is?"

Sara shook her head.

He wrapped his arm around her. "Where exactly were you when you first noticed something wrong?"

She moved to the exact spot, certain of where it was because the mirror had caught the reflection of the moon.

She stopped. Had she seen something outside?

Dave apparently had the same thought. He moved back to the window and ran his hand over the panes. The seals were intact.

The mirror also let her see back into the closet. Sara shut her eyes and tried to remember coming home from work. She had selected jeans to wear, considered a blouse and rejected it, then selected the sweatshirt she now wore.

The cream blouse with rose embroidery. Sara opened her eyes and stared at the mirror.

Hadn't the blouse been put back in the closet next to the sapphire-and-ivory dress? She distinctly remembered the hanger catching on the belt of the dress.

The blouse wasn't there.

She moved over to the closet door, dragging in a deep breath against the gaping fear. The faint smell of the cedar wood she loved lingered in the air.

"Sara? What is it?"

The cream blouse was on the other side of the closet.

She closed her eyes, fighting the dizziness that was encroaching.

"The blouse has been moved," she replied, knowing it didn't make sense but certain it was part of what she was reacting to.

"Anything else?"

She looked around the closet, thinking hard. She shook her head in frustration. "No. Everything else is right."

Dave took out his pocketknife and began to open dresser drawers. "Tell me if anything looks off."

Sara shook her head as drawer after drawer was opened and didn't trigger a sense of alarm.

She hesitated a couple times—when he opened her jewelry drawer...when he opened the drawer where she kept letters from Ellen. Nothing else looked disturbed.

When he opened her bedside dresser drawer, Sara wanted desperately to reach for the gun inside, have it in her hand. Someone had been in her room. Her nerves were screaming it. She let Dave close the drawer.

The others in the detail were arriving. Sara heard them downstairs, spreading out to create a perimeter.

"I don't see anything else, Dave." She knew she was losing her mind. She couldn't be reacting this way simply to a misplaced blouse.

"Move back to the spot. Tell me what you can see."

She drew a deep breath as she did what he asked. "Most of the room. Reflections in the mirror. The window."

"Was your door open or closed when you came upstairs?"

"Open."

"Did you leave it that way earlier?"

She shut her eyes and tried to think. "I'm not sure. I think so. I don't normally close it."

"Where did you put your briefcase when you got home?"

"I left it downstairs. There's nothing else here, Dave. Just a crazy sense that I had put that blouse on the other side of the closet."

He came over to join her and caught hold of her hands. "I'll take your gut reaction any day. I need you to walk through the rest of the house."

Sara hated the idea, but it had to be done. "Let's go."

She hesitated twice, once in the living room beside the mail from that day, a second time by the back door that led out to the rose garden.

She stood, looking out at the night. There was nothing that should be causing this reaction. Her nerves were stretched so taut that anything triggered the fear.

Dave rubbed her arm. "Ben confirmed the sensor logs with a fast forward through the videotapes. They didn't pick up anything."

"I'm spooked from what happened earlier, Dave. I can't explain it beyond that. I have better faith in that security grid than I do my memory. Maybe a bat flew by the window... something in that split second when I stepped into the room.

"Maybe I did hang the blouse by the dress, then moved it later when I went back to select this sweatshirt." She rubbed tired eyes. "I don't know. Everything else in the house looks the same as when we left."

Dave massaged her tense shoulders. "I'll move us up to level four security for tonight, keep a team on the grounds and another in the house. You can sleep in one of the guest rooms, and we'll take another look around in the morning."

Sara nodded, grateful. If he suggested they move locations, it would make matters worse. She would be on the run again.

She had ruined a good evening by frightening herself. She was flinching at shadows.

Sara wasn't surprised that the dreams came back that night. She was surprised that it was Susan holding her arm when she realized where she was.

"Dave went to call the doctor," the agent said softly. "We couldn't get you awake."

Sara blinked against the light. Her muscles were so tight they felt like they would snap her bones.

Her nightshirt was soaked.

It was always so startling to realize she was not being crushed in the darkness.

"I had a bad one."

"I'm surprised you've got any voice left," Susan replied gently. Sara watched the agent key her mike and call Dave.

"Did I say anything?" There was always the hope that she would.

Susan shook her head. "I'm sorry."

Dave arrived at the door to the room. His relief was obvious.

"How long?" she whispered.

He sat down beside her on the bed, taking Susan's place. "Twenty minutes." He brushed back her hair. "Remember anything?"

"Nothing new." The light coming in the window was early morning predawn. "I slept about three hours?"

"Something like that. This one hit fast. You were peaceful one minute and screaming the next."

Sara sighed. It had been so nice to have a few weeks

without the dream. Now, if it ran true to form, there would be a string of nights like this one to endure before the nightmare faded again. She rubbed her face, trying to shake off the aftereffects.

"I'm sorry, Dave."

Her throat was so sore. She gingerly touched it. She could only imagine what it must be like to listen to one of her night terrors.

"I wish we could stop them."

"No. They are there for a reason." Sara rubbed her burning eyes. "Can you help me to a hot shower? This one is going to take a while to wear off."

"Sure. Come on."

When Sara moved to stand up, her legs nearly gave out. It felt like she had run a marathon. She was grateful for Dave and Susan's help.

"Stay away from your bedroom. Susan will get your clothes. I'll bring breakfast up here if you like."

She blinked back tears. "Thanks."

Sara showered, dressed, and managed to eat breakfast while Dave sat beside her. Her brother hadn't slept. Sara hated the fact she had caused that.

The day grew harder as it progressed. Sara faced her bedroom two hours later. With Dave beside her, she drew in a deep breath and stepped inside.

Nothing.

No panic.

She walked over to the closet. In the light of day it looked normal. The cedar paneling lined the walls. Dresses hung on the left, blouses and slacks on the right. The cream-colored blouse was still out of place according to what she last remembered, but it hung with the other like-colored silk blouses. She scanned the carpet, the rest of the bedroom.

She wasn't comfortable here, but she wasn't afraid. Whatever had triggered her reaction last night was not as intense today.

"Anything?"

Sara shook her head. "Am I going crazy?"

"No." Dave didn't hesitate. Sara knew she could trust him to be honest. Even if the answers were painful. When she asked a direct question, her brother would give her a direct answer.

"You reacted to something you saw last night. It's just that…"

She turned to look at him. "What?"

Dave ran his hand through his hair. "I think you reacted to a memory last night. An old memory. Something about coming into this dark bedroom, late at night, the hall light on behind you, hit a buried memory."

Sara slowly nodded. It was a better explanation than any she had put together. "A flashback."

"I think so. You certainly froze."

She sighed. Given how sensitive she was to being in the dark, it made a lot of sense. "How long does this go on, Dave? Why can't I just remember? Why does my mind keep skirting around the truth?"

Her brother drew her into a hug. It felt like she was being surrounded by warmth. She hugged him back, glad he was always there. She needed him today, more than she had needed him in years.

"We'll get through this, Sara. It's just another twist in the road. That's all," he whispered. "Just another twist in the road. There will be an end, I promise you."

Sara wished she had his faith.

"I hear you had a bad night." Adam said from the doorway of Sara's office, not sure if she would welcome the company. Dave had called him without her knowledge.

She picked up her hot tea and gestured for him to join her. "It wasn't much fun." She had to whisper the words; her voice had completely given out.

Adam winced at the sound of her voice. Dave had been factual when he called. Adam understood why, now that he heard Sara. How did you really convey someone had screamed so long she had lost her voice? He had been at his own office reviewing a proposal when Dave called him. He listened, stunned to hear Dave's news. He told his secretary to clear the rest of his day's schedule.

He crossed the room to where Sara sat. It always intrigued him, watching her work, for she normally did it with such complete absorption. Today, he had watched her for a moment from the doorway before he spoke. Her full focus had not seemed to be on the picture in front of her. Her pencil had been almost doodling on the page, coloring like a young child. The distraction from her work told him a lot.

He reached her side and caressed her cheek, searching her face to see how much of the nightmare still haunted her eyes. He didn't like what he saw. She was holding herself together by pure willpower. "Are you going to be okay?"

She nodded, pulling back from his touch. "Dave thinks it was a flashback."

Her movement away from him was not a good sign. An unwillingness to talk about it. A lack of emotional energy to deal with it. A lack of trust to let him in. Fatigue. Probably all of them. Adam took a seat on the stool beside her. He gently interlaced his fingers with hers, overriding her reluctance. He couldn't afford to let Sara shut him out. She needed to lean against the people around her. If he had to force his way in, he would do so. "What do you think?"

"I think he's right. It fits."

A flashback to what part of her nine days of captivity? That was the question Dave asked during their phone call. Adam could understand his concern. Sara didn't need another source driving the terror.

"I'm sorry it happened, Sara. I'm sorry I wasn't there."

She grimaced. "Nothing you could do."

"It would have made me feel better."

He saw the glimmer of tears form in her eyes. They startled him because he rarely saw that kind of emotion get past the barrier she kept so firmly erect. He wished she would cry more than she did, but not over something he said. His fingers brushed away the dampness. "Hey, it's okay."

"Have we had any time together that wasn't touched by this baggage? It's like my own version of cancer. It reaches out and touches everybody around me."

She should be angry at the guy stalking her, the situation she was forced to live in. Instead, she was beating herself up for not handling it better. This was exactly the kind of reaction he did not want from her. "Don't cry. Not over that, of all things."

He didn't need her hiding her past, trying to pretend it didn't exist. It was part of why he cared about her. Her courage was part of what made her so stubbornly attractive. "Do you remember the first time we met in the elevator, when I thought you were a reporter doing a story on me?"

She wiped at the tears that had managed to escape as she nodded.

"The thing I hated was the fact that I thought here's yet someone else lying to me. Sara, I don't need you to cover up the painful facts in your life. I need the real you. That's the person I admire. We should be able to have a full evening without the past intruding, without having to talk about it, be touched by it, be reminded of it. But life isn't always fair. I need you willing to be honest and real; the rest can take care of itself."

He was as tired of riding this roller coaster as she was, but if there was no way to get off, then the only option was to go along for the ride. He needed her to be honest with him too. The last thing he wanted was her bailing out on him, just as he was getting to know her.

"Did Dave call you?" She looked troubled at the idea.

Adam squeezed her hand. "He thought I would want to know. He was right."

He watched her absorb the words, think about them as she finished her tea so she could get a few more words from her strained voice. "Maybe it would be better if you didn't care so much. I wish I could say this isn't what my life is normally like. Unfortunately, it's all too realistic."

Adam framed her face with his hands, smiled, and leaned forward to kiss her. "Don't fret, Sara. I already like you. Live with it." His smile widened at her frown. When she tried to speak, he put a finger to her lips. "Just a minute."

He got up to get her some more tea. "This will help."

She took the cup, a small smile curving her lips. "Thanks," she whispered after taking a soothing sip. "This still isn't fair to you."

Adam ignored where Sara wanted to take the conversation. She was not going to change his position. "It makes me angry to think I contributed to what happened by keeping you out so late."

He watched her close her eyes even as she winced. "Don't. It makes no sense to replay the past. You learn from it, but you don't waste emotional time on it."

Adam folded his arms across the back of the chair. "Then explain it to me. I know this is a lousy time to talk with your voice so wasted, but I need to understand. How do you deal with this? What gets you back to work on the same day a crisis hits? I saw it the first day we met, and I'm seeing it again today."

There was an entire part to Sara that he didn't comprehend. If the trauma of last night didn't knock her down, what if anything ever would?

"I've got great coping skills. Don't mistake that for strength. I deal with the situation because I have no choice. Keeping moving is part of coping. If I let any one crisis stop me, I doubt I would ever move again, they happen so frequently. I have a lifetime of them behind me."

Adam understood part of what she was saying. He knew what it meant to endure for the duration. His twelve-year career in the pros had been that. A long endurance race. He had played hurt, sick, exhausted, defeated. If sacked, he got back on his feet. If losing, he continued to play until the last second expired. If defeated, he focused his efforts on winning the next game.

He understood dealing with the situation and moving on. He didn't understand how she could live under a constant threat and still keep her sanity.

He hadn't meant to ask that question, but he had.

Sara's hand covered his. "Adam, God never gives me more than I can handle." She smiled. "I'm really good at praying, 'God, keep me safe.' "

It drew an answering smile from him.

Adam turned his hand over to grasp hers. "I don't understand why you should have to live like this. It makes no sense that this would be part of God's plan."

She took another sip of tea. "Dave likes to quote that Scripture from Romans 11 that says: 'How unsearchable are [God's] judgments and how inscrutable his ways!' I don't know when this will end. Honestly, I wonder sometimes if it will be old age. He'll get old and die and the threat will be gone. I may get twenty years of freedom at the end of my life. That's what I hold on to, Adam. A dream of someday being free."

Adam looked at her calm face and clear, tired eyes and knew one thing: Part of her strength came from accepting that it would never be over quickly. It was depressing to realize in a way; her strength came from giving up hope for a quick solution. Her hope was in a long term, a last-man-standing-on-the-field victory. The realization sat hard in the pit of his stomach. The duration of that game was not attractive.

"Adam, didn't you once tell me your dad taught you to play football one down at a time? To focus on the moment?"

"Yes."

"That's how I have to live my life. One day at a time. I can cope, as long as I never let the big picture overwhelm me."

Adam smiled. One play at a time. He had spent a career focusing with that single-minded intensity. If that's what it took to live life while under siege, it could be done. He squeezed her hand. "Thanks, Sara."

"For what?"

"Not giving up."

She leaned over and kissed him. Her head nestled against his shoulder. "Adam, if I gave up, I would lose what I do have. Ellen's upcoming wedding. Finishing this children's book. Going out to dinner with you. If I gave up, he would win."

Chapter | 11

King Henry took off down the beach after a seagull. Adam watched him run. The sand scattered as the dog plowed to a stop when a bird rose with a shrill cry into the air.

Adam had come to the beach to see the sunset, let his dog run. He had come to pray.

He tossed the worn ball he held back and forth between his hands. The peaceful evening was not reaching his heart.

He whistled for his dog to come back to his side. With a loping stride, Henry returned.

The disquieting sensation that he was being watched lingered, even though he was alone on the beach. The sensation had been with him ever since he left work, left Sara.

Adam knew what was happening.

Dave's security sweep of his home. Sara's flashback. They had both put him on edge.

God, I can't live my life in fear. I'm not made to function that way. I don't want to live like Sara and Dave, constantly having to look over my shoulder. So what do I do?

He knew that fear wasn't God's plan. God had never intended them to live in fear. Adam had nearly reminded Sara when they were horseback riding that perfect love casts out fear.

So why the sudden uneasiness? Wasn't his faith strong enough for what was happening?

He knew part of it. This was his first real taste of fear where he had no control. His dad's death had been different. He had feared it but had known what to expect, had been able to prepare. The situation now was like grappling with a shadow. The fear was there as this constant threat that at any time could lunge out and strike.

He felt as if he had to restore the dike in what he thought had been a solid faith.

What options did he have? A relationship with Sara depended on him not letting fear gain the upper hand.

He couldn't imagine pulling back and not having Sara in his life. She was too unique a lady. He *liked* her. He wanted to spend the next months getting to know her better.

But he couldn't live in fear.

He had to learn to cope and move on, just like Sara did. He couldn't let the security dominate what he thought about or what they talked about in the future.

Sara had twenty-five years of practice in learning to cope. He had to be a fast learner.

She was right. Her past had intruded into their relationship with great frequency. But there had been brief periods of normalcy in their relationship—watching videos together, horseback riding, going to the movie. Adam knew it was possible to have more days like that with her.

There had to be a way to adapt to this situation so the

relationship still had a chance. He had seen what that flash-back did to her. How steep a price she had paid. He hurt just knowing what she had gone through.

What did she need from him?

Someone to listen, someone to help her cope with the pressure.

He knew he was well on the way to falling in love with her, all the signs were there: awareness, curiosity, attraction, fascination. It had been a long time since he had the simple pleasure of going to a movie and hiding in the back row with a date. The time spent with her was like silver and gold, memories that touched his heart. He didn't let many people get that close.

In small ways the intimacy was beginning. Holding hands. Exploring with a few brief kisses. Risking the vulnerability to be real.

Love would be in full bloom with a little more time.

He had something with Sara that was priceless. He didn't think she even realized what she had let them create or how unique it was. She handled his fame, his wealth, his past, the right way. His accomplishments were respected but not pandered to. She cared a lot more about who he was rather than what he had done. As she put it, it was who he was that had led to what he had accomplished.

Their relationship was equal and balanced. Maybe that was what made this relationship so different. She had a healthy sense of self-respect. He didn't feel like he had to prop up her image of herself. He might desperately want to protect her, might want her to be less reserved about taking a risk on their relationship, but he didn't have to worry about her sense of self. Her casual elegance spoke volumes. She tackled what she had to; she coped and moved on.

She was a joy to look at. He could image a lifetime of days spent with her.

God, You let us cross paths, didn't You? This entire relationship has Your kind of feel to it. Something is required of me—a willingness to help protect Sara, for one thing. With each passing day I better understand just how involved that might be. I said I would be willing to adapt if You gave me the chance. So what do You suggest?

Sara needed to have a life beyond just the security. How simple it was to see that from the outside looking in. The web around her was so tight it had to be claustrophobic. The protection was necessary, but it came at such a high price. Adam nodded. That was something he could do—help her have a life inside of that constant security.

They were going out to dinner together. It was a start. He was going to do his best to ensure it was a nice, comfortable, peaceful evening they both enjoyed. To the extent he could make it happen, there would be nothing from her past to cloud the evening. He knew she needed a break. They both did.

Dave heard Sara up and moving around. He glanced at the bedside clock. Four A.M. He groaned, pulling a pillow over his head. At least she had not woken up screaming today. The last five days had been tough on both of them.

When he heard her move quietly downstairs, he gave up hope of getting more sleep. Sara was up. He was up.

A hot shower helped, but coffee would help more.

Dave found her down in the kitchen, fixing her normal breakfast of a bagel and hot tea. He leaned against the door-jamb as he towel dried his hair. "Couldn't sleep?"

She looked over, smiled, and gave a slight shrug. "Not very well. Can I fix you some breakfast before you leave?"

"Leave for where?"

"The Wisconsin air show. It's been on your calendar for months."

"Oh. I'm not going." He had called and canceled the date with Linda a few days ago. She hadn't sounded that upset; a fact that should have bothered him but didn't.

"Dave, you've been looking forward to this for months. You have to go."

Dave grinned. She had that stubborn look she got when she was determined to win a discussion. She could forget it. He wasn't leaving her today. Not when she had spent the last week flinching at shadows.

He would miss seeing the air show. He tried to go every year if he could. If he hadn't ended up in this line of work because of Sara, he would have probably been a test pilot. He loved everything related to aviation. But he had more pressing concerns at the moment. "I'm not leaving you."

"I don't need a babysitter."

Definitely a touch of mutiny going on today. Good. It was nice to see a little fire in her eyes. He leaned against the counter. Sara had been hiding in the house, using the fact her editor had sent back comments on the H. Q. Victor book as an excuse to avoid even going into the office. He needed to get her out of this house. He folded his arms across his chest. "I'll go if you come along."

"You know when I'm along you don't get to enjoy yourself. You're having to watch out for me."

"Ben and Susan were planning to go along. I bet they would still like to come."

A day of fresh air would do Sara a world of good. He watched her bite her lower lip. He could twist her arm when he had to, when it was for a good cause. "Come on, squirt. I want to go, but I'm only going if you come along. You'll enjoy it. I'll feed you junk food, and you'll get some exercise. You'll have fun."

She looked over at him and he wisely hid his smile. "When do we have to leave?"

"Five. That gives you twenty minutes to change."

She finally laughed. "All right, if I don't say yes you'll just badger me until I agree. I'll go."

Ben and Susan were more than willing to go along. It was the type of day that gave them a good break. They met at the airport as Dave worked down the preflight checklist for the private jet.

Dave watched his sister during the day, saw her begin to truly relax. She was enjoying herself. She wasn't into planes and aviation the way he was, but she was a good sport, trailing him around dozens of planes. He fed her the junk food he had promised, hot dogs and popcorn, and shared the salt-water taffy he bought. She marveled with the rest of the crowd at some of the maneuvers the stunt pilots made during the course of the four-hour air show.

When it was finally time to head home, she had color in her cheeks and the contented look of someone who had spent a relaxing day outside.

Dave was glad he pushed her to come. Sara needed the day away. She sat beside him in the cockpit as he flew home, pestering him with questions. She wanted to do a children's book about an air show. Dave answered the ones he could, tried to deflect others, and wished after a while there was an off switch for her ideas. When she was on a roll, she generated ideas too fast for him to follow her train of thought.

Dave set down the plane, pleased with the nearly flawless touch of the wheels to the runway. He loved this plane and the way it handled.

The airport was busier than it had been when they left at 5 A.M. Sara unloaded their souvenirs from the day, transferring them to the car, as Dave completed his walk around the Lear jet. He slipped his sunglasses back on and nodded to the flight line mechanic. The plane was maneuvered back into its hangar bay.

They had another two hours of daylight. Enough time to get home and start the grill. End a good day on an equally good note.

Sara joined him. "That was worth the trip."

Dave dropped his arm around her shoulders. "Glad you let me talk you into going?"

"Yes."

Dave smiled. "You were decent company." He chuckled at the elbow he got in the ribs.

He dug out keys to the car. "Do you want brats or polish on the grill tonight?"

"One of each," Sara replied, fastening her seat belt.

Dave waved to Ben and Susan and drove through the airport security gate. Tollway traffic was relatively light this afternoon. As he did on most drives, he was watching the mirrors for any signs of trouble while mentally reviewing the security plans for the next few days. "Are you looking forward to tomorrow's date with Adam?"

"Of course."

Dave was surprised to catch her blush. "What?"

"He said formal. Do you think my peach dress would be okay?"

Dave might live with Sara, but he rarely was consulted on her clothes. His hand tightened on the steering wheel. He couldn't decide if this was good or bad. If she was asking a guy's advice, it meant she wanted to make an impression. "You look nice in it." That was like saying the sun was bright.

Was Adam this serious too, or was it just Sara? He should have asked the guy his intentions before now. He liked Adam. The guy had some depth to him to go along with the fame. He wasn't the type to take a relationship lightly. Dave tried to figure out the implications and simply couldn't. This was Sara.

His sister grinned. "Should I gather from the silence you have something else to say?"

"I think I'll keep it to myself, thank you." Dave was grateful he had kept his mouth shut to date. The last thing he needed was Sara getting engaged. That would be a security nightmare to figure out. He didn't mind the occasional date; they were good for her. Something serious…that could be an entirely different matter.

"Are you sure you won't join us for dinner tomorrow? I mean as more than just security?"

She didn't hide her amusement deep enough. He sent her a withering gaze that had her laughing. "You know what Adam would think about that, squirt."

"Sorry, I couldn't resist. I think I like having a social life. I'll have to see if Adam wants to go out more often."

"Just as long as you play by the rules. I don't want you ducking security just for the fun of it."

Her laughter smoothed out as she touched his arm. "I

won't, Dave. You have my word."

He nodded, relieved to hear it. If his sister had to grow up and have a boyfriend, he didn't want to have to spy on her constantly to make sure she hadn't ducked away from security.

It was, however, time to seriously talk to Adam. Besides laying down the strict security ground rules, it was time Adam had security with him. The risk was simply too great. They had to take that basic precaution.

Dave sighed. He hated being the one to bear bad news. Adam wouldn't agree to the suggestion easily. Dave would probably have to force the issue and lay down an ultimatum. Accept the security or don't see Sara.

The dress still fit perfectly. Sara swirled in front of the mirror, enjoying the flair of the peach-colored silk. Adam had said formal, so she would give him formal. The neckline was a high choker collar of peach satin and white pearls. The sleeves were three-quarter length. She wore pearl earrings.

The dress had cost a minor fortune two years ago. It was her favorite outfit when she wanted to make a statement.

She wanted Adam to notice her tonight. She swirled around again. If she was lucky, he would.

She was looking forward to tonight out.

She had done her best with the makeup to remove the worst evidence of her bad nights. With Adam, she hoped to forget the past for a while.

She glanced at the clock. He would be here soon. He had promised her a private, quiet, elegant night out. She was going to hold him to it.

Humming softly, she went to finish curling her hair. She had not intended to wear her hair down, but when she went to get her pearl hair clasp, she hadn't been able to locate it. Normally she kept it in her top left dresser drawer; it hadn't been there.

She couldn't afford to lose the clasp. It had deep sentimental value. Her mother had given it to her. Sara knew she had worn it when she had dinner with Ellen. She couldn't remember having seen it since.

Dave had promised to help her look around when they got home. It was possible she had taken it off downstairs and never carried it back upstairs.

She heard Dave answer the front door. With a last look in the mirror, Sara set down the hairbrush. It was time to go.

Adam's hold on the bouquet of peach roses he had brought about slipped when he saw her coming down the stairs.

Sara grinned and pivoted in the foyer, showing off her dress. "Like it?"

"Absolutely." He was glad she stuck to casual elegance most of her life. This full-blown display took a guy's breath away. He wasn't sharing this lady. Not with anyone from her past, present, or future.

Adam felt himself crossing an invisible line. Engagement and wedding rings were not as much a woman's domain as they liked to think. They represented a man staking his claim. Men only remained reluctant until they found the claim they wanted to stake. Then anyone in their way had better watch out. Sara was *his;* she just didn't know it yet.

"Down, Adam. This is my sister, remember?"

"Relax, Dave. Everything ready?"

"Yes."

"Then let's go eat." He formally offered Sara the bouquet of roses and his arm.

He had chosen a downtown French restaurant, booking its private dining room. He was determined to give Sara an enjoyable, stress-free night out. He could see the shadows under her eyes from the bad nights. Tonight would be different. If he had anything to do with it, by the end of the evening she would have too many good memories for the dark ones to find her.

Dave slipped into the background of their evening. He drove but was the silent chauffeur.

Adam asked about her latest children's book and listened with enjoyment to her tell the story. They might be children's stories, but they were messages about life. Every one of the books told him something new about Sara. He watched the animation in her face, finding delight in the way she gestured, the way she talked....

And with each passing moment, Adam knew this enchanting, courageous, challenging woman was becoming one of the most important people in his life.

Sara found Adam's attention endearing. Dave listened to her children's stories the same way. They were important to her, so they were important to him. It said something special that Adam cared enough to pursue a subject so far from his everyday life. He listened and asked insightful questions. He was learning to appreciate the book business.

She enjoyed every minute of the drive for another reason

too—Adam never let go of her hand. His thumb occasionally rubbed over the back of her hand. Sara had to stop the tingle in her arm from going straight to her heart. He didn't mean anything that profound by the gesture, he was just holding her hand. It was a very nice way to start the evening.

Dinner exceeded her expectations; Adam kept her laughing for most of the night. It was the kind of evening that built on itself, one story spawning another. They were good stories about his sister Mary Beth and his father. He seemed determined to keep the subject off of anything that might dim her spirits. Sara loved him for it.

He was treating her with courtesy, kindness, and compliments, making her feel special, making her laugh. The night was turning into one she would treasure all her life.

She was falling in love with him.

Sara paused in eating her meal just to enjoy the emotion. To have met such a man as Adam by accident could be no accident. God had a hand somewhere in this. The touch was too complete to be unplanned. It was an interesting dilemma. She was falling in love, and it was not after she was free of the past as she had always assumed would be required. She was falling in love at a time the past was very much affecting the present.

Adam showed a remarkable ability to cope with the realities of her life. He brought back to life part of a dream that someday her life would be normal. Someday she would be free. Sara wondered what God had planned and knew she would never be able to figure it out. She was along for the duration, day by day. But life was good. Life was very good.

She hadn't felt so hopeful for years. The love came with a sense of peace. There would be a way through the trouble.

Over it, under it, around it…somehow there would be a life in spite of it.

"I am very glad we got this date arranged."

"So am I." Sara wished the evening would never come to an end.

They were sharing crepes for dessert when Dave came into the room.

Sara froze. She had seen that look of tension on his face only a few times in her life. His hand was on his gun.

"Sara, we're out of here, now!"

CHAPTER | 12

Sara felt the crush of being overwhelmed by security as agents appeared behind Dave. The security blanket came down on her and Adam like a sticky cocoon. They were hustled through the back of the restaurant and into a car she recognized as one from the FBI general security pool, not Dave's car or one from her normal detail.

Ben and Susan were there; Travis was scanning the roofs, looking outward. Dave pushed her head down to help her clear the door frame. She was propelled into the car by the force of his shove.

She forgave him the sound of her dress tearing. Her dignity was not his mission, getting her behind the bulletproof glass was. She could feel his fear, and Dave was not a man to get afraid.

Adam was pushed in nearly as fast; he landed almost on top of her. A fist struck the top of the car, and they immediately pulled away.

Sara picked up three cars with them in the detail. Dave

sat in the front passenger seat, scanning all directions. Ben drove. Within moments she realized they were not heading toward their home. "What's happened?"

Dave handed a folded newspaper over the seat. "Section 2."

It was a week-old copy of a suburban newspaper. Section 2 was local news.

The photo of her and Adam at the ice cream shop, the laughter and closeness between them made the short paragraph in the People in the News column leap out. It didn't say much, just speculated whether a local eligible bachelor was heading toward settling down. They listed her name simply as Sara.

"Your teenager with a crush has been doing summer internships with the local paper for the last two years. She uses their lab to develop her film; one of the employees picked up on the picture."

"It's still just a suburban paper." Sara hoped for something, anything, that was good news.

Dave turned toward the back of the car. "And an hour ago a package got delivered in London." He handed over a faxed picture.

Sara looked at it. She went white. "No!"

"He was in the house, Sara. He was in the *house*."

Her hands were shaking. She was looking at a faxed picture of her pearl hair clasp. It had been a commissioned piece. It was one of a kind. "We checked security. It was clean."

"He got inside. Whatever you picked up last week, whatever he moved, you subconsciously knew it. A sniper rifle could have picked us all off tonight so easily. We walked right out the front door and stood around admiring the nice evening weather."

Instead, the man chose to simply leave that possibility hanging out there. "What did the note say?" Sara asked, her voice dull. There was always a note in the package. He always destroyed her life in the same way. A note and a souvenir.

" 'Want to play again?' "

She shivered, the words echoing in the recesses of her mind she could not access. She held up the newspaper. "Why didn't we see this? We've been scanning all the papers."

"I don't know. Believe me, I'll find out. It's the south region edition of the paper; we should have been covering all editions. But we missed it, and now we are behind the curve. If he can compromise security at the house, he can be anywhere he wants to be. Your name and office are gone, Sara. He knows them. We'll get you to ground and hope he stays in the area long enough for us to finally establish a lead. There is already a team dusting down the house."

Adam was horrified by what he was hearing. He should have left well enough alone when Dave wanted to take the film. But he hadn't. He'd walked Sara straight into danger. His heart went cold. It was rage, iced down; it would flare when he had this madman in his hands, when there was something he could do. Right now the emotion would get in his way. "Where are we going, Dave?"

"The airport. Sara just disappeared."

Adam looked at Sara, could see the resigned acceptance. How many times had she been through this before? three? five? more?

"Adam, you've got to decide what you want to do. I can provide security, but you'll have to assume that for now your condo and your office are both known places where you will be a target. You'll have to stay away from both places. When this guy can't find Sara, he's going to turn his focus toward you."

Adam could feel Sara trembling against him. He made one personal decision. He wasn't adding to her danger. He wanted to stay close to her, but he couldn't, not when doing so would put her at additional risk. His face was too well known. It felt like part of his heart was getting ripped out. *Lord, why are You allowing this to happen?*

"What do you suggest, Dave?"

"You've got friends all over the country. Call one and go spend a few days, then call another and spend a few more days. Stay out of town for the next several weeks. Use cash, not your credit cards. That includes buying the plane tickets. The one thing we have in our favor is that the picture didn't show the ice cream shop's name, but it's only a matter of time before he finds it. That immediately gives him the Little League games and from there, your sister. It's going to get messy."

"What about my sister and her family?"

"There will be security there, I promise you. Agents are already picking up Jordan."

Adam could only imagine what his brother-in-law was feeling right now. He finally understood why Sara tried so desperately to shut people out of her life, even at her own cost. It was frightening to realize you had put someone else in danger. He closed his eyes, sick with dread. He opened them, resolving to cope. Sara didn't need him adding to her own pressure. Adam looked at her, sitting white faced beside him, clenching the fax in fingers that curled. He looked over at his friend in the front seat. Adam didn't like what he saw there any better.

Sara looked scared. He looked dangerous. Dave had the look of a man playing a game of Russian roulette.

"Adam, I'm going to catch this guy. The fact he's suddenly become something more than a shadow is a real break in this case. I'll get him."

Her suitcase landed on the bed with a thud. The safe house bedroom looked like many others Sara had slept in during her life. She was somewhere in Colorado. It was after 2 A.M.

Fatigue and fury fought for dominance.

She had lost Adam. The pain would come later. Right now, anger controlled.

She unzipped the suitcase. She called it her hot case because it was always waiting for just this contingency. Every item inside had been chosen with care. Every time they had to abruptly relocate it hit her hard, was a disorienting shock to her system. She needed *something* to be familiar when she was tossed into a new location.

Since the man had entered the house, everything she owned was possible evidence. It could be weeks before anything could be sent on to her here.

She unpacked, having learned to do it as soon as she arrived. Coping skills dictated she put her stamp on this room as soon as possible, make it her own turf.

A Bible, the leather cover worn from handling. A pearl necklace. A black sweatshirt to match her mood. Three shirts, a sweater, two pair of jeans. Three books—she had learned, once the adrenaline faded, she would be facing endless days of isolation and boredom. A sketch pad and a full set of colored pencils.

The stuffed bear from Dave went on the nightstand.

It did not take long to unpack. Sara sank down on the side of the bed and rubbed her face with her hands. She could go to bed and face a probable nightmare or she could stay awake and wait for dawn to arrive.

Dave. It hurt knowing her brother was in danger. He would be doing a full-court press tonight, looking for the lead that would break open the case. These first forty-eight hours were critical.

Adam. She hoped he would one day forgive her. She had just managed to destroy a chunk of his life.

The black despair hit.

The sense of being alone was overwhelming. Her heart felt ripped out. Unless the man was caught, Adam was gone for good—and he'd taken a part of her with him.

She had no choice. She could either flex with the blow or let it break her.

The pain was intolerable.

God, You have to give me the strength to hold this together.

The killer was back....

CHAPTER | 13

"How are you doing, Sara?" Adam's voice sounded tired tonight, rough and emotional.

Sara pushed back her hair so she could cradle the phone against her shoulder. The last two weeks had been tough on them both. Dave had arranged for Adam to be able to call her every evening at ten. It had become an intensely lonely, isolated wait—waiting for news from Dave, waiting for these brief chances to talk with Adam. She missed him so much she ached inside.

"I'm fine." If he could see her, her lie would be apparent. Dave and Adam weren't there to offer comfort, and the dreams terrified her. She didn't want to add to his stress by talking about something he could do nothing about.

She rubbed her temples, her tension headache gaining the upper hand. She could hear Susan moving around in the next room. Susan and Ben were good about giving her as much privacy as they could. It wasn't much, though. The safe house didn't allow for much freedom of movement. "How are you doing?"

"Missing you."

Sara curled her feet farther up under her on the alcove ledge. It was her favorite place to sit in the rustic home, for its three bay windows allowed her to look out over the back patio to the woods. She could watch the animals come from the forest to nibble on the corn Ben put out, see the birds pick up seeds from the feeders. She knew she was only allowed to sit here because the original window glass had been replaced with something that could stop a sniper's bullet.

"It's mutual, Adam." Not having him nearby left a hollow ache inside. "How's your family doing?"

No matter how many times Dave reassured her that every precaution was being taken, Mary Beth, Jordan, and the children continued to weigh heavily on her mind. They were in danger because she had made a bad decision. It always circled back to that common denominator. She had been stupid enough to go to a public park with a public figure. Why not just paint a billboard for the guy and announce, I'm right here. Everyone around her was paying because she'd relaxed her guard.

"Sara, quit blaming yourself for this situation."

"I'm sorry, but I can't help it. In two weeks we should have at least been able to turn up a lead, something. We've got nothing. So you live with no life, and your family lives under a cloud of security. Do you know what that is doing to your nieces? Your nephew?"

"Sara. Calm down. I speak to them every day, to Mary Beth, Jordan, and the kids. They are fine."

"I didn't mean to drag you into this." She never should have extended that first invitation. That had been a bad decision as well. There was no reason for Adam to be in the middle of this. It was her own arrogance to think she could avoid the risks that had set up this crisis.

"Stop beating yourself up, Sara. You didn't drag me into this. You're not the one playing games." He bit back something he started to say. "How did you spend your day today?"

She knew the rules. Nothing that said location, time of day, type of weather, type of clothing, towns near or far, local news. "I read a book."

"You've been doing a lot of reading. Have you been able to work on your next children's book?"

"No." It was dangerous to say more.

"I will be so glad when this particular separation is over. I owe you dinner."

She closed her eyes. *Don't you understand, Adam, you may never see me again? Don't you understand how security works? It may be months if not years. It may be a new identity.*

"When will I get to see you again?"

"You won't. I can't put you at risk."

"Come on, Sara. You can't hide forever."

"Dave sets my agenda."

How she wished she could admit to Adam how stir-crazy she was getting, stuck here in a beautiful place but without productive work to do, without her life.

The isolation was eating at her and nothing brought relief. When Dave called, he seemed to sense that, and all he was able to do was urge patience. Sara's ability to be patient was running out. She had no outlet for the emotions beyond the sketches she could do. She could not work through the intricacies of putting a book together in this place.

God seemed content to make things more confusing. Her devotions kept leading her back again and again to

Ecclesiastes 3 that starts: "For everything there is a season, and a time for every matter under heaven."

She kept getting stuck on the third one, "a time to kill, and a time to heal." She wished it were prophetic but had a feeling it was wishful thinking.

Despite efforts to make the safe house comfortable and restful, it was not home. She wanted to be home again, surrounded by her own things, able to go back to her office where she could bury herself and her emotions in work. But the killer had robbed her of her home. Few things could strike quite that close to her heart. *God, he robbed me of my home!*

She needed to change the subject. "How are you really doing?"

"You don't need to worry about me. I've got two shadows on my every step." He tried to make light of it, but she could tell he wasn't comfortable with the security being so tight. "I'm doing fine. I'm busy."

She wasn't sure where he currently was. She knew he had initially been in Montana, then New Mexico.

"Is there anything I can get you?"

His concern reached deep inside her heart. The man cared. He probably cared too much. It was going to be hard to convince him to step back and get on with his life.

"I'm okay, Adam. They are good at providing whatever they can."

"Everything but freedom of movement."

"That they can't provide."

She didn't want the conversation to end. But the clock said they had been talking for half an hour. Her time limit on the secure channel was up. "Will you call again tomorrow night?"

"Every night. No matter how long you're gone. It's a promise."

Tears welled up in her eyes. She blinked them away. "Thank you, Adam. Then I'll say good night. Keep safe."

"You too, Sara."

She hung up the phone. How long was this intolerable situation going to last? It was a pretty prison, but it was still a prison.

She worried about Adam. He had never lived under the cloak of protective security before. It took a toll—emotionally, mentally, physically. Living under the stress was incredible. How was he adapting? She heard his frustration. He tried to downplay the situation, but she knew what it was really like, knew what he was going through. And all of it was because he had the misfortune of meeting her. She owed him for destroying his life.

Lord, how do we catch this guy? Give me something I can do that will end this situation once and for all.

There were people she loved who were in danger. There had to be a way to catch this guy, even if it meant she had to break security to do it.

She pushed to her feet. Didn't that passage in Ecclesiastes say something about a time for war? She sure felt like waging one. How, she didn't know. Even if it was just trying yet again for that face she knew lingered somewhere in her mind, it would be better than this endless waiting.

Adam let the phone drop back into its cradle. Sara sounded frustrated. He couldn't blame her. He couldn't imagine what it was like on her end of this nightmare. He wearily rubbed the knee he had bruised earlier that day while unpacking. The hotel room was like thousands of others he had stayed in over the years. He thought he was done with this nomadic lifestyle.

A hotel was better than placing a friend in danger. He had a bedroom in the suite, the two FBI agents literally outside his door. They changed hotels every four days. He missed his dog, but Jordan's kids liked taking care of him.

He had told Sara not to worry about him. He did enough worrying for the both of them. The night Dave had done the security sweep of his condominium, Adam had known he would eventually face a day when the threat to Sara would invade their relationship. He wondered then how he would handle it. Now he knew. He wasn't handling it very well at all.

He was concerned about his own safety, but he could do something about his situation. Sara's safety was not in his hands. He went to bed at night praying she was safe, got up the next morning with the same worry.

The emotional toll on her was incredible. The man had gotten into her house, into her room. Short of a face-to-face encounter, it didn't get more terrifying than that. Sara didn't have to tell him the nightmares were back. He could hear it in the huskiness of her strained voice.

Adam tried to keep her spirits up, tried to use the phone calls to remind her she still had a life, she still had him. He didn't know if his efforts were enough to stem the tide. The loss had been so abrupt and complete. Her home, her work, her friends.

Unless Dave got a lead in the case soon, Adam didn't know how they were going to deal with the situation. He needed to see her. He could do so little to help her while he remained at a distance. Somehow, he had to convince Dave that it was better for them to be together than it was for them to be apart.

After five weeks, anyplace began to feel like home, even *this* place. Sara inverted the cake pan carefully. It was Adam's birthday, and if Dave got his act together, he and Adam were going to be here for dinner.

The news had brightened everyone's mood. Four more agents had joined Susan and Ben, reuniting most of the team working on the case. The day was bright, sunny, and taking on a festive air. They would be her first visitors since she had arrived here.

Sara kept herself busy in the kitchen. She couldn't get out to buy a gift, but she could ensure Adam got a good meal. Ben had agreed that fixing steaks out on the grill was an acceptable risk. No one had a line of sight to the back patio without being in an area his team patrolled.

Sara had been able to find a few balloons tucked in the back of a drawer and four candles for the cake. She tied the balloons to the back porch railing where at least the breeze would make them dance. She wished they would be able to eat outdoors but knew the answer without having to ask.

"Relax, Sara. They'll be here soon."

Sara realized she was pacing the kitchen, watching the clock. She forced herself to settle on one of the kitchen bar stools. "I know, Susan." The agent had become a friend in the last five weeks. "I'm just nervous."

"Security is good. You don't have anything to worry about."

"It's not that."

Susan smiled. "He's going to be glad to see you. I wouldn't worry about the rest."

Sara smiled back, hoping Susan was right.

The car finally arrived. Sara watched Adam look around the area and over at the house as he followed Dave up the walkway.

She bit her lip and forced herself to wait, standing in the living room doorway.

They came into the house.

Adam had a little more gray in his hair, and his face showed the price of five weeks of stress, but he was here. To Sara, that was all that mattered.

She rushed to meet him, not caring who saw, overwhelmed by emotion as she buried herself against his chest. Feeling his arms come around her ended so many doubts.

"It's good to see you, Sara." His hug was tight.

At a quiet word from Dave, the security detail left them alone. Sara barely even noticed their exit. She told herself she was not going to cry, but she couldn't stop the tears.

Adam rubbed her arms. "Hey, it's okay."

"Sorry." She swallowed hard, brushing away the tears. "I promised myself I wasn't going to do this."

Adam wiped at a few more of them. "I don't mind. I'm glad you talked Dave into letting me come. He's been a brick wall the last five weeks."

"I'm so sorry you can't spend your birthday with your family, Adam."

He smiled. "I'd rather spend it with you."

Sara was grateful to know he meant it. She slipped her hand in his. "It's not much, but I've got a nice dinner planned."

"Sounds like a good birthday to me." He let her lead him toward the kitchen.

Dave was at the patio door, talking with Ben and Susan. Sara crossed the room and gave him a long hug.

Dave hugged her back. "How are you doing, squirt?"

She didn't even mind his affectionate use of her nickname; she was glad to have him here and unhurt. It was her worst nightmare, leaving her brother in Chicago, knowing he might end up in a shooting match with the man they were after. "Better now that you're here."

So far, everything had been quiet. Too quiet, which concerned Sara deeply. Nothing had been uncovered at the house to show how he'd gained access. No one had made inquiries at the newspaper. Surveillance of Adam's home, his office, her home and office, and the ice cream shop had resulted in no leads. Hundreds of car plates had been checked but revealed no suspicious hits.

The trail was cold.

Her brother was working himself into the ground trying to break the case. She only had to look at him to see the price he had paid during the last five weeks.

"Adam and I are going to put the steaks on the grill." Sara clutched Adam's hand and dragged him toward the back patio.

Dave glanced at Ben and got a nod in return. "Remember I like mine medium rare."

Dinner was everything Sara had hoped it would be. Adam helped her grill the steaks, one arm casually tucked around her shoulders as they leaned against the porch railing, talking, waiting to turn the steaks. It was good to laugh with him, to have him close by.

She had set the table inside for five. When the security details rotated, she would fix a second round of steaks.

She had been worried about the birthday cake, but when she cut the chocolate cake after Adam had blown out the candles, its two layers held its shape.

With a soft plea to Dave, she got permission for them to move to the back porch where they could watch the sunset over the mountains. Dave came with them, carrying his soda can.

The evening was just beginning to turn cool and the breeze was picking up.

Adam watched the sky begin to change colors. "It's a beautiful view."

Sara smiled as she leaned against the porch rail, balancing her cake plate. "It's awesome. Sunsets are always spectacular here."

Adam touched her arm to point out an owl he had spotted in a nearby tree. "You're cold. Where's your jacket?"

"The utility room off the kitchen."

"I'll be right back. Want another soda?"

"Sure. Thanks."

Adam nodded and went into the house.

Dave joined her at the railing.

"Thanks for bringing Adam. I know you probably took some heat to make it happen."

"It distracted you for a few days, so it was worth the effort."

"I'm here indefinitely, aren't I?"

"Something is wrong, Sara. It feels like New York again. We're missing something."

Sara paused, then nodded. "Thanks for arranging today then."

"I've got some ideas we're kicking around. It's not hopeless yet. Give me a couple more weeks, okay?"

Sara forced a smile. He didn't need another burden. He was already doing everything he could. Her nightmares were her own problem. "Sure."

The sound was loud and startling. Sara felt something hit her cheek. The next second Dave took her over the rail of the patio with one sweeping arm. She couldn't breathe under his weight but knew it didn't matter. She heard his gun cock beside her ear.

All was quiet for several long moments. Dave took a deep breath. "Sorry." The gun safety went back on.

It had been a balloon popping. A balloon…that was all. It must have been blown by the breeze to touch the hot edge of the grill where it had instantly exploded.

"You got cake on my favorite shirt," Sara remarked, trying to shake off the disorientation. She had been taken to the ground too many times by Dave to overreact to a false alarm. Given the tension level they had been living with for the last five weeks, it had been due. She moved very carefully and began to assess how many new bruises she had just picked up. Dave had taken her over the railing in a sweeping, instinctive move. From the deck railing to the ground was not a minor two-feet fall.

Dave extended his hand.

Ben and Susan were there, standing almost on top of them. Two other agents had come in view, signaled in by the radio call.

"Clear! We're clear!" Dave called out.

Sara looked around at the agents, then at Adam who had rushed down the deck steps. She started to laugh. It was either that or cry. She slugged her brother lightly on the arm. "Good reflexes."

"If it had been a sniper, we would have both been dead." He was looking at the red welt on her forearm where she had struck the hot grill.

"Always the pessimistic one." She lowered her head and dropped one hand on her knee as the lightheadedness overwhelmed her.

Dave's hand was warm on her back. "What did I break?"

"I don't know, maybe a rib. I'm just out of breath." She closed her eyes, but the darkness overwhelmed her, and she forced her eyes open again.

Adam was at her side. "Sara."

She went down on one knee. She tried to laugh, but it was too hard to get her breath.

"Susan, call an ambulance."

"No. It's not that serious," Sara gasped.

"Go," Dave ordered.

"Hold up, Dave. She just got the wind knocked out of her," Adam interceded. "Give her a minute."

As her breathing eased, Sara became aware of the fact Adam's arm was around her back, his other hand resting against her abdomen. He was warm, strong, and holding her steady.

"She's going to be fine, Dave."

"Come on, let's get you inside and make sure nothing else is hurt." Dave helped her to her feet. She gasped in pain and quickly looked at her right hand. She had picked up a splinter in the center of her palm and had just embedded it nice and deep when she put her hand down to push herself up.

"I'm fine. It's a nuisance." Sara scowled at the blood. It

would have to be her drawing hand.

"Have a seat at the kitchen table and let me look at that hand," Susan directed. "Dave, can you find tweezers?"

Sara dusted off the spots of icing that she had managed to pick up during the fall. Adam held out a kitchen chair for her, and she sank gratefully into it. He squeezed her shoulder.

Susan took a careful look at Sara's hand, wiping away the oozing blood. "It's embedded up into the center of your palm. Would you rather have us let a local doctor do this?"

"No, your help will be fine. It's the bruise between my ribs I wish you could make go away. I think Dave had a can of pop in his hand when his arm came around me."

Susan glanced at Sara's back. "Looks like the remains of a diet cola. Hope this shirt wasn't your favorite."

"Dave is getting used to having to replace my wardrobe."

Dave came back carrying what they would need to deal with the splinter, as well as cream for the welt that had risen on her forearm.

"Take these," Adam offered, holding out two aspirins. "They'll help with the bruises."

Sara took them with a nod. "Thanks."

Adam sat beside her and held her good hand while Susan considered how to remove the splinter.

Sara didn't make a sound as the jagged piece of wood was removed from her palm. The antiseptic sent tears streaming down her cheeks, but finally the wound was bandaged.

If it had been a sniper, the two people she loved most might have paid with their lives today. Adam had been with her moments before; Dave had been right beside her.

The decision Sara made settled inside, irrevocably set.

This was *not* going to happen again. No matter what the cost, this was never going to happen again.

Adam didn't like the look in Sara's eyes. It wasn't just shock. Her eyes had gone flat of all emotion. As soon as Susan was done, Adam took Sara's good hand. "C'mere." She didn't protest as he helped her to her feet.

Adam led her away from Dave and the others to the relative privacy of the living room. She had that alarming look of terror that he had seen only once before. The day when the elevator had gone dark. The look in her eyes was frightening. It was like her world had just gone dark. He rubbed her arms, hoping to break her out of it. "Don't get spooked, okay? It was an accident."

"And if it had been real?" She shifted away from his hands. "I can't afford to have you near me, Adam. I couldn't bear it if you got hurt. It's bad enough I put Dave in constant danger."

Adam felt the surge of the tide breaking against him and had so little to fight with. It was a helpless feeling. He'd never told her the most important thing of all, the one thing he couldn't stand her not knowing—that he loved her. "Don't tear us apart just because we can't find this guy. Then he *will* win."

"Don't ask me to live with the risk. I can't. I can't continue to put people I care about in danger. I'm leaving here. I know how to disappear, not just hide. It's time to take that step."

Disappear. Leave his life. Adam tried to imagine life without her and couldn't. She would be ripping out a chunk of his heart if she left. "Sara, you're overreacting—"

And try as he might, he couldn't keep the slightly desperate note out of that attempted reassurance.

Sara's heart constricted at Adam's almost frantic words, but she had no choice.

"Adam, trust me. I'm not." She refused to let the emotions win. *God, give me the courage to do what I know has to be done. You said there was a time for war. It feels like that time has come.*

Adam wanted to slay her dragons for her, but if she let him try, her dragon would slay *him*.

Her hands on his shoulders, she reached up and gently kissed him on the cheek as she had done months before on a cold, wet July night in the middle of a concrete parking garage. "Be happy, friend, okay?" She walked swiftly toward the back bedroom, afraid to let her steps pause in what she knew she had to do.

Dave would fight what she had in mind, but he would have no choice. Her course was set. She knew one way to catch the man. She didn't care anymore about the high price she would have to pay.

It was time to catch a dragon....

CHAPTER | 14

Dave, don't give me that same line." Adam paced in Dave's office. He juggled the paperweight he had picked up. "I've heard that excuse for three weeks now, and I don't buy it. You refuse me her phone number. You refuse me her location. You refuse me any information on how she is doing." He turned to glare over at his friend. "Quit stonewalling."

Adam had been back in Chicago for five days, days with constant surveillance covering his movements. The three weeks since he had last seen Sara felt like an eternity.

She was haunting his sleep.

Moving home had just made the troubled sleep worse. The stalker knew where he lived. It didn't matter that security was nearby, watching every entrance to his home. The sense of being hunted followed him into his dreams. He wondered if he was getting a taste of what Sara lived with in her dreams. In hers, she wasn't just hunted, she was caught. Just imagining it was terrifying.

"Adam, she is the one refusing to give you the phone number. She's the one refusing mail. She's the one refusing to allow any information to be given to you." Dave rubbed his hands across his face. "I'm sorry. I can't give you what you're asking for."

Adam didn't believe him. "You're saying as her brother you have no sway one way or the other over her decisions?"

"Sure I do. I can cross her and she'll do what she's threatened to do—pull off the FBI coverage team. She can place one phone call and within a day, every bit of protection I have around her will be gone. People, dogs, surveillance, all of it. Do you think I like this situation? It's untenable. But she's serious."

"Why is she doing this? It makes no sense."

Dave met his hard gaze. "You know why she's doing this."

That was the problem. He did.

Adam ran a hand through his hair and reached a tough conclusion. "Then you convey a message to her: I've had it. This is a two-way relationship, and if I have to set private investigators on her trail to find her, I *will* do it. I am not going away. I will do my absolute best not to give away her location to the man who's after her, but since my investigators will know a whole lot less about the details of the case than yours do, the stalker may just learn what he's after. I sure hope if that happens, your security is as good as you say it is."

Adam turned to walk toward the door, then stopped and pivoted. "You tell her if she doesn't agree to see me, she is intentionally choosing to put her entire security detail in harm's way."

It was a threat but a calculated one. Adam could no

longer go on like this. He had no means to force her hand. All he knew for certain was he *had* to. He would do whatever it took to make her see him.

He'd spent weeks wrestling with the decision, feeling the deep emptiness inside without her there with him, debating which was best—both of them living life apart and miserable, or accepting the risk of both being in danger. He would rather live in danger than live without her.

She had made her decision in order to keep him out of danger. He had finally decided it wasn't hers to make. He loved her. He wanted to be with her. The fact she was in danger simply made that decision inevitable. He wanted to be there to help protect her. It went along with loving her.

His money had to be good for something. Finding one Sara Walsh, buried somewhere in FBI protective custody, was going to be money well spent. He wondered if she would thank him for it and knew she probably wouldn't. She'd see it as too much of a sacrifice. He couldn't demand she accept him or the fact he loved her. But he was going to give it his best shot. He was not walking away without trying.

The call came at 6 P.M. as he sat at his desk at home. He was clearing paperwork so he would be able to leave the business in Jordan's hands for a period of time. He was hoping for the day to end even though he knew he wouldn't sleep that night. It would be another night spent staring at the ceiling and wishing for what he didn't have.

Dave's voice came over the phone line, his words abrupt. "I'm flying down to see her tonight. Pack a bag and you can come along. She doesn't know you're coming, so don't count on a warm reception." Dave hung up.

Adam rubbed the bridge of his nose, and for the first

time in weeks felt some of the tension drain from his shoulders. *Thank You, God.*

He packed only the essentials, figuring the odds were more toward blue jeans than suits for wherever they were going.

Dave drove and Adam could see the deep weariness in his friend's face. The man had been working nonstop to try to track down every lead from the package that had come in. They had uncovered precious little.

Adam was surprised to find them taking a back entrance to O'Hare. They drove along a row of corporate jets. Two men were waiting at the steps to the Lear jet.

Dave parked the car and handed the keys to a waiting agent. "After you, Adam."

Adam walked up the steps into the plane and stepped into the luxurious interior that could seat eight comfortably. The seats looked to be the best any plane in the world could offer.

"Store your luggage while I check with my crew." Dave slipped his bag and briefcase into one of the storage lockers.

"Preflight is done and the flight plan is filed. You've got clear weather all the way," one of the men who had been waiting for their car told Dave.

"Thank you, Richard."

Dave was flying the jet. Adam didn't know whether to be relieved or distressed. The man was tired and this aircraft was not a toy.

Twenty minutes later, the plane lifted off. Adam still didn't know where they were heading, but the moon gave him the sense they were traveling southwest.

It was a nice jet. He had spent years flying on the team

plane, flying first class to speaking engagements. This plane gave a smooth ride, the seats were comfortable, the view clear. This was a nice way to travel. If he weren't so tense, he would probably be able to rest his head back and get some sleep.

"Dave wants to know if you would like to come forward." It was the copilot, the agent Dave had called Richard.

Adam undid his seat belt and moved forward. The copilot stayed in the back, having volunteered to see about sandwiches. None of them had taken time to eat.

Dave gestured to the copilot seat. "Have a seat. How do you like Sara's little plane?"

"She owns this?"

"She likes her security team to travel in comfort."

How did Sara afford it? She was this wealthy?

Dave was constantly scanning the skies, reviewing the dash for indicators slipping outside optimal range.

"Where is she?"

"She went back to the lion's den. She went back to the one piece of land that madman knows she owns."

"Frank Victor's ranch."

"Yes."

It made sense, Frank leaving the ranch to Sara. "She's been there ever since the birthday party?"

"She flew down the next day. She's trying to recreate what happened."

"How?"

"The case files. Her memory. Sometime in the next couple days, she's planning to revisit the farmhouse where they were held."

Adam closed his eyes. He desperately wanted them to be

able to do something that would find the guy, end the nightmare, but this? "Please, tell me you're kidding."

"She's stopped caring about the risk, Adam. She just wants this guy stopped at any cost. And she's paying…heavily," Dave said grimly. "Her nightmares are becoming extreme. Her security detail reports she is sleeping less than four hours a night."

Adam wanted something to rage against but had no enemy to face, only a man that never came out of the shadows. "Can't anything be done?"

"She refuses to be medicated. She says that under sedation she still lives the nightmare but can't force herself awake, so she has to endure it playing over and over in her mind. You can't comprehend one of her nightmares until you see one. She is absolutely petrified. It can take an hour or more to work her out of the hysteria. Because of that fact, she long ago agreed that I would hold medical power of attorney for her."

Adam understood the dread in Dave's voice. "You're going to have to step in."

"I might. I sincerely hope not. She has worked hard with some of the best trauma counselors in the country. They're split on what to do at this point. If I have to intervene, it won't be pretty. I don't want to go that route."

"So I'm the catalyst."

Dave nodded. "I'm counting on the shock value and any pride she has left to force her into listening to reason."

Adam gave a heavy sigh. "If this doesn't work, she's never going to speak to either one of us again."

"You've got that right."

They landed at a small private airstrip that Dave said belonged to the neighboring ranch. There were two pickup trucks parked by the hangar, keys tucked above the visor. The co-pilot headed to town, less than ten minutes away, where a hotel room had already been booked for him. Adam and Dave went toward Frank Victor's ranch. It was desolate country. More brown shrubbery than grass, predominately dirt.

"The ranch makes quite a nice profit because of the breeding stock Frank had acquired, so while the number of head the land can support is few, the stud fees the bulls Sara currently has more than adequately pay all the bills."

It was a long drive down a rocky road to the ranch. There were several stables and two large barns, the house itself a sprawling L-shaped ranch. Around it, providing shade, were a surprising number of trees that had grown to maturity. The house and the fence around the two corrals were painted white, the barns blue and white.

"Frank's dad planted all those trees, and they've survived every attempt by nature since to kill them by drought, flood, or wind. Sara calls them a study in the sturdiness of God. You would be surprised how many sketchbooks she has filled with images of those trees."

Their arrival attracted several security agents whom Dave had radioed from the truck several times during the course of the drive, alerting them of their location.

Adam turned to get his bag from the back of the truck and froze when he found a man with a rifle cocked and aimed at him standing less than three feet away. "Would you state your name please, sir?"

Adam felt the sweat run down his back as he answered a dozen questions politely put to him while the gun stayed leveled at him. When he answered the last question in an acceptable fashion, the gun was lifted and the safety slipped back into place.

"Dave may be primary for the government, but I am primary security for Sara's person on this ranch. We keep motion sensors through the house; we make rounds in the house and grounds at all hours; we know every movement across any boundary of her land; and we'll ask questions after the fact, not before, are we clear?"

"Perfectly."

"Then welcome to the H. Q. Ranch. I hope you have some luck in helping the lady to get some sleep."

The shadow of a man was gone.

"Quinton Scott. The best security man we ever found. He may be getting on in years, but he knows more about protecting someone than anyone else I know. We convinced him to come out of retirement when we told him Sara was determined to come back and stay at the ranch for a while. You'll see about twenty men who work for him mingled among the full-time ranch hands. Come on, let's go see Sara."

It was after midnight, Adam was fighting sleep. They went through the back door and into the kitchen, setting down their luggage. The coffeepot was full and recently brewed. Dave poured them both a mug.

"Are you sure Sara's up?"

"Her office light was on. She's up." Dave led the way through a modern, Southern ranch house, the colors pleasing and coordinated from the color on the walls to the ceramics on the tables.

Dave used the edge of his hand to push wide the half-open door just past the formal dining room.

Adam's first impression was that Sara had a massive office. It was full of memorabilia: carvings, Indian pottery, books, and sculptures. The room had been built to hold an impressive library. Adam guessed that this had once been Frank's office. It appeared Sara had changed very little of it.

She was sitting behind a large desk, clear except for a laptop, one high stack of papers, and a thick open file she was reading through. Adam could barely believe it was the same person he had seen three weeks ago. Her cheeks were hollow, her face gaunt. She rubbed her wrists as she read, first one and then the other. She had not heard them enter.

"Do you really think going back over the case files is going to solve something we haven't been able to break in twenty-five years?" Dave stepped into the room.

She looked up and her hand jerked as she saw who it was, sending pages scattering. Adam could see the instant desire to flee rise in her eyes, and he hated that fact. Anger followed by despair slammed into his gut. It was not the greeting he had hoped for, not the greeting he had gotten at the safe house.

"Go away, Dave, and take Adam with you. I don't want you two here."

"Tough. I own part of this place too, even if it's only one share of the stock. Sit down. We didn't come to pressure you, just to say hi. We've missed you."

When Dave sat down in one of the deep chairs and Adam in another, she returned to her seat. "Why are you here?"

"I was curious to see if you had decided on your next

book project or not," Dave replied.

"You know what I've decided." She rubbed her eyes. "Have you told him yet?"

"Not my secret to tell."

"I write more than children's books, Adam. Those are also my books." She gestured toward a bookcase to the right. It went from floor to ceiling, and every book spine was black with one word written in blood red. *Shawn. Tara. Benjamin. Scott. Jennifer.* All books by H. Q. Victor. Translated into dozens of languages.

"I am two people, Adam—the children's author and illustrator who can still feel the innocence of being a child and the person who at age six met evil face-to-face. Through H. Q. Victor, the part of me that saw the evil gets to have a voice."

Adam stared at the books, feeling chills creep up his spine as he recognized and remembered those he had read. They were best sellers because the stories were detailed, complex, and vivid. They packed an emotional punch that made you feel like someone had robbed you of your breath.

Sara was H. Q. Victor. The insight it revealed into who she was made it difficult to keep his perspective. There was rage in those books, controlled, focused, but there. A deadly rage.

It was out of step with everything he had seen in her to date.

It wasn't that he thought of her as a victim. She handled the situation she was in with too much courage and dignity for him to think of her that way. But he had never thought of her as aggressively angry, and now he wondered why he hadn't. It was the logical reaction to her situation. In fact, not seeing her anger should have been a red flag that something was wrong. No one in her situation could sit back and accept it, not if she were to stay sane.

The books were a direct attack against the man who had killed Kim and who still stalked her.

It was like being handed a dictionary and suddenly understanding what the words meant.

Sara was being driven by this stalker, her life controlled for twenty-five years by this faceless man. She was fighting back by giving him a face, letting him try to win, and always having the law catch him in the end.

Adam scanned the books, counting the titles. Nine. How many more would it take before she could finally release the memories? Would the anger ever fade?

No wonder she was forcing a distance between them. She was fighting a war with this man, and it was taking everything she had. She was back in the past; there wasn't room for the present, wasn't room to plan a future.

"Dave, you know I'm doing Kim's and my story as the next H. Q. Victor book. I have authorization to use all the case material the FBI gathered as I write it. I'm going to nail his face. It's in my mind. I know it. Writing this book, reliving it in careful detail, is going to give me that face."

"Sara, are you crazy?" When Dave had said she was reviewing the case files it was one thing, but to write a book and force herself to literally relive what had happened?

Adam's exclamation earned him a scorched look from her and a warning one from Dave.

"Hypnosis couldn't bring back that face. All you're doing is adding to your suffering."

"It will work, Dave. It has to. The buttons on the first man's shirt—nothing in these reports or all the therapy afterward ever mentioned them, but I know what they look like now."

She dug through a stack of paper and found a sketch. "They were metal, the type that could be shined, and the third button had a flattened edge to it on the left side. I can get the images in my mind accurately onto paper now. I didn't have the technical skills to do that before. I do now."

Dave looked at the sketch. "You think you can remember the same details of the second man?" There was real hope in his voice.

"Yes."

Adam got up to pace the room as Dave and Sara talked, not liking where their discussion was heading. Sara was in no shape to be doing this.

He stopped to run a finger along the spines of the books she had written.

Her first instinct when she had seen him had been to flee. She didn't trust him. She might like him, even love him, but she didn't trust him.

He needed her to trust him, to be able to say anything to him, not to be worried about his reaction. He had seen it in her eyes—the fear of rejection, had seen it in her stiff spine and heard it in her tight words. Her rejection hurt.

What do I do, Lord? How do I reach her?

She needed him. If she was determined to walk into her nightmare, she needed someone to talk to. Not surface level talk, but gut level talk. Someone to share the memories that made her panic. The fear. The rage. Dave was too close to the case; he would push for details without realizing it was time to pull back.

Adam looked back at Sara talking with her brother. She thought she could do it herself by directing the memories to paper. He knew she couldn't. He had watched his father's peaceful death less than a year before, and the memories of that day were still vicious. If Sara got close to her complete memories of what had happened during those nine days…she was not going to be able to walk alone through that minefield.

He was staying until she got her answers or was ready to let it go. His mind was set. She would hate it, but he didn't intend to give her an option.

The discussion between Sara and Dave had turned into a semiargument.

"You've got to sleep, and it's apparent you are not."

"The memories come," Sara replied, stacking papers.

Adam decided it was time to interrupt before Dave threatened her with medical intervention. That would be a match to dry timber right now. "What did Frank do when you were a child and these dreams plagued your sleep?" Adam asked her, hoping there was an answer to the question.

"He'd saddle his horse, set me up in front of him, and we'd ride for hours. I'd eventually fall asleep." Sara's face tinged momentarily with a distant smile, the memory a good one.

"The old-fashioned way of taking a crying baby for a car ride," Dave remarked.

"Something like that."

"Okay, then. Let's go riding," Adam decided. "Sara, you are going to get a good night's sleep tonight, and it can be through sleeping pills or a horseback ride. Your choice."

"That's hardly a safe thing to do at the moment," Dave protested.

"You can arrange it."

"Why take the risk?"

"Dave, find us a couple horses. You can come along if you like," Sara said, ending the discussion.

Adam followed Dave and Sara to the barn. Twenty minutes later, with a quiet word to Quinton to lay out their path and the security that would accompany them, they were riding.

Adam kept his arms loose on the reins. Sara settled comfortably against him, and he gave her a gentle hug in appreciation. "I've missed you something fierce," he told her as they followed Dave.

"I missed you too, but it's immaterial. We can't have a future, Adam."

He didn't reply, thinking through what he had seen and heard that evening.

"There's something else you haven't told me, isn't there? Something pretty big," he concluded. She was too intent on separating them for there not to be something else.

His question surprised her. He felt her stiffen. He prayed she had the courage to tell him.

The minutes passed as they rode. He felt the moment she finally made her decision; her head bowed forward and her shoulders sagged.

She shifted in the saddle and leaned her head back against his shoulder, looking up at the vastness of the night sky. Through the silvery moonlight he could see tears slip down her cheeks.

"I used to imagine having children—four, five, with dozens of grandchildren. We would have family barbecues and Fourth of July celebrations, and it would be a family who fought and cared for each other." She was silent as she cried.

Finally she said, "I can't have children, Adam."

Her eyes looked toward him. "I can make books for them, tell them stories, bake cookies, and babysit, but I'll never have children of my own."

Adam couldn't reply. He had no reply. He could barely breathe. Not have children with her? It was one of his core dreams for his future, being a father, raising his children.

Why hadn't she told him sooner? He didn't need another sucker punch tonight. She had already delivered one with the H. Q. Victor books.

Anger surged inside him, but it had nowhere to go. When should she have told him? Before his heart had been involved? It had been involved from the earliest days of having met her. Getting angry at her now would only injure himself. He was hurt. He could imagine how she must feel.

Time slipped by as he fought to keep his emotions in check.

She can't have children.

He felt sick.

"Sara, I am so sorry."

His arms closed gently around her midriff, his hands splayed across a womb that would never carry his children. He wanted so badly to have somewhere to direct his pain.

Why this, God? Why have You given her a life where everything good is denied her? Safety? Loving parents? Stability? Marriage? Children?

He had to get his anger under control. Life didn't come on his terms. If it did, they wouldn't be in this situation. God allowed much more pain to enter their lives than Adam would ever understand. Was this revelation worth losing Sara over? That was how important a matter this was.

Adam turned her into his shoulder, brushing away the tears that continued to fall, taking a deep, steadying breath.

"It doesn't change anything. I don't love you any less," he said softly.

He felt her jerk.

"You surprised me with the H. Q. Victor books, but that's okay. They weren't exactly something you could just mention."

"Adam."

"Shh." He eased her head back down on his shoulder. "Give me some time to adjust. I can hear how raw the issue of children is in your heart. You've made a decision that we can't have a future together because of that fact. Maybe you're right. But it's a decision we will both have to make. You can't make this one unilaterally."

"You would resent a marriage where you couldn't have children."

"That's an awfully big assumption."

Sara rubbed his arm. "Am I right?"

Adam didn't know how to answer her. The pain cut too deep for there to be a simple answer. "I'll have to think about it, Sara. I don't know."

They rode in silence for a while, following Dave.

Her hand pressed against his chest. "I'm glad you came to the ranch."

Adam answered her whisper with a soft kiss against her hair.

Ten minutes later, she was asleep.

Adam moved his embrace, a hand around her waist, the other supporting her shoulders and neck, content to hold her as she slept.

Dave had dropped back to join him when the quiet words between them had died away. "She asleep?"

"Yes."

Dave shifted in his saddle. "It is beautiful country, isn't it? The heavens unlike anything someone who lives in the city would ever see."

"It is magnificent." Countless stars stretched across the horizon. Adam tried to keep his attention on the here and now and not on the bomb Sara had just dropped.

Did Dave know Sara couldn't have children? It was a hard question for Adam to consider. It surprised him, but he almost thought Dave didn't know. Sara was a lady who kept her secrets deep. She wouldn't like pity. She might not have told her brother.

"I think this is why she comes to the ranch, to see the panorama, to feel closer to God."

"Is she going to be okay, Dave? Reliving what happened?"

"I don't know. The files that have been released to her are only the factual files: the depositions of witnesses, the physical evidence. But there are other files—the speculations, the options—that were used to help put context to the facts she had been able to recall. Frankly, most of the child psychologists who worked with Sara were against pursuing her memories."

"Dave, she's already split into two people—Sara Walsh and H. Q. Victor. We've both read her H. Q. Victor books. She's been reliving those nine days of captivity in different ways with each one."

"I know. So maybe now is the time for her to try to remember the rest of it. But I've been through these flash-backs with her. It's not pretty. There is little I can say that is going to prep you for what they'll be like."

They turned and rode in silence back to the ranch. Dave took a sleeping Sara from Adam's arms. Stable hands were there to take the horses.

"Her bedroom is the last one on the right," Dave said softly as they walked down the hall. Adam turned down the blankets and helped Dave ease her down.

Dave turned on the bedside light. Adam stopped his question. Of course Sara slept with a light on.

"Come on, I'll point out a guest room."

Adam wearily opened his suitcase and prepared for bed. He was exhausted.

"I can't have children." The statement ran as a refrain in his mind, adding another reason to why Sara had been trying so hard to distance herself from him. His love of kids and desire to have a family had not exactly been a tightly held secret.

The bed was comfortable; the ceiling above was wooden timber to continue the theme in the house.

"I can't have children." There was something about the way she had said it that lingered at the edge of his mind, refusing to let the words slip away. He puzzled over what was disturbing him but found no answers. It was the most emotional statement she had made to him since telling him Kim died; maybe that's what was troubling him. He shifted restlessly on the bed. *God, I missed something. I don't know what. But I missed something critical. Help me out. Please.*

He drifted off to sleep thinking about Sara.

CHAPTER | 15

The morning was overcast, a heavy blanket of low altitude clouds hanging in the air. Adam stood at the kitchen window studying the sky as he listened to Dave and Sara argue.

He had known them since early July and had never heard them seriously fight before, with voices raised and cupboard doors slammed.

Listening to it hurt.

He needed Dave to win, but his friend was going to lose. Sara had decided her plans for the day, and no one was going to change them. There was so much focused anger in her, not at her brother, although he had made himself a target by getting in her way, but at the man she feared.

Today she was revisiting the sites where it had all begun.

Adam had tried to discourage her, only to discover he wasn't welcome to come along. That stung.

She didn't want him in danger.

It was a convenient excuse. He knew the truth. She didn't

want him to see the places that haunted her.

She had about as much chance of convincing him to stay behind as Dave had of convincing her not to go. If she wanted to revisit the places that tore her apart, she was going to have a lot of company.

Dave slammed the back door on his way out of the kitchen.

Adam turned.

Sara's color was high, her face taut.

He finished his hot coffee, hating what he was seeing. She was so brittle. He feared today was going to break her. He set his cup down by the sink, squeezed her shoulder, and gave her privacy for her tears.

He found Dave on the back patio.

"Ben, get three people to the park. I'll *try* to keep her in the van. Have two people sweep the old farmhouse and put a spotter on the entrance road. At least there we've got a line of sight for miles around. We'll travel in three vehicles."

Adam stopped beside Dave to look at the map spread out on the table. Dave's frustration was obvious. He was nearly drilling the paper with his finger.

"Can you give me an hour to get it set up?" Ben asked.

"Even if I have to lock her inside." Dave's voice was firm, final.

He was coiled too tight to do anyone any good. Adam wondered if Sara realized by taking this trip, she was forcing Dave to go through it again too.

Dave may not have been in the cellar, but he had spent the nine days blaming himself for not being able to stop what had happened. He had never seen his sister Kim alive again.

Adam knew Dave was still not over the grief. Sara was

choosing to relive it. Dave wasn't given a choice.

"Are you going to be okay?" A lousy question, but there was no good one.

Dave grimaced. "Security is an illusion. If he tries something, all we'll be able to do is react."

"Dave, can *you* face it again?"

His friend rubbed his face with the heel of his hand. "I don't know. I've got no choice. The park is the point the nightmare starts for both of us." He folded the map. "Stay close to her, Adam. I've got that tight feeling in my gut that says today is going to be a dangerous day. We still haven't figured out how he compromised security at the house in Chicago. That guy could be anywhere."

They left the ranch an hour later in three vehicles. Adam sat beside Sara in the backseat of the van. Travis drove while Dave sat in the passenger seat. Dave was in constant motion, scanning the road and talking to the lead and chase cars over the radio.

Adam could feel Sara's tension. She sat stiff, a sketch pad resting in her lap, her hands tight around the cardboard spine.

There might as well be a wall between them. High. Impenetrable. Her thoughts today were private.

Adam watched the passing countryside, hoping there would one day be an opportunity to come back and explore the country Sara had loved as a child without this threat hanging over them. He could understand why she called this place home. It was a great expanse of open land. It fit her need for freedom.

The interstate eventually led into the city. They slowed and entered city traffic.

No one had to tell him when they reached the point of town near the park. Sara and Dave both sat up straighter, tense.

It was an upscale neighborhood. They turned a corner. Up ahead on the right was an oasis of trees.

"It's changed. They've widened the streets. There were not stoplights before," Sara said, looking around.

The park was large. The van slowed and drove along the quiet street. They entered the park from the north. The road wound past picnic benches and small parking lots.

Sara touched Travis's shoulder. "Stop up there by the bridge over the pond."

The van pulled to a stop.

There was silence as Sara and Dave looked around.

"There was playground equipment there on the grassy knoll. Mom was there, to the right. The van drove right over this curb."

Sara was back in the past. Adam could hear the memories, the raw pain. His hand gripped hers. It was hard to listen to the quiet words.

The scene was peaceful. The sun had come out making it a beautiful day. It looked nothing like what it really was— a place nightmares had been born.

"Dave, I want to get out."

Her brother didn't argue. Several agents had already formed a perimeter.

Sara stepped from the van.

Adam stayed beside her as she resolutely walked across the grass. Her steps didn't hesitate until she reached the grassy knoll. She turned and looked back toward the van.

She studied the view. "This is about where Kim and I

were," she decided. "Where were you, Dave?"

Her brother pointed. "There."

Adam watched her close her eyes, swallowing hard. She opened her eyes and looked around. "It's been, what, five years since we last came here?"

"About that. Anything new strike you?"

"The trees have grown." She shivered. "The place gives me the creeps."

"It should. Come on, let's get back to the van." They had been outside ten minutes now, and it was obvious Dave wanted her behind the tinted safety glass.

Sara was reluctant to move. "There has to be something here. It's those first few moments that hold the most promise. Before I realized the threat was directed at me, at Kim, at you. What's here that I'm missing?"

Dave squeezed her hand. "Don't, Sara. You haven't been missing anything."

After another two minutes, Dave tried again. "Come on, Sara. This isn't safe."

This time she let Dave tug her away from the danger.

The town traffic was heavy with the lunchtime rush hour. Sara barely seemed to notice. Adam watched as she drew a sketch of the view from the grassy knoll. The lines conveyed a sense of menace beneath the peaceful appearance.

When her sketch was finished, she leaned her head back and closed her eyes.

It was a long ride to the farmhouse.

What had it been like for her and Kim, riding over this or similar roads, not knowing where they were being taken? Every minute must have seemed an eternity.

Adam tried to flex muscles stiff with tension. He didn't look forward to what they were about to see.

Sara abruptly sat forward, momentarily unclipping her seat belt so she could reach the briefcase by her feet. She withdrew a thick folder.

Adam watched her, curious. Her face was intense.

Pictures.

Adam knew in a matter of moments what the pictures were from. He had seen one of them before. The faxed photo of her pearl hair clasp.

The stack was deep. She turned through them in order, looking for something Adam could only guess at. Each sent memento represented another source of terror. Letters. Objects.

Dave had told him the packages had become more frequent and more personal over the years and were arriving now on almost a preset schedule.

She stopped at one picture, pulled it from the stack, and looked at the date on the back.

Blue hair ribbons.

Sara looked ready to cry.

Adam grasped her hand as she looked at the picture of the evidence.

"He marked my sixteenth birthday with this package," she whispered.

A lifetime of anticipating every important date in her life with dread rather than joy. Adam wrapped his arm around her and tugged her to his chest. He carefully took the photo from her hand. He didn't have to ask if the hair ribbons had been something special to her as a child. The man would have chosen the cruelest thing he could.

"I'm sorry, Sara." There had been a lifetime of birthdays and Christmas holidays ripped apart by packages. Someday he would be able to start making those memories up to her.

"So am I," she whispered.

Her hand against his shirt suddenly clenched. Adam felt the tremors she fought off. His hand smoothed her hair, his arm around her shoulders tightened. She wasn't strong enough to do this. The past was too big an abyss.

He had no hope of changing her mind. *Help her survive this, God. Please.*

They eventually turned off the highway.

Dust, heat, ruts in the road. That was Adam's initial impression of their destination. The land was barren, rocky, the ground a pale brown clay. Dirt devils swirled in the air.

If this had once been a farmhouse, time and nature had reduced it to an uninhabitable remnant. Their van pulled to a stop beside the other two vehicles. Dave left them to sit in the van while he spoke to the other agents.

"I don't suppose I can ask you to stay here." Sara sat up and ruthlessly cleared her face of any emotion.

Adam simply shook his head. "No." She was afraid to show him this place. The fact she couldn't yet trust him with the deepest wound of all was hard to accept. He had no choice. She did it in self-defense to avoid his rejection. He was going to have to show her that her fear was unfounded. No matter what she told him, he was not turning away from her. He loved her too much; to turn away would be to rip out his own heart.

Dave opened the door. The dry heat rolled into the air-conditioned interior. "Are you sure about this, Sara?"

She stepped out of the van. "I'm sure."

She walked with purpose across the uneven ground and around the dilapidated house. Adam found the coarse grass was sharp even through his socks. They passed a well, red-colored slivers of rust dusting the ground at the base of the pump handle. A hay barn, part of its roof collapsed, leaned in the distance, pushed by wind.

Desolate. Forsaken. The wind a lonely, hollow whistle. The sounds intensified the emotions.

To be left here, forgotten... Adam looked over at Sara and saw her jaw was locked. This place was having its full effect.

A good fifty feet behind the house, Sara came to a stop.

The cellar.

Boards in one of the two doors had rotted. One of the hinges had given way. The slide bolt no longer bore a padlock.

Dust drifted around in the sunlight.

She looked down at the rotting boards of the cellar door, wrapping her arms around her waist. "Open it, Dave."

The doors came back with a loud creak.

She didn't step near for several minutes, just stood look-ing at the dark chamber the sunlight struggled to penetrate. Dave stood by, watching her like a hawk.

She finally stepped forward, put her hand on the door-sill, and ducked her head to step inside. She didn't pause to let herself think about it.

The root cellar stank with the smell of decades of rot. She could stand after a fashion. Spiderwebs smeared her hands and dried-up bugs crunched under her boots. The shivers were not from the sudden coolness.

The cellar was deeper than she remembered, more narrow. Her hands could reach out and touch both walls.

Scarred into the side of the cellar wall were the distant traces of her struggle to get free. She had dug out quite an impression with her bare hands trying to yank from the wall the source of her restraints. She rubbed her wrists as she looked at that reminder.

She had thought she could get the restraints free, but her best effort had not been good enough. She had failed.

If she had been able to get free, Kim would still be alive. That fact still ate away inside her heart every day. She carried the guilt. She had failed to keep her sister safe.

She had seen this place many times before in the crime-scene photos, had been brought back here as a child. She and Dave had returned here on two previous occasions. She looked around carefully, forcing the fear not to overwhelm her. There had to be something here.

It was only a place now. The taste in her mouth was bitter. This was reality.

This was where life as she had known it had ceased to exist. This was her cross to bear.

Sunlight filtered in, casting her shadow across the place Kim had been.

The tears were too deep in her heart to fall. Like the park, there was nothing here to remember, only to relive. The darkness gripped her and this time it did not let go.

He had won.

"Is she asleep?" Adam asked.

Dave wearily sat down in the nearby office chair. "Yes. She finally cried herself to sleep." His voice was ragged.

Adam looked over at his friend. They were feeling the same pain. "She'll leave with us in the morning, give up this quest?"

"She said she would."

Adam had never spent a more horrible day in his life. They had watched Sara shatter. It had been a slow fracture as they drove back to the ranch.

Neither one of them could do anything but watch. Adam still felt the hit his heart had taken. She had rested her head against his shoulder and just started crying.

She had never stopped.

"Where does she go next?" He looked over at Dave. He saw the man hesitate, then take a drink from the soda can he held.

"Seattle. They are finalizing arrangements now. They found a private place on the coast, a loft with good sunlight for her studio. Remote. She can walk for miles along the shore."

It was as good a fit as Dave could create. Even so, Adam could hear the sound of defeat in his friend's voice. Dave would take a bullet for his sister. To watch what had happened to Sara today had ripped him to shreds. Uprooting her again, even for her own protection, was tearing at his soul.

"Will she be okay?"

Dave squeezed the bridge of his nose. "If she starts to sleep again, stops fighting, starts accepting. It's the same process for every move. She'll do it because she has no other choice. Her will to fight is still there. Today was an exercise in hitting her head against a brick wall. She does it occasionally." Dave leaned his head back. "What about you, Adam?"

"It sounds like I'm moving to Seattle." It meant leaving

family, conducting his business via frequent conference calls and faxes. So be it. He wasn't leaving Sara.

He had made that decision this afternoon. He had spent twelve years living life as a nomad. If he had to spend the next ten doing the same, at least he knew what to expect.

Sara dreamed of one day being free but had to accept the loss.

He dreamed of having a family. His dream would have to die.

His heart had already decided Sara was his choice for a wife. He could stay single and have no children or marry Sara and have no children.

If that was his choice, it wasn't a hard one.

Dave looked over at him. "Don't do this to be heroic, Adam. The shining armor starts to tarnish after about the first year."

Adam gave a brief smile. "I've got my eyes open. A few weeks in protective custody quickly took off the rose-colored glasses. I know what I'm getting into."

Dave flexed the side of the soda can. "More trouble is going to follow us to Seattle. He knows you are with her."

Adam had weighed that risk at length since they had returned to the ranch. "She doesn't have a life if she keeps losing everyone who's important to her. That's part of the problem. He's driving her. Her actions are going to get more and more desperate unless we put a zone of relative normalcy around her."

"She can't take another emotional blow right now."

"I know she can't. She's so bruised right now she's going to try to retreat, exactly as she did after Colorado. If we let her, she's going to tuck herself so far away she'll never let someone get close to her again. You have to get her out of here, safety demands that. But I'm coming along."

"You're that serious about her."

"Yes." There was no joy in that word, only sober acceptance of what it meant. Sara was living under a prison sentence, Dave beside her by choice. Adam had just committed to join the two of them for the duration.

"She's not exactly going to be thrilled with the idea, Adam."

"She protects those she loves. I've already figured that part out."

"And she feels responsible for the situation. Please understand and don't take this the wrong way. You will be another burden to her. You can tell her she isn't responsible, but that won't keep her from shouldering the weight of putting you in this situation."

Adam hesitated. "Just like she did with Kimmy."

"Yeah. She still thinks it was her fault."

"Any idea why?"

"Twin stuff, I think. They were close to each other. Sara lost more than just her sister, she lost part of herself. In many ways they were two halves that made a whole."

Adam hadn't thought of that. Born the same day, playmates, confidants, soul mates. Sara *had* lost part of herself.

"Why didn't she talk for such a long time after the kidnapping?" He had already asked Sara that question, but he needed Dave's perspective. Those years were his best indication of how the trauma had affected her.

"Fear. She thought he would come after others in her family. He had threatened retaliation. And she didn't want to talk about what had happened. Didn't want to talk about

Kim. I think that was what frightened her the most. Remembering Kim."

Adam closed his eyes, seeing a terrified six-year-old girl who didn't know what to do. "Didn't anyone ever tell her it was okay to be afraid?"

"You have to understand the times. An ambassador's two daughters had been kidnapped; one of them had died. There was a fury to find those responsible. Sara was the only lead they had. They pushed her for information in every possible way they could."

Adam's hand clenched.

Dave flinched. "She used to creep into my room and tuck herself under my school desk so no one could find her. It was awful."

Adam could see it only too clearly.

"Mom wasn't strong enough to stand up to the pressure. She was a wonderful lady, but even if she had steel in her backbone, I don't think she would have been able to stop the onslaught. I think that was one reason she left my dad—to give Sara some distance. It tore me apart the day I watched them get on the plane to move permanently back to the States."

"Sara mentioned one time how much she wished you could have stayed together."

"It was mutual. I hated our father for a long time after the divorce."

"Is that why Sara is still at odds with him?"

"Part of it. She was always trying to please him, and he is a hard man to please. After the kidnapping, there was no chance of a relationship between them. It was the money, the accusations, the events. Too much to repair."

Dave pointed to a picture on the end table. "Frank Victor. Now there is a guy you would have liked. Mom met him totally by chance. They were married soon after they met. Frank was just the person Sara needed. He was as different as night and day from our dad. She used to follow him around like a shadow. I think he was the first one to get a smile, definitely the first one to get a word out of her."

"The new foal."

Dave smiled. "Yeah. Frank never did sell that foal. He had a sentimental streak in him, Frank did. The time I got to spend here was the happiest of my life. It was always too brief."

Dave went quiet. Adam knew there were certain memories that would always be private.

"How close has this kidnapper gotten to Sara in the past, Dave?"

"Into the house on two occasions we know about. It's not about killing her, although he has shown a willingness to take a shot at anyone around her, as I know from firsthand experience. No, he wants her back in his control. That's what all those packages are about. He would kill her to protect his identity, but if he did, he would destroy the thing he wants most. So he keeps playing this game. The ironic thing is he's probably using the ransom money as a way to cover his tracks and make this possible."

"Are there any new leads?"

"No. A lot of theories. A lot of time on the ground trying to piece together the packages. He has sent enough of them, though, that we are possibly beginning to have a handle on his travel patterns.

"The handwriting is still our best source of evidence. The

words he chooses give some clues. We can almost tell which newspaper articles he kept from that era when the search was going on. We've gone so far as to cross-index newspaper subscription lists from those years. We just need a break somewhere where he tips his hand.

"As traumatic as Chicago was, it did open a new direction for the case. He had to travel to a known destination within a known period of time. That helps."

Dave thought for a moment. "The best lead has always been the one kidnapper in jail. By tracing everyone he had been seen with in the six months before the abduction, we thought we might find a link. In the initial years of the investigation, that was the focus of the legwork. It didn't pan out then, but I've put Susan and Ben back on it to take another look."

Adam could hear the discouragement. "Dave, you will find him one day."

"I pray we do. I pray it ends because we know who the suspect is, not because he gets close. We can't afford to be playing defense when this finally ends." Dave sat forward in his chair, setting down his drink. "Don't be surprised if we end up with a short night."

"Sara?"

"Probably. I'm going to make some coffee, trade off shifts with Quinton."

"Do you want me to stay up, take a turn?"

Dave grimaced. "No need. If she wakes up, you'll hear her."

CHAPTER | 16

D ave wished he hadn't been right this time. Sara's screams woke him. They were chilling in their shrill-ness.

His bedroom was directly across from hers. He literally ran into Adam at the door to Sara's bedroom and shoved him back from the doorway against the wall.

"Dave, what the—"

"Be quiet!" Dave peered around the door frame, then pulled back.

Quinton was in the hall with them now. "Go to the east window," Dave ordered Quinton.

"What's going on?" Adam demanded.

"She has another gun hidden somewhere in the room. Quinton and I thought we had them all removed. In this state of terror, we're going to be digging bullets out of the woodwork if we're not careful."

There was a commotion in the bedroom, the sound of things falling.

"Talk to her," Adam urged.

"Doesn't work. She hears a man's voice and it's not us she's hearing. Believe me, we've tried before."

Dave took another cautious glance around the doorway. The screams had stopped, but there hadn't been a word from Sara. "I don't see her," he whispered. He keyed the security radio. "Quinton, do you see her?"

"She's not on the bed; her closet door is open. I can't see the end of the bed."

"What do you suggest? Wait? Go in?"

"Go in. She's a levelheaded lady, but there's no telling what she just remembered," Quinton replied.

Dave entered the bedroom and saw her seconds later. She was crouched beyond the dresser in the corner of the room, the closet door open to hide her as best she could. The gun had been set down on the floor, away from her reach. "Don't let him reach me, Dave. Don't let him reach me."

Dave eased the gun on the floor farther back with his foot, relieved to see sanity in her eyes beyond the terror. Very carefully, he reached out a hand and her left hand came up to clench his.

There was blood on her shirt. Her right arm was bleeding from a gash near her elbow. Most everything on the dresser had been knocked off it, including dozens of pictures. Now that he realized it, he was kneeling in broken glass.

"The last time he came, he wanted me to see his face. He purposely wanted me to see him," Sara said, her voice in the past.

Dave didn't like the way her eyes were beginning to close. "Adam, shake out that comforter. I'm going to lift her out of this mess of glass to you."

Dave tried to ease Sara away from the shattered glass as he picked her up. Her eyes were closed, and it was clear she was letting herself see the details her mind had never wanted her to see. Dave looked at Adam and shook his head as he handed his sister over. Only after he was sure Sara was safe with Adam did Dave bend down to pick up the gun. His foot was on a picture of Kim. A silent tear dropped to the floor as he carefully retrieved the picture from the shards of glass.

Adam shifted Sara up in his arms as he turned to the hall. Just as she had during the episode in the dark elevator, she had mentally slipped away from this place, was lost somewhere that terrified her. He could see the clenched hands, the bit lip. She wasn't shaking yet, but he felt the tremors coming. Adam brushed a kiss across her forehead, hugging her tight, as he strode down the hall. "Hang in there, honey. Hang in there."

They had to stop the memories before they overwhelmed her, get that bleeding stopped.

Quinton was beside him. "The kitchen. I can get the glass out and stitch the cut if it needs it."

Adam nodded and followed him and, when they got to the kitchen, kept Sara in his lap. Her left hand had curled into his shirt, and her head was resting against his shoulder. She didn't want to be moved and he wasn't in favor of it either.

She stirred as the medical supplies were gathered. Adam was relieved to see her blink against the light.

Dave joined them, pulling up another chair. He gently brushed back Sara's hair. "How are you doing, squirt?"

A wisp of a smile crossed her face. "Kim named me that, didn't she?"

Dave closed his hand around her clenched one, easing it open. "Yeah. When you were about four." He looked up and gave a rueful smile. "My own little way of prodding a memory, I guess."

Sara reached over to touch his cheek. "Thanks." Her voice was a whisper. "I always liked the name, but I could never figure out why. I remembered tonight."

Dave ruffled her hair. "I'm glad. Look away; you don't like needles."

She looked at Quinton as he loaded a syringe. "I like drugs even less."

"Novocaine, Sara. You'll need it. That cut is deep."

Quinton removed the glass with care. The gash bled heavily, soaking the towel he used to apply pressure. He closed the gash with five neat stitches.

Sara closed her eyes and rested her head back against Adam's shoulder as Quinton worked.

Adam watched each stitch go in and wanted badly to have something, someone he could hit. He had nearly lost Sara tonight. It wasn't an easy thought to accept.

"I need a pencil," Sara said, her voice clear and grim.

It was nice to know they were both feeling the same emotions.

Adam set a mug of coffee beside Sara as she sat curled up on the corner of the couch and got an absentminded thanks in return. She had been working for four hours. The sketches were being drawn with a black charcoal pencil, seven of them now, each one a slice of time from her memory.

The first sketch was the most critical, for it depicted the one time she had directly looked at the kidnapper's face. With precise lines and sharp detail, she had drawn him as he looked twenty-five years ago.

Dave picked up the sketch, his mouth tightened, then he went to Sara's office to make some phone calls.

The other sketches were of other instances she had seen the man's face, some in side relief, some glimpses only of his eyes, but together the sketches were drawing a face in such detail it was going to be a literal photograph of what the man looked like twenty-five years ago.

The sketch she was drawing now was the composite of everything she had seen. She had his face down to the literal number of stitches he had in an old cut above his eye, the exact part of his nose that showed an old break, the exact pitch of his cheekbones.

For an hour after Quinton had closed the gash on her arm, Sara sat at the kitchen table, not saying much, drinking the coffee Dave brewed. Adam recognized the slow way shock wore off, as it had after the elevator ride, and Dave did too. That she had remembered more details than she was willing to tell them was obvious, but neither of them pushed her to talk. She told Dave a few new details about the van and about the order of events during the nine days. Then she had begun to draw.

Adam left Sara sketching and went to join Dave in her office. He found her brother pacing. It instantly put him on guard. "What's wrong? This should be good news, yet you're as tense as a threatened rattlesnake."

"We have always known, or at least strongly suspected,

that the mastermind of the kidnapping was actually part of the law enforcement community, that he somehow had access to what was going on."

"You're serious?"

"A distant connection but enough to keep him in the information loop. There were too many instances where negotiations would change directions without a reasonable explanation.

"Whoever carried out the kidnapping knew this part of the country and knew it well. It was his partner that got sloppy and left the evidence at the farmhouse, not the man we're after. I suspect we're looking for a man who probably works for one of the surrounding county sheriff's offices. Sara just handed me that man's picture." Dave held up one of the sketches.

"We've got to spread out, find him, and get him into custody before he learns the truth. My biggest fear is that he has an information source here on the ranch, someone who is going to pass on the news that Sara remembered a face."

"Can you trust Quinton?"

"Yes. But we don't trust anyone else. The housekeeper, the ranch hands."

Sara came into the office carrying the final sketches. She handed them to Dave. "Are they enough?"

"Yes." Dave squeezed her hand. "It's enough. It's going to finally end, Sara."

She nodded. Unsteady on her feet, she grasped the back of a chair to hold on to. "I am so tired."

Adam wrapped his arm around her waist. "Come on, you need to eat a little; then you can sleep for as long as you like."

She tried to smile. "You've got a deal."

He sat across from her at the kitchen table as she ate and tried to tell from the expressions on her face how well she was coping. The exhaustion was vying with strain, but she didn't look afraid. That had been his biggest worry.

She put the plate and soup bowl into the dishwasher when she was finished. She had managed to eat; that in itself was good to see.

Adam got up to fix hot tea for her. "Can I get you anything else?"

She joined him at the counter, wrapped her arms around his waist, and leaned her head against his shoulder. She had initiated the contact. Adam loved it. He gently wrapped her in a hug of his own.

"I'm fine. You've done exactly what I needed. Thank you."

He was pleased to see the look of a fighter coming back into her eyes. She was pulling herself back together with the same determination she had done after every crisis. "You're welcome. Want to take your tea into the living room?"

She half smiled. "I'll be lousy company. I'm going to fall asleep."

"I won't mind."

She settled on the couch and finished her tea, then stretched out with a quiet sigh. She was asleep in minutes.

Settling into the chair beside her with one of her H. Q. Victor books, Adam alternated between watching her sleep and reading a few pages. He had read this book before, but now he read it in a totally different light.

Dave stopped by to watch her for a moment, then quietly said he was going to the downtown office.

Adam didn't expect Sara to awaken that day, not after the turmoil of the last twenty-four hours. She slept through the afternoon stretched out on the living room couch. Quinton came by frequently. Adam doubted he was ever far away.

The end was in sight. Adam knew it. Dave was determined; he had the lead he needed. Adam had no doubt about his succeeding. But there was a big issue that still lingered.

Children.

"I can't have children." Her voice had been so raw as she had said the words.

Adam didn't consider adoption to be something with a stigma to it. They could still have children, but she had not mentioned that option.

Part of it was obvious, as soon as he realized she also wrote as H. Q. Victor. Sara was terrified of having one of her own children snatched and held for ransom. He was wealthy, but Sara herself was extremely wealthy, each H. Q. Victor book bringing in millions of dollars. She wouldn't want her children to grow up surrounded by security, but neither would she want them put at risk. Adam could feel himself being squeezed between a rock and a hard place. There had to be an option, but he couldn't find one.

He really did want a family. Sara knew that. What had Dave said last night? *"She will still shoulder the weight of having put you in this situation."* Yes, Sara would do that if they were to marry, knowing they would never have children. She would carry the guilt even if it was his decision.

There had to be a solution that met both their needs without placing a new burden on Sara.

Her matter-of-fact statement for Dave to call the counselors she had used in the past was the most encouraging thing he had heard short of seeing those drawings. They had to find this man but Sara also needed to heal. Now, if she could just include him in that list of people she could trust with the raw truth....

He knew how hard it would be to hear what she had to share. It didn't matter. He loved her, no matter what.

Dave returned as the sun began to set. "Has she stirred at all?"

"No. I think if we let her, she'd sleep another full day right where she is," Adam replied with a slight smile.

Dave slid off his jacket and tossed it over a chair. "We've got a strategy in place for how to do the search. I'll take Sara in with me tomorrow. I know there is no way to keep her out of it, so I might as well head it off. I would appreciate if you could keep an eye on how it's hitting her."

"I'll keep an eye on her."

"Thanks."

They talked quietly as Sara slept, both of them needing a chance to let go of the stress. Adam figured out that Dave had about six hours sleep in seventy hours, but he gave up trying to get the guy to see reason and go to bed. If he were lucky, Dave might fall asleep right where he sat, but his friend just sat working an old tennis ball with his hand, watching his sister sleep.

Was this what love did to you, made you willing to walk between the one you loved and danger? It was Dave's way of showing his love. Adam couldn't fault his friend for that. It showed dedication on Dave's part to have hung in there for such a long duration. He was going to like having this guy for a brother-in-law.

Sara finally woke at ten that night. She mumbled a sleepy hello to Dave, teetered a bit as she gave her brother a hug, and whispered a foggy good-night to Adam. Then she promptly went to crash in her bed for the rest of the night.

"Satisfied?"

Dave had a sleep-deprived smile on his face. "Yeah. She's okay."

"I told you she was." Adam couldn't help the grin. "Come on, Dave." Adam had to haul the guy to his feet. "I don't want to see your face until after nine tomorrow. Sleep is now a priority, got it?"

"This is like looking for a needle in a haystack."

Adam turned to see Sara rub her eyes. He knew what she meant. It was dusty work looking through the newspaper archives. The clippings smelled musty, making her frequently sneeze.

They were the lucky ones. At least they were not on the microfiche team, having to read white text on a black background.

Around various parts of the conference room were groups of agents going through old television film footage, yearbooks, military IDs, driver's licenses. Anything that bore a photograph of someone listed in the case index. In the center of the room, agents were going through the actual case files.

The man they were after had stayed on top of the details of the case. They knew that from the letters he had sent over the years. If he had been trying to stay on top of the details during the search…there was a reasonable chance he had been photographed. A good chance if his desire for attention had been high. He would have enjoyed taunting the searchers by actually staying close to the investigators.

Sara's sketch had been computer aged by twenty-five years. That idea was truly a long shot, but the agents were showing a unique determination to try anything that might succeed.

Just to make sure no possible match was overlooked, two different agents independently reviewed all the material. Anything that looked like a possible match was routed to Sara.

After a long day of work, they had barely made a dent in the amount of material they had to go through.

"Adam, take Sara home. This will all be here tomorrow." Dave stopped beside them.

"I can do another hour more."

"Sara, we're talking at least a week of solid work. This can't be done in a day. I need you rested."

"I'll take her home," Adam agreed. "Ben and Susan will take us?"

"Yes. I'll send two other cars as well."

It was a quiet ride. Sara had been quiet all day.

Adam followed her into the house, considering what he should do. His hand on her arm stopped her in the foyer. "Sara, how about we make a deal. For the next four hours, we can't think or talk about the search. It will still be there tomorrow."

Adam watched the tension in her face drain away. He hadn't realized his comment would have such a profound impact.

"Really? Not at all?"

"I think we both deserve the break."

She reached up and kissed him. "Thanks. We'll have it."

Adam smiled. "Why don't you select a video? I'll bring in dinner."

There were Texas-size hamburgers and french fries ready for them. Dave had called ahead. Adam fixed two plates and carried them back into the living room.

After Sara finished rewinding the videotape, she accepted the dinner plate.

Adam had brought her another couple aspirins to help with the throbbing arm. She hadn't been complaining, but he knew it had to be hurting.

"Thanks." She accepted the glass of water.

She started the comedy she had chosen for them to watch, and they ate dinner sitting on the couch.

It was good to laugh. Sara curled up on the couch, settling her weight against his shoulder. Adam made her comfortable, loving the chance to have a stress-free evening with her.

She fell asleep before the movie was over. Adam wasn't surprised. He brushed her hair back from her face, idly watching her.

It was a reminder of other evenings spent with her. He didn't want it to end.

Dave finally came home shortly before midnight. He shook his head as he settled into a chair with a soda. Adam paused the movie. "Did you really expect to find a match in the first day of the search?"

Dave gave a rueful smile. "No, but I can hope." He looked down at the soda can, and when he looked up, it was with an expression Adam had never seen before. "How's she going to handle it if we can't find a match?"

Adam felt his gut clench. He hadn't thought about that. His jaw tensed. He had better start thinking about it. He loved her. He had often wondered if anything might be able to break her. What Dave had just told him would. Remembering the kidnapper's face had always been her one thread of hope. If they couldn't find a match, how would she cope without a thread to hold on to?

"Dave, she'll cope by going to Seattle and starting a life with me. God has gotten her this far. He'll give her the strength to start over." He should have realized he had better start tempering her expectations. Part of his job was to protect her. Dave might watch out for her physical security, but that didn't mean Adam didn't have a critical role to play as well. She had suddenly seized on the hope that this would be over quickly. She had only been able to endure in the past because she had focused on a long-term hope. He had better start preparing her for the possibility they would not quickly find a match. "I'll start easing into the subject tomorrow, prep her for the possibility."

"One of us needs to. I can, if you'd like."

Adam shook his head. "Let me. I need to introduce the idea of my going along with her to Seattle. She'll be bothered enough by that; it may take the sting out of why I'm bringing up the subject."

Dave nodded. "We've got about a week of work to do before we run out of first-source material and have to go back to the drawing board for how to do the search."

"She'll be as ready as I can get her for the bad news, if you have to tell her."

"Thanks, Adam."

"We both love her. If I can soften the blow, all the better. What are the odds that we'll find a match for the picture?"

"It depends on how arrogant the guy was at the time. He was careful, or we would've already found him. He knows she saw his face; he purposely let her see it. Did he expect her to remember his face? He had to. He probably didn't expect her to seize up the way she did, to shut out the memories.

"He would have been far away from the area by the time she was found. But with time? When he realized he was safe? He used the original packages to taunt us that he was still free. He probably returned to his old life—same address, same job, same friends. I would guess that there is maybe a 30 percent chance we'll find a match."

"No higher?"

Dave shook his head. "That may already be too optimistic. He stayed tied into the case somehow; his negotiations show that. But I doubt he let himself be photographed at the crime scene of all places. There are over two thousand names in that index of people remotely associated with the case through the years. When those names are exhausted, the search could go on indefinitely."

Adam carefully brushed back Sara's hair, watching her sleep. He did not enjoy thinking about Seattle. "We had better find a match in those names, Dave."

"I hear you, friend."

The conference room was quiet except for the sound of paper turning. It had been six days. Adam knew he had an ulcer forming. Every day that passed made the stress worse. They were down to the very last of the material.

Dave had been silent during the drive into the district office this morning. Adam didn't have to ask. By midafternoon, they would be facing the inevitable. The decision to move to Seattle.

Dave had convinced Sara to stay at the ranch. She didn't need to be here when the last page was turned and hope was gone. She hadn't protested. Adam watched the hope begin to slip away over the last two days. She was retreating into silence rather than talking about it.

Lunch had been brought in, but Adam's sat beside him, untouched.

There were still open names in the index file, people they had yet to find a picture for. There was still hope after this afternoon. But it grew more distant with each day. The agents were too efficient in finding ways to rule out people who were on that list.

They would leave for Seattle first thing in the morning if they drew a blank today. Adam dreaded telling Sara that news. She would absorb the blow like she had every other one and set herself to deal with the move. She didn't like the idea of his going along, but she had resigned herself to it.

The search would start all over with an even broader mix of names. The wait would be open-ended again.

Adam worked through the thick list of names of volunteers who had participated in the nine-day search. In nine days, with a large area to cover, there had been a lot of volunteers. He was one of many working through the list.

The long drawer in front of him held old driver's license applications with last names beginning with the letter *K*. He was looking through the list and eliminating those he could. Unfortunately, he was marking them off one right after the other. He had not even generated a faint possibility to hand off to another agent.

He pulled out yet another card to match to a name. His hand stilled. "Dave."

His voice said it all.

Dave came over from the other end of the table. Adam set down the driver's license application next to the sketch Sara had made. Dave's hand on his shoulder tightened.

Dave started moving. "Ben, call the team in. Silent alarm. I don't want anyone attracting attention getting here.

"Susan, get this guy through the airline records. Tell me if we've got a match to Chicago. Travis, find out his current address—and do the computer search yourself; don't ask someone in records. He's going to have contacts. This guy signed the log as a sheriff's deputy."

Adam looked again at the sketch and circled a name. Thomas Krane. He had taken part in the search.

Adam handed Dave a cup of coffee. "Do you take him into custody tonight?"

The guy had traveled to Chicago. They had a match to New York as well as two other locations where packages had been mailed. A team was keeping him under surveillance now.

"It's enough evidence for a search warrant but not enough to make the case. It's the memory of a six-year-old child. Any good defense attorney would tear Sara to shreds with only the circumstantial evidence. We need more. We need the money. We need his partner to name him. Somewhere he's got evidence from the crime scene he has been using to send in the packages. Ideally, we have to get all of it."

"The longer you wait, the more likely he's going to realize he's being watched."

"We won't let him slip out of the net. The agents on the front line will prevent that; they know what's at stake. Hopefully we will have a lead on the money in the next few hours." He glanced at his watch. "Sara is going to be wondering. We should have been back to the ranch an hour ago. Let's go tell her." Dave smiled. "It feels good to be ahead of the curve for a change. Ben, call me as soon as the bank traces are complete."

The agent nodded.

Adam reached for his jacket. The ride to the ranch was spent discussing possible options for how they might proceed.

Adam realized to his surprise that he was seeing a different side to Dave. He was beginning to see his friend relax deep inside. Dave had been good at hiding the burden, but now that it was lifting, the difference was noticeable. Sara was likely going to be the same.

Sara was stretched out on the couch reading a book, or had been. She was fast asleep.

Dave sat down on the edge of the couch beside her and gently shook her shoulder. "Sara, you want to drift toward opening your eyes for a moment?"

She yawned as she woke up. "Dave." She didn't look pleased to be awakened; she still looked too battered for that.

"I've got some news for you."

She pushed herself up and ran her hands through her hair.

"His name is Thomas Krane. He worked for the sheriff's

office over in Jefferson County. He's retired now."

She blinked, her face not showing any emotion.

Dave waited for the news to sink in. "Adam found the match. The sketch is incredibly accurate. His photo came up when we were going through the volunteers who helped with the search. He was volunteer eight-seven."

"He took part in the search," Sara said in disbelief.

"He took part in the search," Dave confirmed. "He was assigned an area about fifty miles north of where you had been hidden."

"We've already confirmed he flew to Chicago, was there for two weeks. We've confirmed New York as well, and two other locations where packages were mailed. We should know about the money by morning."

"What happens now?" Adam was surprised at her calm. He had expected elation.

"Now that we know his identity, we are quietly going to take apart his life. He's under surveillance and will be until we take him into custody. Sara, I want to catch him sending another package. If his pattern holds, another one is due to be mailed next week. We'll use the time to build up a profile on his movements. A week, ten days, and this will all be over. He's going to jail for the rest of his life. I promise you that."

Adam saw the moment Sara's composure broke. She leaned forward against her brother and the sobs began to fall. Adam reached over and laid a hand on her back. They were sobs of relief. A lifelong prison sentence had just been lifted. They let her cry until there were no more tears to shed.

She finally rubbed away the last of the tears. She looked up at her brother. "I don't want you there when they take him down."

Dave's jaw tightened. "I have to be there, Sara; you know that."

"You want to be there. You don't have to be."

Dave raked his hand through his hair. "I know why you're worried. Yes, I want this guy at practically any cost. But I won't put my team in danger to make it happen. It will be handled by the book."

"Can you promise that?"

"I'll do everything I can, but you know I can't make promises. They don't exist in our world."

Adam didn't reply. He was too busy praying to the only One who could make—and carry out—every promise.

Adam watched Sara pace the living room. She had not sat down in the last three hours.

"Why isn't he back yet?"

"Dave said not to expect him until late this evening." Adam couldn't change the anxiety. Word came two hours ago that Thomas Krane had broken his pattern of travel and was apparently heading to a neighboring town. Dave left to join the team shadowing him. They had been slowly building the case over the last six days, tracking the money trail, his past travels, watching, waiting. Today might be the main event.

She rubbed her arms as she paced. "Why hasn't he called?"

"He probably has nothing to report. This is a matter of patience, Sara. Let them do their job."

"He's going to get hurt. I know it."

"Sara..." He stopped what he was going to say. There was no way to remove the fear. He was worried too. He crossed over to her side and pulled her into a hug. "Stop. Don't panic. That won't help anything. Let's pray about it."

She turned into his hug. "I couldn't stand it if something happened to Dave."

Adam understood that only too well. She had already lost a sister. She couldn't handle something happening to Dave too. "He'll be okay. You want to pray or should I?"

"My brother." Her hands wrapped around his as she took a steadying breath. "God, please keep Dave safe. Don't let him do anything foolish. Don't let him get hurt."

Her hands tightened. "This man, Thomas Krane, doesn't deserve Your mercy, not with innocent blood on his hands, but keep him safe too. Bring him to face justice for what happened to Kim.

"Help me to finally forgive him."

"Amen." Adam said quietly when it was clear she had no more words. How did you forgive a murderer? It was a good principle until you were faced with living it. He wasn't doing very well with that problem either.

Sara stood quietly for a long time. She finally nodded and gave him a hug. "Dave will be hungry when he gets home. I'm going to go see what I can fix."

Adam kissed her forehead. "That's my girl. Come on, I'll keep you company."

They settled on fixing chili.

He watched Sara focus on the task with intensity. The ground beef simmered in the skillet while she diced the onions. The onions made her cry, tears she brushed away with the back of her sleeve. After the chili was put together, Sara started looking through the cupboards. "I could fix cornbread to go with the chili."

Adam paused as he wiped off the stove. "That sounds good." Anything to keep her occupied.

She fixed the cornbread, then a chocolate cake, starting to search the cupboards again.

"Sara, let's go find something on television to watch." She let him pull her away from making pudding.

She settled on the couch and picked up the remote to flip through the channels. "There's nothing on."

Adam settled beside her, grasping her hand. "News will be fine." He doubted there would ever be a more stressful day in her life. She was struggling to wait it out, but she was handling it. Dave had been too focused after the call came in to realize Sara needed a few minutes with him before he left, just in case. Dave's hug had been brief and then he was gone. Adam knew what was on the line today. He wanted Dave back here safe, unhurt, and with good news. Anything less was going to put unbearable pressure on Sara.

The tension continued to build as the afternoon passed without word.

Dave listened to the security radio as the cars handling the coverage of Thomas Krane passed responsibility back and forth. There were six cars involved. They were changing off so one car never remained in sight for long. Another four cars were on side roads, ready to intervene if necessary. This case had a lot of resources assigned, but all were carefully chosen. There would be no whisper to the local law enforcement that the FBI had a high-profile case coming to a conclusion.

"Ben, take us to within two miles. Do we have someone at the post office in Mayfield?"

"An agent is stationed in the sorting area. You really think this is the day?"

"Yes, I do." He keyed his radio to confirm his team was ready. His anticipation was high. After days of waiting, this felt like payday.

Thomas Krane was driving a new blue pickup. Word came that he was pulling off the highway into town.

He was parking at the post office.

"Take us in, Ben."

Dave radioed Travis to keep Krane in sight so that he couldn't slip out of the building another way. They couldn't risk an arrest while he was surrounded by civilians. They would have to wait until he was back on the highway.

"It's a package to London. We've got the evidence."

The radio mike suddenly burst with a flurry of noise. "Dave, he saw me. He's heading into the grocery store next door."

Elation tore down to dread. "Stay back, Travis. Don't give him cause to grab someone."

Ben punched the gas. As they pulled into view, they saw Krane coming out of the west grocery store entrance, gun in hand, dragging a clerk with him. Ben stopped across the road, blocking traffic, as did the other cars joining them. Dave watched as the man crossed back toward his pickup truck. If he got in the truck with that hostage, odds were the clerk would be dead before this was over.

Procedures said contain the situation and let a negotiator deal with it. Reality said the man was crazy. Sara would never forgive him if someone else got hurt.

He didn't have a choice. Dave picked up the radio. "Pull back and give him the road. Let him go." They would end up in a high-speed pursuit, possibly risk losing him, but a free corridor would give him one less reason to take the hostage along.

They watched the truck start and begin to move. The clerk was shoved aside. Only Krane didn't head toward the road, he hit the gas with the truck in gear and headed for the post office front window.

Shattering glass rained down around the wreck. The truck had hit a steel column, preventing it from going right into the building. In the initial confusion it wasn't clear if Krane had been inside the cab of the truck or had bailed before the collision.

Agents surrounded the wreck, guns drawn.

He wasn't inside.

"He's on foot, heading west." Travis's frantic call came over the radio; from his voice it was obvious he was in pursuit.

Dave started running. Krane might be crazy, but he knew what he was doing. The other highway. He could grab another vehicle and be gone. If he had time to accomplish it, it would work too.

Dave spotted Travis ahead of him, and a block beyond him, Thomas Krane. The man chose a route through the city park. Agents were pouring into the area, sealing it off.

The foot chase ended by the town fountain.

One shot sent Travis diving for cover.

Dave hit the ground behind a concrete flower planter an instant before a shot chipped a piece of the concrete away.

Krane was cornered, if being mutually pinned down meant anything.

They had to take this man alive. So many questions

depended on it. "Give it up, Krane. There's nowhere to go!"

Another shot came right over the edge of the planter.

It was hard to tell how many bullets Krane was carrying, but Dave suspected the last one would be used to ensure he didn't get taken alive. Waiting for him to run out of bullets was a bad idea.

Sara would also never let him hear the end of it if he got himself hurt. Dave tried to keep that in mind as he thought through options. He wanted this man.

Sara would deal with it. She had Adam.

He keyed his radio. "Travis, cover me."

He moved away from the planter with a burst of speed. Shots were fired from the west.

Two people could play at this unexpected game. He went right for Thomas Krane. Hit the pavement. Pulled the trigger.

The sound of a vehicle pulling into the driveway had Sara leaping to her feet.

Dave walked in the door and Sara hit him moving full speed.

He wrapped her into a tight hug. "We got him, Sara."

"He mailed a package?"

"Yes. And gave us a merry chase to catch him."

Sara drew back. "Your forehead is bruised."

"Concrete does that." Dave's fingers unfurled her brow. "I'm walking, talking, and all in one piece. He's in surgery with a bullet to the shoulder. Fair trade."

"Anyone else hurt?"

"Seven people got hit with flying glass when he put his pickup truck through the front window of the post office.

The injuries are minor. They've all been treated and released."

"Why haven't we heard anything on the news?"

"You will soon. The search warrant is being executed as we speak. The DA is on site with the forensic team."

"It's over."

"It's really over, Sara."

She had to brace him up as he weaved a bit. "You're exhausted."

Dave smiled at her. "It was a long day. What smells so good? You've been cooking?"

She smiled. "Chili. I had to keep busy."

"Lead me to it, and I'll tell you the long version of the day."

CHAPTER | 17

I'm staying here at the ranch, Adam."

He looked over at her, not entirely surprised by the announcement. They had been riding that day, across barren land, then to lush valleys where water came from underground springs. They were eating lunch perched on two large rocks where they could look down and see in the stream extremely large catfish swimming at their leisure around the bottom of the clear pool.

It was over. One step into the home of the reclusive Thomas Krane had been enough to ensure the case against him would never go to trial. The obsession was everywhere.

They had finally figured out how he had circumvented security at the house in Chicago. The FBI badge had been a decent forgery, good enough to get him a copy of the alarm schematics from the company that maintained the system.

There had been no grand motive to his kidnapping plan, just greed, and opportunity. The local sheriff's office had increased security patrols in the neighborhood when they learned an ambassador's wife and kids were visiting. It tipped Thomas off to someone of wealth and importance coming to town. With access to the new routes, Krane was able to arrange the snatch and avoid the patrols. He was counting on the increased security being considered an asset, not a liability, and it worked. Attention never focused on law enforcement personnel until he had both the money and the evidence from the crime well stashed.

Adam looked at Sara as she looked over the valley. He wished he could say something, anything, to change her mind. But in the last ten days, it was a different Sara that had emerged. She still had security around her, tight security for the man was not yet sentenced. But she was sleeping again, spending long hours walking with Dave in the evening, spending her time during the day with Adam riding the ranch or working with the ranch hands.

When she came back from sessions with the counselor, drained of emotion, he would fix her a sandwich, give her a tight hug, and see that she spent a few hours out in the sun getting her equilibrium back. He didn't ask questions and she didn't volunteer anything because it wasn't time yet, and they both knew that. He needed her trust in him more than he needed the information he still hesitated to hear.

"I'm going to complete the H. Q. Victor book that tells Kim's and my story."

"You can't do that in Chicago?"

"Chicago is a place, this is home. This spacious land helps me feel free. I know how difficult this is for you. It's difficult for me too. But I need you to understand how deeply I need what I've never had before—freedom."

"And when the book is finished? What then?"

Sara reached into her back pocket and slid a wallet-sized photo from her pocket. She handed it to him. "I can't have kids. And you can't imagine life without them."

It was a small snapshot of him and his niece Bethany.

"Then we will adopt." He watched her bite her bottom lip. So his speculation had been right. Had his guess been right as well? His hand reached for hers. "Come here." She followed his gentle urging, letting herself come under his arm, to be held by his linked hands. "Sara, it's not that you *can't* have children; it's the fact that you can't *risk* having children. That's the real problem, isn't it?"

He had called her on her lie and she stiffened then, trying to retreat. He tightened his grip. "Easy. I understand why you said what you did. You're petrified of having a child go through what you did. That is perfectly logical. You don't need to justify that fear to me."

"You want a family."

"Very much so."

"I can't risk having one."

"Sara, you're ten days past something that has kept you terrified for twenty-five years. I wouldn't call our case hopeless at this point."

"I can't change who I am, Adam."

"I promise you, I won't pressure you into having kids, but I won't lie about how much I want them. This is one of those times God has got to work for there to be a solution. And at this point, that is what we're both going to have to do, give God time."

She drew back. "I think you should go back to Chicago and start looking for a wife who can give you a family."

"Sara."

"I mean it, Adam. Before you decide to go buy a ring and ask the question, I'll give you my answer. It's no. I won't marry you. I won't deny you your dream of a family. I cannot become the wife of a public figure. I cannot by choice accept to ever again live my life in a cage of security. I'm sorry."

The words pierced his heart, but he didn't respond. He knew she was breaking her own heart to say those words. They were a reflection of her present state of mind. He didn't intend to add to the stress on her by pushing her into a debate. He watched her mount her horse and turn back toward the ranch house.

God's love is deeper than this problem. Any problem. The soft reassurance echoed in his heart. Adam closed his eyes and rubbed at the tension headache. *I know that, Lord. But how long until she realizes that? I love her.*

Her concerns were well founded. He couldn't argue against her position. It broke his heart to think about leaving her here with this subject unsettled. What if she retreated again like she did after Colorado? He couldn't afford that.

He sat a long time looking at the water, wrestling with what he should do. He finally rose to his feet, mounted his own horse, and returned to the ranch.

He returned with Dave to Chicago two days later.

"Adam, you've got to make a decision on the commercial deals. We can't stall them any longer."

Adam turned from considering the skyline to look across his office at Jordan. "I'll renew only the sports apparel line. I'm not interested in the others."

"You're sure? We are talking about a lot of money."

"Yes, I'm sure. It's what Dad always said—do what you like to do. I like the commercial proposal they pitched, I'll enjoy doing that deal—I'll pass on the rest."

Jordan gathered up the papers. "You've been…quiet the last couple weeks since coming back from Texas. Is there anything I can do?"

"No. But thanks for asking, Jordan. I'm fine. Really."

Adam meant it. There was a peace inside that had not been in his life a few months ago. He could vividly remember the stormy July night he had stood in this office, unsure of what move to make next in his life. Those worries seemed so distant now. The challenges he faced now were bigger, but they were simpler. On that July night, he had met Sara. The decisions he had to make now regarding his career were minor compared to everything else.

Dave had come by the office yesterday to tell him before the news broke to the public about the second kidnapper being sentenced. What Dave told him still lingered: "I'm seeing Sara taste freedom for the first time in her life. And it's a priceless treasure we should never have denied her. I held Sara the day she was born. I know what her life was like with my father, with Frank Victor, then with Peter Walsh. I've been entwined in her life for the last fourteen years as chief of her security detail. She's changing, like a captured eagle suddenly given the heavens to fly in. She doesn't talk much, and she spends fourteen hours a day working on that book laying memories to rest—but she's living again, free."

Adam walked back to his desk and looked down at the photo sitting there. Dave had taken it for him when Sara wasn't watching—the picture of Sara leading her horse back to the corral after an afternoon's ride. She was smiling, and

Adam found even in the picture the attraction he had felt since the beginning.

He hadn't called her in the last two weeks even though he longed to hear her voice. He would overrun her decisions if he wasn't careful; so for now, he kept his distance. Part of it was in honor of her request that he not call. Part of it was his own recognition that giving her space and freedom right now was the best thing he could do for her. She needed time, and he would give her what he could. But it wouldn't be forever.

She was afraid to have children.

He had asked her to give it some time, to see if that fear changed…but he wasn't placing much hope on that happening.

One event had made Sara who she was. It had set the tone of her personality, the entire focus of her life. He expected remnants of fear would always be there.

He had been ready to sacrifice his dream of having children when he had known there was no choice, when he had known they would be living under a daily threat.

He could still accept that if he had to. But if Sara could change just enough to accept the risk…

He didn't want to pressure her.

He did want a family.

His friends from his football days had the same problem. Wealth, fame—yet they managed to keep their families safe in the midst of the media attention. Money could buy security, privacy. They would just have to find a compromise.

Adam knew what it had been like during the days he had been in the spotlight, having security around him. The risk had been there, but it had not stopped him from having a life. He had been free to move about, to spend time with his family, his dad. His privacy had still been intact.

Sara had tasted the other extreme. Twenty-five years of someone hunting her. To keep her safe, the protection had been forced to be smothering.

Maybe with time, she would be able to see the difference.

Adam let out a deep sigh as he ran his hand through his hair. *Lord, am I simply being stubborn about wanting to have a family? What do You want for us?*

He sat down at his desk, reached back to the credenza, and picked up the red folder. The list he had written with his dad was dog-eared now; it had been read so many times. His ideal wife. There was a new item on the page.

A name.

The sky was clear tonight, the stars brilliant. Sara sat on the rocky outcrop that had been her favorite observation point as a child and listened to the night flow around her. It was so utterly peaceful here.

God felt so far away.

Sara didn't understand what had changed. For years she had been so aware of God's constant presence. It was different now. Less tangible. The realization had been troubling her for the last few weeks.

She had brought a flashlight along with her Bible, and she soberly turned pages in Psalms, looking at the verses and notes she had written going back to her teenage years. She suspected the problem, and what she read only helped confirm it. Passage by passage they told a journey built around one theme: a plea for protection.

It was the freedom.

She had clung so tightly to God for safety because she felt so afraid. She had never learned how to relate to Him in a broader way.

Gradually as she read, her tension began to fade. She should have realized the change that would naturally occur. She hadn't moved. God hadn't moved. Her life had moved.

Everything had been touched by her past. The entire basis of why she loved God had been built around her need for Him to protect her. He was her strong security, her refuge, and she had let that be enough. God had so many more qualities she should have been adding to that list over the years. Instead, she had let time slip by, content to know God in only one way.

All her dreams she had prayed about through the years—her children's books, her home, her family—had all been in one way or another filled with worry about the man pursuing her.

She was looking at ripples from her past that led to the very heart of her relationship with God.

Anger and sadness both vied for her emotions.

There was so much to rebuild.

Lord, I don't need to pray for safety.... How many times have You heard that plea from me over the years? Thousands? I am so sorry I never understood. I thought I was trusting You. Now I see I never got past being scared. I just kept coming back time after time to hear Your reassurance. Will I ever truly grow beyond this fear?

Sara quietly scanned the wide-open land. She was still seeking that reassurance, coming back to the haven God has provided from her childhood where she had felt the most safe.

She couldn't change the past. Whether she liked it or not, the need to feel safe had been paramount throughout her life. That need wasn't going to change in the future. The threat might not be a specific person, but the emotional need would still be there.

The last few weeks had been heart wrenching without Adam. It would be a delight to spend a lifetime with him. But to deny him children would be to rob him of his own dreams. She loved him too much to do that.

Can't you trust God with your children?

She wanted children. She wanted to trust that it would be okay, but years living with security had torn away the illusion that there could be a normal life.

If you trust God, why are you so afraid?

Kim died.

The fact sat immovable in her path. She was afraid because life had taught her to be afraid.

Have all the verses and all the prayers just been words?

Sara closed her Bible. She wrapped her arms around her knees and stared at the night sky.

How deep had faith taken root? Deep enough to accept the assurance God was offering?

She was at a crossroads.

She had envied her best friend getting married. Now, she had to make a choice. Was she going to walk away from marriage with Adam because of her past?

It always came back to that. Her past. Would her future forever be held prisoner because of it?

The wind began to stir, causing Sara to pull her jacket tighter around her shoulders.

Was the past still controlling her, or was she learning

from it? It was hard to distinguish where that line was. She needed to figure out what was driving her actions.

God had kept her safe through a lifetime of threats. That should be worth something. It was as real as the fact Kim had died.

Where did courage come from to take a step of faith? Children would be that kind of ultimate risk.

She didn't want to take that risk. It went against everything she felt right now.

She wasn't the only one in the equation. Adam and God were too. She looked at the stars spread above her. God was big.

She had never felt so small.

The grandfather clock in the hallway announced midnight. Sara continued to work on her last H. Q. Victor book, to tell her story…Kim's story.

Day 9.

Sara struggled to find the words to let readers know what it had been like. This was the pivotal chapter. She set down her pen.

"Why did You let her die?" The whispered prayer came from her heart.

It was the core of her struggle.

The number of days for Kim's life were different than yours. Do you want to carry the guilt forever? It wasn't your decision.

The bitterness she wanted to direct at Thomas Krane instead turned toward God. She had buried the doubts with her sister rather than let them surface. Now they were starkly laid out on the pages before her. She felt so helpless.

Make the decision. Are you going to trust God or not? Would you deny yourself a future with Adam because you can't predict what God will allow?

She did want children. Dreamed about having a family someday. The only thing holding her back from that future was her fear.

A cautious hope was born even as she considered what it would mean to take that step, to say yes to Adam. She had to learn to handle the risks and precautions that went with being free, and do it without overreacting. Security would not have to be as oppressively tight as it had been in her past. She no longer had reason to fear a specific bogeyman in the night. Surely there was a compromise possible that would keep children safe?

There was a future waiting for her—her choice for a future, not one forced upon her by events of the past—if she had the courage to reach for it.

The words from a favorite psalm flowed into her heart, bringing a smile, and with that smile, tears she reached to brush away....

"I waited patiently for the LORD; he inclined to me and heard my cry. He drew me up from the desolate pit...."

Thank You, Lord, for lifting me out of that cellar. For showing me the past can be left behind.

"He set my feet upon a rock, making my steps secure...."

There is solid ground for the future. Solid ground with Adam. I can see it now. I can feel Your hand steadying my doubts.

"He put a new song in my mouth, a song of praise to our God."

Thank You, Lord, for rescuing me. Joy bubbles up inside for what You have done. Adam loves me. I could never have imagined such a wonderful answer to prayer.

What had happened in the past was just that—in the past. It was time to move on.

From the hall came the sound of a door closing. "Quinton?" Besides the housekeeper, he would be the only one in the house at night.

There was no answer. She got to her feet.

In the middle of the night, a ringing phone brought fear. Adam reached to his left to pick it up. "Yes?"

"Adam, I'll be at your door in five minutes. Krane escaped."

"How?! Krane was supposed to be under lockdown in a secure mental facility."

"They were transporting him to the hospital after what they believed was a suicide attempt. The guard thought he was unconscious, turned his back, and was nearly killed."

"Sara?"

"No one at the ranch is answering. Teams from the regional office are on their way now."

Adam could barely breathe. Chicago to Texas. Whatever was happening would be over before he could get there. He had left Sara there, considering her safe. "We're hours away."

"I know." Dave's voice was rough. "Meet me downstairs. We'll get there as fast as we can."

"Thomas."

"Hello, Sara. I told you we would meet again."

The fear held her frozen by her desk. He was in the

house. She looked nervously past him to the open door.

Krane smiled. "Don't worry. We won't be interrupted. Quinton should learn to watch his back."

She was on her own. The handgun was in the top drawer. Dave had ensured she knew how to use it.

He followed her glance and gestured to the chair. "Sit down."

To put the desk between them, she moved to the chair.

He pulled open the drawer and withdrew the handgun. He set it down on the desk, temptingly close, taunting her to reach for it. "I hear you did a very flattering portrait."

"I did a portrait."

He flipped open a folder lying on the desk, scanning a page. "About me?"

She nodded.

"Writing a book?"

He smiled at her silence.

"Truth or fiction?"

Rage had overtaken the fear. "There are no words for your evil."

His laugh made her skin crawl. "I'm mad. All the doctors say so." He gestured to the doorway. "After you."

"No."

"Sara. Shall I kill Quinton first? You are coming with me."

He would kill to make her come. He had always wanted her, only her. It was the past all over again. Only now she wasn't a child.

Lord, give me the courage to trust Your security! If the days of my life have already been numbered by You, then You decide what happens, not this man I fear so much.

Dave would stop him. Adam. Someone would.

And God was here. With her.

She wasn't going to fear Thomas Krane. Not anymore. Not at the price of her faith. Whatever the outcome, she'd already won this fight.

Sara moved around the edge of the desk, keeping her distance, walking toward the door.

"Drop."

The terse order came from in front of her.

Sara hit the hardwood floor and heard the shot fired.

She didn't look behind her. She didn't want to see the result. "Quinton." She knew the outcome from the fact he lowered his gun. He was bleeding from a gash on his temple.

"Sorry to be late to the party."

She reached his side and helped him sit down. "Thank you."

The phones were dead. By the time she found her cell phone, she could hear the approaching helicopters.

"Adam." Sara walked into his arms, closed her eyes, and held on.

The conference room in the hospital had become her private sanctuary. She had been watching the dawn lighten the sky. Waiting for Adam and Dave to arrive.

Her long night was over.

In every way.

"I'm sorry I wasn't here."

She tightened her hold. "It's okay. God knew what He was doing." It could have been a long standoff, another set of memories to give her flashbacks, a crisis that would have pushed away any hope of a future. Instead, it was over. God had removed the threat forever. She had seen the man she feared. He was different than the childhood memories she had of him. Not as tall, not as big…and he bled, he died.

Already the past had a different emotional feel. She thought about the cellar, and it was Kim she remembered, not Krane. They were memories of a childhood spent with her sister. Good memories, no longer blocked by the event that had shut everything else out.

There wasn't a reason to fear what would happen when God was the One taking care of her.

Dave rested his hand on her shoulder. "Quinton said you have already given your statement."

"I have." Concerned at how shaken her brother looked, she reached for his hand. "I sent you back to Chicago. Will you please let it go? There won't be any images to forget. I never looked back. It's finished."

Dave stroked her cheek. "Come back with us?"

Sara looked back at Adam and smiled. "I was just waiting for an invitation."

CHAPTER | 18

Adam met Ellen at the door with a smile and eased back King Henry who had come to greet her too. "You made good time." He took her coat, draping it over a chair. Since they had arrived back in Chicago two weeks ago, Sara had been helping Ellen with her final wedding preparations.

"Sara thinks I'm doing some shopping while she has lunch with Dave. Are you sure you want to do this?" The package she held was thick.

Adam had thought about it long and hard before he had made his request. Sara had finished the final chapter of her book. "Yes, I'm sure." He accepted it, felt its weight, and set it on the end table. "How are the arrangements coming?"

Ellen laughed. "She doesn't have a clue." She leaned down to greet Henry.

"I appreciate what you're doing."

"It's been a pleasure. I'm having such fun. Anything else you have thought of?"

He already had the list written.

Ellen glanced through it. "Not a problem. I'll just conveniently have another 'I forgot about' stumble tonight. It's driving Sara crazy."

"Be careful not to tip your hand. If she suspects, I'll really land in the doghouse," he said with a rueful glance at his husky.

"Don't worry. I've been waiting a lifetime for a chance to set her up. She won't suspect a thing." Ellen glanced at her watch. "In keeping with that, I had better run. If I'm not loaded down with shopping bags, she'll be wondering what I've been doing."

"Thanks, Ellen."

She gave him a knowing smile. "Would you quit worrying? Sara's head over heels in love with you. I'll call if I have any questions."

Adam walked with her to the door and showed her out. He hoped Ellen was right. He was taking an awful gamble with this plan.

He paced back to the couch and looked at the box Ellen had brought. Now or later?

He rubbed the back of his neck and went to get himself a soda. Now. If he put it off, he would only wonder more.

He settled at the dining room table and cut the tape sealing the package. Sara's latest manuscript. Ellen had made a copy for him while Sara was otherwise engaged. Adam didn't like going behind her back, but he had weighed the options and accepted the risk. He needed to know the truth.

He would prefer to know what he was asking Sara to talk about before he raised the subject. The fact that Thomas Krane was dead did not remove the need for them to talk about her past. He didn't want to walk her into a minefield without knowing what was there. If he could lessen the impact of her words by learning the details now, it was worth the price.

She had titled the book *Kim*.

He started reading, turning pages of the manuscript slowly as the afternoon wore into the evening.

Several times he had to stop and walk away, heading to the living room to get away from the words. The truth was even worse than he had feared.

When he turned the last page shortly after eight, dusk had long since descended on the city and the lights twinkled back at him.

God, I can't handle this.

There were the facts of what had happened, there was the turmoil that had gripped Sara's life since then, and there was the hit it had made to her faith.

There was a point in time when Kim died that Sara thought she was going to die too. And she wanted to die. The guilt of not being able to save her sister had been overwhelming. Sara spent a lifetime fighting the guilt of being the one to survive.

It was clear from her epilogue that with the death of Thomas Krane a chapter in her life had closed. Kim was part of her past. A twin. A friend. She had faced the options when reviewing the evidence, looked at what had been possible for her to do, and finally accepted as fact that she had done all that could have been done.

Adam straightened the manuscript pages he held.

He didn't love her any less; he probably loved her even more.

Did he need to change his plans?

God, if this isn't going to work, I need to know soon.

He had set the plans in motion, gambling that he could get the answer he hoped for. Now, knowing what he would be asking Sara to overcome…. He had never made such a risky move in his life.

Sara came back from Texas ready to compromise, to find a way to have a future together. He had set in motion preparations for a day he hoped she would never forget. But he was hesitating, postponing the conversation they needed to have about children.

It had shaken him to hear Sara was in danger again, to know he was too far away to help. Having suffered through those long hours of uncertainty, he now understood Sara's hesitation to have children. He had to weigh his desire to have children against the risk he would be asking her to accept. If something ever did happen, he would be putting her in a position that would break her heart.

Father, I want this to work. It's released to You—all of it. Children. Marriage. You know what she can handle.

He loved her enough to let that go if God asked it of him.

He knew now what he needed to tell Sara.

It was late. Dave would be annoyed. Adam reached for the phone anyway. "Dave, how are the plans going, buddy?"

Laughter came back from Dave. "Would you relax? Everything is under control." It reassured Adam just to hear his friend's voice. Dave at least thought his plan was good.

"Ellen, hold still or we are going to have to redo your tiara. Trust me, your train lays out fabulously."

Ellen stopped moving so Sara could get the last bobby pin in place. "I don't know what I would have done these last couple weeks if you hadn't been here, Sara."

"Gone crazy by the look of it. You're only getting married, you know. It's not something really big or anything," Sara teased back.

The dress was beautiful. When Ellen had first started looking for a gown shortly after her fiancé proposed, she knew exactly what she wanted. She had a picture of a gown from a designer collection, and she spent days looking for something similar. Sara showed up at Ellen's apartment one day with a box, opened it, and produced the original. "Consider it a commission for all those books you've helped me write." The dress won over Ellen to accepting the gift.

The time helping Ellen with her final wedding plans had been filled with laughter. Their days had been hectic with last-minute details. They often crashed on the couch late at night to commiserate and laugh about the complexity of it all.

Sara was grateful for a reason to be busy. Adam had her confused. There was a distance between them she didn't know how to deal with. They needed to talk about her past. Talk about children. Neither discussion would be easy. It felt like he was deliberately avoiding time when they could talk privately. Sara didn't understand it. After the wedding was over, she would have to pin him down and find out what was wrong.

There had been one profoundly sad day in the last two weeks, the day Ellen set aside to read the book Sara had finished, the same day Sara returned to Kim's grave to say a final good-bye. It was hard to do, for in writing the book she not only wrote about the kidnapping but about her friendship and fights with her twin. They were so close. The need to remember Kim was never going to fade, but the loss was finally being accepted.

There were flowers on Kim's grave the day she visited. The card bore Adam's signature. Sara sat down on the grass and grieved in a way she had never done before. There were so many things she missed having with her sister. The double dates. The talk of boyfriends. The joy of growing up together. It was a necessary grief. She left the cemetery carrying one of the flowers from the bouquet Adam had left.

Ellen's mother came to join them, indicating it was time for them to move upstairs. The bridesmaids, all from Ellen's extended family, went to meet their escorts. The music was starting. "Ready?" Sara asked Ellen.

"Yes. Maybe. Sara, if I stumble over the words, you've got to cover for me. Drop your bouquet, something."

Sara had to grin. "Your nerves are showing."

"They're dancing. Listen, Sara, when you eventually get married, take my advice, make it a short engagement."

"I'll do you one better. I'll probably elope," Sara replied, half serious, thinking about the last few hectic days. She walked with Ellen up the stairs, holding the train of her wedding dress.

Dave smiled as they joined him. "All ready?"

"Yes."

She didn't see Adam as she walked up the aisle and wondered where he was. He had brought her to the wedding. He looked fabulous in his tux.

To her relief, the wedding went smoothly. Ellen's voice was calm and clear, the photographer covering the wedding, discreet.

Less than an hour from the start of the service, they were standing together in a receiving line at the back of the church. Sara was very aware of Dave in his tux standing directly behind her. Security was quite tight all around the wedding since there were several dignitaries in attendance.

Halfway through the line of people, Sara was beginning to hope for any sort of commotion or distraction to occur just to give her hand a break.

The line eventually began to dwindle, but she knew the night was far from over. Her duties as maid of honor had barely begun. At the reception, she was going to be swamped with details to ensure Ellen didn't have any hassles.

She turned to greet the last guest, her smile one that had been politely pasted on her face for the last hour.

"You look like you could use a break." Adam caught her hand in his and smiled. "Ellen, we'll be back in a couple minutes."

Sara didn't protest. She would take any time with Adam she could get. "Where have you been?"

"Finishing some details."

She found herself being led back into the church, to the padded pews at the front of the sanctuary. Adam tugged over the pianist's bench so he could sit facing her.

"I've got a simple question for you." His smile made her heart lift. "Will you marry me?"

"Adam…"

"Hear me out." He bent his head and took a deep breath. "I've read your book. Ellen got me a copy. I know what you've been through."

Sara flinched, not prepared for that news.

"I can deal with what I've read, Sara. It doesn't change

what I think about you…what I feel. I love you. I love you more deeply than I can figure out how to put into words."

Tears welled in her eyes; Adam gently brushed them aside. "I know how hard it's going to be for you to trust me in the way I am going to ask, but I need you to think about something for a minute. You've believed the truth of Isaiah 41:10 all your life. 'Fear not, for I am with you, be not dismayed, for I am your God; I will strengthen you, I will help you, I will uphold you with my victorious right hand.' You've held on to it as your source of strength. I'm offering a compromise. We let God decide if we have children. He will be fair to both of us. He knows your fear, and He knows my dreams.

"I trust God enough to have Him say to me, 'Adam, I'm sorry, but for the good of your wife, you will not have children.'"

His hand brushed along her face. "Are you willing to trust Him if He says, 'Sara, you can handle the child I'm giving you'?"

"It may still be months or years before I can take that risk."

"I know that, honey. But I think God can work out any miracle He desires to. Please, say you'll marry me."

Sara closed her eyes, considering everything God had taught her, and when she opened them, her eyes were shining. "If you'll have me, for better or for worse, then yes, I'll marry you."

Adam kissed her.

They broke apart when Dave made his presence clear with a chuckle.

Sara looked up and Ellen was there beside her. "Congratulations! But there is no way I'm letting you elope."

Sara couldn't help the laughter. She glanced back at

Adam. "When do you want to get married? Just so I can officially put it on Ellen's calendar."

"Today," Adam replied smoothly.

Sara was stunned. "Are you serious?"

"I've got the license in my pocket, and Ellen just happened to call the designer who made her dress to find out which one had been your favorite when you were looking for hers—it's waiting downstairs."

Sara looked from Adam back to Ellen. "You didn't."

Ellen smiled. "Adam can be quite persuasive. Come on, I'll help you change."

"But guests, family, friends?"

"By the time you get changed, the important ones will be here," Ellen assured her. "Our best man is going to keep the reception at the country club moving along until we all arrive. Come on, Sara. This way you'll have all the finery and not a single bit of the hassle. You won't even have time for prewedding nerves. We are all prepared. Why do you think I've been running around so much the last two weeks? We've even got napkins printed for the occasion."

Sara started to laugh. "Yes, okay." She leaned forward and kissed Adam again. "This is crazy, but you're on. I rather like the freedom to be impulsive these days."

Ellen helped her change, and there was a lot of laughter as they both tried to move around in wedding dresses, but eventually Sara was ready, her hair swept up, her makeup done by Ellen's expert hand. Sara stood at the top of the steps, the organist playing the song Sara had helped pick out.

"Ready?" Dave handed her a beautiful bouquet.

She smiled and did her best to still the trembling in her hands. "I think so."

His amused smile as he offered his arm helped. "Come on then, Adam's waiting."

Sara walked down the aisle on her brother's arm.

Adam's family was there. Sara's friends. The people she had depended on to keep her safe through the years.

When her hand was transferred to Adam's, it was taken in a reassuring grasp. "Thank you for this. You make an absolutely gorgeous bride."

"Did I get you a ring?" Sara whispered back.

Adam's grin was instantaneous. "Dave is holding it."

Sara loved the ceremony, the music, and the fact she was winning her heart's desire. When Adam slid the ring on her finger, it felt like God had just handed her a present she had been dreaming of for a lifetime. She leaned into Adam's kiss at the end of the ceremony, felt his arms come around her. She didn't want to move.

It took some maneuvering to fit her dress into the back of the limousine so they could go to the reception. They did it with laughter as they were showered with rice.

Adam settled her against him, holding her hand. "Mrs. Sara Black. I like the sound of that."

She relaxed against him. "I love the ring."

"I enjoyed the search to find it. You like the one you bought me?"

Sara got a good look at it before she slipped it on his finger. A solid plain gold band. It suited him quite well. "Who helped you pick it out?"

"Dave."

"I can't believe I never had a clue all the fuss these last two weeks was about us."

Adam tugged a curl. "Arrangements kept you busy?"

"It was exhausting. Thank goodness I didn't know it was for us, or I would have been a nervous wreck."

"I was afraid you would say no."

Sara leaned back and considered him. "I love you, Adam. I'm just sorry I come with so much baggage."

He brushed her hair back. "I'm not worried about it. You don't need to be either. We'll take it one day at a time. Just enjoy today."

"Do I get to feed you cake?"

Adam grinned. "And let you mess up this new tux? We'll take some with us on the plane."

"We're taking the jet? Where are we going?" She hadn't thought about the honeymoon. She wasn't packed for it.

"Somewhere private."

Sara laughed softly. "So far it sounds excellent."

"It will be," Adam promised. "Don't worry, those shopping bags Ellen has been carting home are for you."

"You're serious?"

He smiled. "Yes."

Their arrival at the reception as a married couple sent quite a surprised murmur through the crowd. They mingled, making their way through the room.

Adam eventually pulled her onto the dance floor. Sara was more than willing to stay cocooned in his arms and let the talk drift around them.

After a few dances, though, she leaned close to his ear. "How long before we can escape?"

He chuckled. "I thought the bride always liked to linger."

"Not this one. I want to give my roses to Mary Beth and slip away." She linked her hands behind his neck, smiling. "I haven't seen much of you in the last few weeks. I don't want to share."

Adam kissed her softly. "Good point. Come on."

Sara laughed and followed his lead. She was going to love following this man for a lifetime. The future had never promised so much joy.

The publisher and author would love to hear your comments about this book. *Please contact us at:* www.deehenderson.com

Dear Reader,

Thank you for reading *Danger in the Shadows*. As an author, I fell in love with Adam and Sara and the story they had to tell. Getting to share their story with you is a pleasure.

Each book is a journey, an opportunity to learn something new about God. This story brought the words from Isaiah 41:10 to life. "Fear not" are two powerful words. Hearing those words is a comfort I have come to treasure.

If that were the only lesson I learned while writing this story, it would have been enough. It was only the first. I also learned God likes to surprise us with joy. He makes love show up in the most amazing places and under the most unlikely circumstances.

God cares about us when we are afraid.

He is bigger than our biggest fears.

He surprises us with joy.

He is the One who says, "Fear not, for I am with you, be not dismayed, for I am your God; I will strengthen you, I will help you, I will uphold you with my victorious right hand." Take Him at His word and let Him lift your burdens.

As always, I love to hear from my readers. Feel free to write me:

Dee Henderson
c/o Tyndale House Publishers, Inc.
351 Executive Drive
Carol Stream, IL 60188
You can also find me on-line at: www.deehenderson.com,
or e-mail: dee@deehenderson.com
Thanks again for letting me share a special story.
Sincerely,

Dee Henderson

The Protector

Jack O'Malley is a fireman who is fearless when it comes to facing an inferno. But when an arsonist begins targeting his district, his shift, his friends, Jack faces the ultimate challenge: protecting the lady who saw the arsonist before she pays an even higher price. . . .

ISBN–10: 1-4143-1059-5
ISBN–13: 978-1-4143-1059-6

The Healer

Rachel O'Malley works disasters for a living, her specialty helping children through trauma. When a school shooting rips through her community, she finds herself dealing with more than just grief among the children she is trying to help. One of them saw the shooting. And the gun is still missing. . . .

ISBN–10: 1-4143-1060-9
ISBN–13: 978-1-4143-1060-2

The Rescuer

Stephen O'Malley is a paramedic who has been rescuing people all his life. His friend Meghan is in trouble: Stolen jewels are turning up in interesting places and she's in the middle of it. Stephen's about to run into a night he will never forget: a kidnapping, a tornado, and a race to rescue the woman he loves. . . .

ISBN–10: 1-4143-1061-7
ISBN–13: 978-1-4143-1061-9

And visit **www.DeeHenderson.com**
to find first chapters and more!

THE DEEP HAVEN SERIES BY SUSAN MAY WARREN

Happily Ever After

She thought her hero was just a fairy tale . . . .

ISBN–10: 0-8423-8117-1
ISBN–13: 978-0-8423-8117-8

Tying the Knot

Anne was at the end of her rope . . . until her hero came along.

ISBN–10: 0-8423-8118-X
ISBN–13: 978-0-8423-8118-5

The Perfect Match

Ellie's life was under control . . . until he set her heart on fire.

ISBN–10: 0-8423-8119-8
ISBN–13: 978-0-8423-8119-2

Visit **www.heartquest.com** today!